P9-EMP-784
AURORA
SCHOOL

Steinbeck's Ghost

Steinbeck's Ghost

LEWIS
BUZBEE

FEIWEL AND FRIENDS
NEW YORK

A FEIWEL AND FRIENDS BOOK
An Imprint of Macmillan

The author and editors gratefully acknowledge Jan Neal of the John Steinbeck Public Library for her gracious help during the research for this work.

Thanks also to artist Owen Smith, who traveled to the Steinbeck House in Salinas, California, to collect images and impressions as reference for his painting on the jacket.

 Printed in the United States of America. For information, address Feiwel and Friends, 175 Fifth Avenue, New York, N.Y. 10010.

Library of Congress Cataloging-in-Publication Data

Buzbee, Lewis
Steinbeck's ghost / by Lewis Buzbee.
p. cm.
Summary: Unhappy after his parents move to a weird subdivision and become workaholics, thirteen-year-old Travis returns to his old Salinas neighborhood and becomes actively involved in saving the John Steinbeck Library and, at the same time, begins seeing characters from Steinbeck's books who seem to have a message for him.
ISBN-13: 978-0-312-37328-3 / ISBN-10: 0-312-37328-7
[1. Books and reading—Fiction. 2. Characters in literature—Fiction. 3. Libraries—Fiction. 4. Political activists—Fiction. 5. Family life—California—Fiction. 6. Moving, Household—Fiction. 7. Steinbeck, John, 1902–1968—Fiction. 8. Salinas (Calif.)—Fiction.] I. Title.
PZ7.B98318Ste 2008 [Fic]—dc22 2008005625

Feiwel and Friends logo designed by Filomena Tuosto

First Edition: September 2008

10 9 8 7 6 5 4 3 2 1

www.feiwelandfriends.com

for Maddy
a promise

✦ ✦ ✦

I READ ALL OF THESE WHEN I WAS VERY YOUNG AND I REMEMBER THEM NOT AT ALL AS BOOKS BUT AS THINGS THAT HAPPENED TO ME.

—John Steinbeck

I

THE LIBRARY

ONE

FINALLY. He finally found the word he had been looking for.

Camazotz.

The moment Travis Williams stepped out of his house into the warm September afternoon, the word came to him. For months, ever since he and his parents had moved into the new house, he'd been trying to figure out what was so creepy about this place. Now he knew.

He stepped off the porch into the bright sunshine and whispered the word.

"Camazotz."

A Wrinkle in Time was one of Travis's favorite books. He'd first borrowed it from the library a couple of years ago, when he was eleven, and had probably borrowed it three times since, read it he didn't know how many times. Whenever he thought of the book, he pictured the planet Camazotz.

On Camazotz, everything was perfect. Every house was exactly like every other house, every lawn like all the rest. Every garden grew the same kind of flower, and the exact same number of those flowers. Everyone in Camazotz dressed like everyone else, and they all did the same things and at the same times. One child played ball in front of each house, and each ball bounced to the same beat.

Camazotz was supposed to be a perfect planet. And in a way, Travis thought, it was perfect. Perfectly creepy.

Bella Linda Terrace was supposed to be perfect, too. At least that's what Travis's parents told him. The house was big and brand-new, much bigger than the old house. Bathrooms galore, huge bedrooms, and in the living room, cathedral ceilings. His parents said "cathedral ceilings" in breathy voices as if these were the magic words that might open Aladdin's cave.

Before they'd moved in, Travis also thought that Bella Linda Terrace might be perfect. It was a spanking-new subdivision surrounded by a high stone wall. The houses had just been built, many of them still waiting for their lawns. The first time Travis toured Bella Linda Terrace with his parents, the fresh smell of the sunbaked earth was everywhere. He loved that smell. The streets were wide and clean and newly coated with black tar. Travis loved that smell, too, hot asphalt.

When they walked through the model of the new house, his parents showed him which room would be his. Travis would have the enormous bedroom at the front of the house, with two high, wide windows and a vast expanse of floor. His bedroom on Riker Street was about the size of the closet here, cramped but cozy. His new bedroom was palatial.

"All of it?" he kept asking. "All of it mine?"

Travis loved the view from these windows—his desk would go right in front of one. He could see all the way across the valley, past the freeway to Oldtown Salinas, and beyond that the dark Santa Lucia Mountains, and beyond that the ocean.

But his parents had saved the best for last that day. When they left the model home they drove to the far side of Bella Linda Terrace and parked above the community pool. A pool! It was Olympic-sized, the water as bright as a sapphire; there was a high dive and a three-story waterslide.

"You can go every single day if you want," his mom said. Travis felt like he was going to fall out of the car.

They moved in just after school let out for summer. Travis tried his best to decorate his room, not sure he had enough stuff to fill it up. He made sure to swim *every* day, mostly twice a day, and made a great friend, Hilario. But he never quite got over how weird Bella

Linda Terrace felt. Waking up in Bella Linda Terrace was like wearing a shirt that was too tight; he couldn't get used to it.

"Camazotz," he said again, standing on the porch. The word sounded too loud. "It's just like Camazotz."

The hot afternoon wind pushed against him, trying to blow him up into the hills.

At the old house there were big trees that offered shade and cut off the afternoon wind, but in Bella Linda Terrace all the trees were saplings. The trees here were like a kindergartner's drawing of what a tree should be, stick trunks with stick branches. There was no shade at all, and every afternoon the wind was fierce and steady.

"I live on Camazotz," Travis said.

It was true. Everything here was exactly the same as everything else. Nothing was out of place.

There was one huge difference, though, between here and Camazotz. At least on that tedious planet, children played in the streets. The streets of Bella Linda Terrace were deserted. Nothing moved except the wind.

Creepy. He'd better get going to Hilario's.

✦ ✦ ✦

Hil's bedroom was always dark. He kept it dark because it made playing video games easier—no glare on the screen—but Travis didn't understand why it had to be dark when he wasn't playing.

Travis and Hil basically lived in the same house—Camazotz again. Although Hil's house was three twisting blocks from Travis's, both had the same floor plan. Hil's bedroom was the same size and in the same slot over the garage as Travis's. And both houses had the same footprint, as his dad liked to say; they faced the same direction, west across Salinas. But you'd never know it because Hil's curtains were always closed. The curtains were heavy and black as night—couldn't get much darker.

Travis fingered the bottom edge of the thick curtain. He was almost afraid to open it; the perfectly bored children of Camazotz might be on the other side of the glass playing their reasonable games.

"So, Big T?" Hil said. "What's it gonna be?"

Hil clutched a fan of video-game boxes in one hand while he gracefully swept the other across them, like the hostess of a TV game show.

"First up," Hil said, his voice now an announcer's baritone. "For your gaming pleasure, Triumphant Weasel, a riveting journey through a forest of evil-eyed rodents. Next is Going Going Gong II, whose mysteries of the Far East are not for the squeamish. And today's final selection, Icon, where contestants scramble to create world-crushing corporations. All items sold separately."

Travis didn't want to play video games today, but he had to laugh. Hil was a funny guy, that's all there was to it. Sometimes Travis laughed just looking at him, as if he could almost hear the funny things cooking in Hil's head. Even his name was funny. Hil, Hilario, Hilarious.

Travis nudged the curtain and peeked out the window. The world was still there.

"I don't know, man," Travis said. "Whatever. Or I mean, don't you want to go outside or something? There's no one out there. We could do anything."

"Oh, dude," Hil said. "You know I'd love to, but my delicate skin, she is so pale."

Hilario's skin was as brown as a walnut.

"No, really," Travis said. "Let's ride bikes or something. Get outside. The dark in here, it's so cold. Sooooo coooooold."

"Maybe tomorrow. I gotta be here at four sharp. I set up an Icon session with the guys. Have to be online by then."

Hil cued Triumphant Weasel and leaped onto a sofa two feet from the TV. Travis shrugged and fell onto the sofa, too, and began blasting net-bombs at evil ferrets and vile stoats.

Afternoons with Hil weren't like this at first. They'd met at the pool a few weeks before school started, and Travis liked him on the spot. He remembered the first time he saw him, Hilario walking off the high dive as if taking a stroll, only realizing halfway to the water where he was, and then running like crazy in midair to save himself. Travis was already laughing before Hil's big splash. When Hil got out of the water, he took a regal bow, but the only one in the audience was Travis. Everyone else was splashing and screaming.

Travis got in the high-dive line behind him, and just as Hil was about to go out onto the board, he asked him to do his funny walk again.

"Check this out," Hil said. He ambled to the edge of the diving board, turned and looked into the distance as though he'd forgotten something. Then he pretended to lose his balance and windmilled all the way to a big sploosh! About the funniest thing Travis had ever seen.

After that, they were together every day. Which was a good thing because Travis had been worried about making new friends. Not worried, really, more like uninformed. He'd never moved before, and even though Bella Linda Terrace was only four miles from Riker Street, everything had changed—new school, new friends. He wasn't really sure what to do, as simple as that. Did you sit at home and wait for a welcoming committee to come over for a snack and sign up to be your friends?

For the first two months at Bella Linda Terrace, Travis went to the pool every day. He swam and dived and slid down the slide, and occasionally got into a thirty- or forty-kid game of Marco Polo. It wasn't like all the other kids here had friends already, it was a new place for everyone. Some kids did have friends, but they traveled in small groups, twos and threes, groups that were harder to break into. There were a lot of brothers and sisters, and they formed their own little knots. The rest of the kids seemed as uncertain as Travis. But he figured friends would happen, eventually.

Travis and his best friends from the old house, Rich Davis and Anthony Gonzales, had made a solemn pact to stay in touch—no matter what. They spat into one another's palms and shook, swore on it. Something always came up, though, vacations or baseball practice, and then Anthony and his family up and moved to Albuquerque in July.

Rich did come over once for a day of swimming. It was fun, but Travis found there wasn't much to talk about anymore. He and Rich used to talk nonstop about everything—baseball and music and which girls they thought were cute and might actually talk to them—but that evening after dinner, while Rich and Travis sat in his room, a great big empty silence sat there with them. Every time Rich brought up something, Travis didn't know enough about it to know what to say next. And every time Travis thought of something to say, Rich only smiled and said, "Yeah, pretty cool."

When Rich's parents picked him up that night, they both promised to call each other the very next day. But Rich didn't call and neither did Travis.

By August, Travis had to face the facts: He was lonely. His parents were always at work these days, rarely home before eight or nine. Even on weekends they sometimes went to work, and when they were home, they were too tired to go to the pool with Travis. The pool they worked so hard to afford. Travis didn't get that at all.

Then there was Hil. For the last few weeks of summer, he and Travis were at the pool every day. In the afternoons, when it got too hot, they'd go to Hil's and play video games, and in the evenings, when the wind died down, they'd ride their bikes all over Bella Linda Terrace. Then back to the pool for night swimming.

But when school started, everything changed. Turned out you couldn't go swimming *every* day. Once school started, only one lifeguard was on duty, and children had to be accompanied by a parent.

His new school, Torgas Middle School, was tucked into Bella Linda Terrace, and like everything else out here, it was brand-new and too shiny. Because it was new, the other eighth graders seemed as lost as Travis, but Travis had Hil to hang out with, which really helped. They had homeroom, history, and math together, and ate lunch together every day in the cafeteria.

Travis liked hanging out with Hil, but afternoons had fallen into a serious rut. They started every afternoon with sodas and cookies in Hil's kitchen. They goofed around for a while—that was the only word for it, *goofing*—which usually involved running around the house and jumping over furniture. And that was great, really. But then the video games came out. After that, it was just video games—chasing weasels or elves or robots or strange creatures Travis didn't recognize.

And here they were again.

"Take that, Señor Weasel," Hil said. "Feel the fury of my furry slingshot."

Travis couldn't help himself; he laughed.

But the games were boring, always the same. Hil and Travis captured what was supposed to be captured, blew up everything else. No matter how many times they played, the story was always the same. Nothing changed.

A bell pinged in the room, and Hil's computer sprang to life, the screen glowing blue in the darkness.

"That's them," Hil said. He shot off the sofa and tossed the joystick aside. "We got eight guys on Icon at once. You gotta help me, T, my infrastructure needs some serious work."

Hil was already glued to the computer, clicking his mouse furiously. He was mumbling.

Travis couldn't do it. He couldn't spend another three hours hunched over his best friend's shoulder worrying about the sanitation system of a digital world.

"You know, man," Travis said, "I just remembered. I got some extra homework. I better get going."

He waited for Hil to say something.

"Cool, T, check ya later," was all he said.

He didn't look up from his computer when Travis left.

The kitchen was spotless; the countertops actually gleamed. When Travis opened the refrigerator, the white-blue light was so bright and the food so neatly arrayed, he couldn't imagine making a snack. It would be like eating plastic.

He padded through the rest of the house, looking

for something to do. But it was all too perfect, way too Camazotz.

The carpet hushed under his feet. The furniture looked painted in place. When they moved out of Old-town, his parents purchased all new furniture, so new and clean that Travis was almost afraid to touch it. Even the garage was immaculate, the boxes of their old life stacked tidily on stainless-steel shelves.

The old house on Riker Street wasn't big or perfect. It was crowded and messy, full of life. The new house was a magazine advertisement.

The only sound in the house this afternoon was the wind pushing, whistling in doorways and windows. That sound, the wind, made the whole world seem even more quiet than it actually was.

He could almost hear his mom telling him to go outside and get some air. But the wind and the heat and the stillness kept him inside. Besides, he wasn't allowed to leave Bella Linda Terrace, to take his bike beyond the big stone wall. He was only allowed to ride his bike up one perfect street and down another.

Travis found himself at his desk. He had homework, but it stayed in his backpack, and his backpack stayed hung on its hook on the back of his door. His parents wouldn't be home till past eight, and Travis had no idea how he was going to get through the long, quiet hours.

So he stared. West, toward the ocean, which was a band of blue fog on the horizon. He stared past the other streets of Bella Linda Terrace, past the golf course and the dark sharp ravine of El Toro Creek, past Highway 101. He stared at downtown Salinas, at Oldtown. He thought maybe if he stared long enough, he would spot his old house on Riker Street.

Then he remembered the library. Whenever he thought of his old life, the library was the first thing that sprang to mind. Every Saturday, Travis and his parents went to the nearby public library, the John Steinbeck Library. This was their weekend ritual; they'd spend the whole day there, and always go home with stacks of books. "As much as you can carry," his mom used to tell him.

Although the library was only a few blocks from Riker Street, and it would have been a lot easier to go home for lunch, Travis and his parents always had a picnic on the library's front lawn, right at the base of the statue of John Steinbeck. This made it more like a hike than a visit to the library.

Travis had always liked hanging out by the bronze likeness of Salinas's most famous citizen. Steinbeck was one of the most popular writers in the world, and tourists came from all over to see the places he wrote about, although Travis found it hard to imagine anyone wanting to spend a vacation in Salinas. But when you grew up here, Steinbeck was a part of the landscape, always there, like the wind or the mountains. Even before you read any of his books—Travis had been reading him for a few years now—he was a part of you somehow.

There was something about this statue that was very special to Travis, something that didn't have to do with fame or tourists. The bronze figure was tall, lanky—he was pretty sure that was the right word—dressed in work boots, jeans, and a shirt with the sleeves rolled up, ready to get to work. The statue's smile, under a short beard and moustache, was soft, slight, but Travis sensed that behind the smile, Steinbeck was really smart and funnier than he was letting on. And his ears, those great big sticking-out ears—that's how you knew it was Steinbeck.

The statue always seemed alive to Travis, almost breathing. Steinbeck looked like the guardian of the library, a knight protecting his castle. Whenever they passed the statue, Travis and his parents always greeted it, "Hello, John," and each of them tapped his writing hand three times. They tapped the hand for good luck, good luck in finding the exact right book. It didn't have to be a new book, or a great book, particularly, but the exact right book, the one you needed on that given day.

The library suddenly seemed more real to Travis than his desk and his room. He could see the pale yellow-painted cinder-block walls of the kids' section, the short shelves of books there, the old beanbag chairs he sometimes fell asleep in, and the wall of windows that flooded the room with warm light.

Travis realized he had to go to the library, and right now. He needed to read *A Wrinkle in Time* again, and tonight. Maybe if he read about the planet Camazotz, his own world would feel less Camazotz.

He shouldn't go, he knew that. But he had to, the urge was boiling inside of him. Could his parents actually get mad at him for going to the library? Probably. That is, if they ever found out.

He raced into the garage. The tires on his bike had plenty of air, a sure sign he should go.

Even with the hot wind blowing in his face, it felt great to be out of Bella Linda Terrace. Natividad Road was crowded with cars and trucks, and noisy, but it felt like the real world. Travis stayed on the cracked, bumpy sidewalks, flying past trailer parks and liquor stores, churches with peeling paint, greasy-smelling auto shops, chain-link fences that had trapped scraps of paper.

He pushed up the Highway 101 overpass, zoomed down onto Market and over to Main, headed toward the library. Past Dick Bruhn's A Man's Store, past Beck's Red Wing Shoes, Chang's Nails, La Fogata, and Shogun Sushi, and past Sheila's, the bar where his father used to work before the new job. There were people everywhere in Oldtown. Packs of kids hanging out in front of the Maya Cinema, men in tight black jeans and crisp white Stetsons, moms lugging pink plastic bags of groceries, tourists on their way to the National Steinbeck Center.

He leaned into the turn at San Luis, and there it was, the library. It was a squat white building, not very pretty at all, but it made Travis smile, especially when the statue of Steinbeck came into view. He locked his bike in the rack, then crossed the gold-green lawn and tapped the statue of Steinbeck three times on his writing hand—good luck for a good book. The statue was almost exactly as he remembered it, those laughing, wise eyes and great big ears. If anything, it seemed more alive today than he remembered, almost glowing in the long light of the afternoon. "Hello, John," he said as he and his parents had always done. "It's good to be back." Travis looked around, embarrassed to be talking to a statue.

Then there was shouting, from behind him. Travis turned. Across the alley, in front of a sepia-tone mural of what Main Street looked like a hundred years ago, an old man was yelling something. The man was dressed in a dirty, blue denim jacket and tattered jeans, and he carried his belongings on a stick over his shoulder. His hat was straw and ragged. Underneath the baggy clothing, Travis could tell, the man was all skinny arms and legs. He wasn't just old, though, he seemed old-fashioned, as if he'd stepped out of the mural, out of another century.

"I am Gitano," the man was shouting, "and I have come back!"

A lot of homeless people lived in Oldtown, and they hung around the library a lot. Travis was used to that, had grown up with that. Often one of them would be screaming, but angry screams, painful ones.

This man was not angry at all. He looked tired, but he seemed happy, relieved.

Everyone else going into the library ignored the man as if they couldn't see or hear him.

"I am Gitano," the man yelled, his face to the sky, "and I have come back!" He dropped his bindle on the ground and sat down next to it. He looked like he meant to rest on that spot of grass forever.

Travis smiled at Gitano, then turned and entered the library. How strange. Travis had just been saying the same thing, kind of, but to a statue. Maybe it was a special day, the day of returning to the library. "I am Travis," he whispered, "and I have come back."

TWO

"It's about time, Mr. Williams. Nice to see you again."

Charlene Babb was Travis's favorite librarian. If she weren't an adult, he would have thought of her as a friend. He'd known her since he was a little kid, from family Saturdays at the library. Over the years she had put a hundred different books in his hands, and no matter what book she suggested, he always loved it. Travis didn't realize how much he'd missed her until he saw her behind the main checkout counter.

"Hi, Miss Babb. How are you?"

"I'm fine, now that you're back. It's been months, way too long. I was afraid you'd been sucked into some endless video game. It happens, you know. But I knew you'd be back; you couldn't have read every book just yet, Mr. Williams."

Travis felt himself blush. Miss Babb always called

him Mr. Williams, and while he knew she was just being polite and funny, he couldn't help feeling a little nervous when she called him that; it made him feel like a kid and a grown-up at the same time.

"Well," he said, leaning against the counter. "See, we moved to the east side, and I—"

"I knew that. I've been standing here for months waiting for you. Your folks coming?"

"No, ma'am," he said. He always seemed to get extra polite around Miss Babb. "They're still at work. I rode my bike over."

"Very good," she said.

Miss Babb hadn't changed at all. But why should she have? It had only been a few months. She was tall and thin, with a mane of wild blonde hair. She held her head high, as if she could see something behind you that no one else could see. She was a little older than his parents, he knew that, but he couldn't tell how much older. Adults were confusing that way; you could never get their ages right. Miss Babb was married and had two kids, but was always Miss, even to Travis's parents.

The library was the same, too. It had never been brand-new, as far as Travis could tell. The carpets had always been beige and worn. The shelves were still the same old brown metal shelves they'd always been. The cinder-block walls the same white, on the grown-up side of the library, or yellow on the kids'. Even the newest books on the new-arrival shelves looked worn because of the plastic covers over their bright dust jackets. And the smell was exactly the same—the dusty odor of old books.

Travis was relieved to find the library unchanged. On the ride over, he had the weird thought that since he'd last been here, the library might have become brand-new, shinier.

"Well," Miss Babb said. "Tell me all about it, your new house and everything."

The library seemed extra quiet today. To one side of the checkout counter, past the new arrivals, a few adults sat alone at different tables, hunched over books and newspapers. To the other side of the counter, near the big windows that looked out on the street, a young girl, probably a fifth grader, sat alone in the kids' section, curled up in a beanbag chair. A bulging backpack of homework sat next to her, but she was reading a novel.

Travis told Miss Babb all about Bella Linda Terrace. Except the part about it being like Camazotz and how the word had popped into his head that day. If anybody would understand, she would; she had given him the book in the first place. But he felt like he wanted to keep that to himself a bit longer, as if the word were still echoing in his head.

"What's it called again?" Miss Babb asked.

"Bella Linda Terrace."

"Ha." Miss Babb slapped the front counter.

"Is that funny?" Travis didn't get it.

"Kind of," Miss Babb said. "It sounds like one of those made-up names. Do you know what it means?"

"Uh. Bacon, lettuce, and tomato sandwich?" Travis remembered the first time he saw the initials BLT on the front gate of the subdivision.

"Ha." She slapped the counter again. "Touché, Mr. Williams. Touché."

"But I'm pretty sure it doesn't mean that."

"Probably not, and that's a shame." Miss Babb typed into her computer, then scribbled with a pencil on a piece of scratch paper. "Here. If you've got time, you can look it up. This is a dictionary with five different languages. That's your clue. Come back later and tell me what it means."

Travis looked at the call numbers; they started with REF. The reference section.

"Now," Miss Babb said. "What brings you here?"

"Just looking, hanging out. You know."

"Take your time. And now," she said with a flourish, "if you'll excuse me, my public awaits."

She bowed to Travis, then took a pile of books from an old man with a white goatee.

"Hello, Mr. Ray," she said, winking at the man. She began to scan his books into the computer. "Hydrology again, I see. Well, you gotta dig that."

She and the old man both laughed. Travis was pretty sure he understood the joke they shared—it had something to do with water.

Travis was looking at books. And not looking. He was pretending to look, but mostly he was letting the library wash over him. It felt great to be here—like being home again.

It was strange to be so happy to be here. This was, after all, just a library, a very common place to most people. He remembered Ray Bradbury's *Something Wicked This Way Comes,* an awesome and terrifying book about a mysterious carnival that arrived one October day in a small Midwestern town. The two boys, Jim and Will, hid in the town's library; they were being chased by Mr. Dark and the Illustrated Man. Despite his many powers, Mr. Dark was afraid of the library and anxious to get the boys out of there. Travis pictured the boys where they hid high in the shelves between the novels of Dickens and Dostoevsky;

he wasn't the only one who thought the library an important place.

After grazing the new arrivals, he went up the short steps to the main adult collection and browsed the aisles there, enjoying the hush of the place. Then he wandered back to the kids' section—Miss Babb was still busy—and roamed, head tilted to the right, past his favorite shelves, fiction.

The books he'd read and loved seemed to jump out at him, as if waiting for him. *The Teddy Bear Habit, Henry and Ribsy, The Chocolate War, M. C. Higgins the Great, Bridge to Terabithia, Tuck Everlasting, Homer Price.* Oh, *Something Wicked This Way Comes*—funny to find that one now. On and on. Every book he recognized opened up the world of that book to him. These weren't stacks of paper bound together with glue or string—they weren't items or products. Every book was an entire universe.

Corral de Tierra by Ernest Oster. He hadn't thought of this book when coming to the library, but there it was. Of all his favorite books, this might be his favorite ever. He slipped it from the shelf and held it flat in his hand. In the foreground of the cover illustration, a young boy, about Travis's age, stood with his back to the reader. In the distance was a mysterious valley, painted in somber greens and blacks, where a shadowy figure lurked near the opening to a deep path. Travis thumbed the pages; they were soft and old. He opened the back cover and looked at the checkout card in its paper sleeve. The book had been checked out twenty or so times in the last few years. Travis had probably checked it out half those times, and he knew that the other readers had checked it out because Miss Babb had given it to them. She loved *Corral de Tierra,* too.

The first time he checked it out was in sixth grade. It must have been a Saturday because he remembered being at the library with his parents that day. He asked Miss Babb, as he'd done many times, if she would recommend a book for him.

"I've read about everywhere," he said. "London, Paris, Russia, Kentucky, Los Angeles, Mars, places that don't exist. But I've never read any books about Salinas. Do they make any books about Salinas?"

"Oh my, Mr. Williams. Oh, yes."

Miss Babb stomped off to the kids' section, and Travis scurried behind her. She found a copy of *Corral de Tierra*—the only copy the library owned—and handed it to him.

"Corral de Tierra is a real place," she said. "Do you know it? It's off 68, on the way to Monterey. A beautiful valley back up in the Santa Lucias. Anyway, this is a book about John Steinbeck, when he was a boy. You know, Steinbeck the writer? He was born right here, just a few blocks away. It's all about how he used to go up into the Corral and create adventures for himself. It's funny and spooky. You'll love it."

Travis plopped right down in a beanbag chair and started reading. It was a black-gray day—the memory of the day was as real as the floor he stood on now—lots of rain, and the ink-dark sky went perfectly with the yellow cinder-block walls of the library. He scrunched into the beanbag and read, and was almost halfway through the book when his parents dragged him home.

What captured him about *Corral de Tierra,* that first day and every reading since, wasn't the plot or the characters, really, although the book was, as Miss Babb said, funny and spooky, a great combination for any book. No, it was something bigger than that. Travis's dad often said, when he would sit down to read, that he was about to "get lost" in a book, and Travis understood that plainly. When Travis started *Corral de Tierra,* he wasn't reading about a place. He was there, in the book, in the valley. And when they walked home that rain-soaked Saturday, and Travis saw the Santa Lucias only a few miles away, he knew exactly how Corral de Tierra looked, and more important, what it felt like to walk there.

Miss Babb was right, as usual. He did love the book, and read it three times before it was due again.

Now Travis tucked it under his arm. It had been almost a year since he'd read it.

He was headed to the L's in the fiction shelves, for L'Engle, when he nearly stepped on a copy of *A Wrinkle in Time*. It was lying open, pages down, right where some kid had left it. He looked around; the kids' section was empty. This was the book he'd come for, and so no surprise to find it. But to find it like this, as if it had been left for him? He picked it up and turned it over. The book was opened to pages 98 and 99, in the middle of the chapter called "A Happy Medium." One word leaped out at him: *Camazotz*.

Ever since he'd remembered the word this afternoon and whispered it, the world seemed changed somehow, like when Alice went through the looking-glass. The world still looked the same, pretty much, but it was also different, no two doubts about it, as his mom liked to say. And Travis liked the change. In the months since they'd moved to Bella Linda Terrace, he felt he'd been living in some vague dream, cut off from sights and sounds, everything muffled. But now, since this afternoon, he'd felt alive again, a part of the world. When he said the word *Camazotz*, he'd been able to escape Camazotz.

He tucked *A Wrinkle in Time* under his arm, too.

Time had evaporated. Dusk was coming on. The shadows outside were purple, the buildings pink and orange. He had to get going; it was almost seven.

In the REF section, he found the dictionary Miss Babb had scribbled down for him. It was a big red book as fat as a loaf of bread, *A Dictionary of Five Languages into English*.

He leafed through it, looking up the words Bella and Linda and Terrace. Bella was from Italian and meant "beautiful." Linda was from Spanish and also meant "beautiful." Terrace was from a bunch of different languages, but it all boiled down to one basic meaning: a place.

Beautiful, beautiful place. Now Travis knew why Miss Babb laughed when he said Bella Linda Terrace. The name was nonsense. It didn't mean anything. Bella Linda Terrace was a fake.

At the front counter, Miss Babb swept his books toward her.

"Beautiful, beautiful place," he said.

"Exactly," she said. "Isn't that nuts? Hooptedoodle, if you ask me. Nice work, Mr. Williams."

Miss Babb waved the electronic scanner over the bar codes on the backs of the books.

"Again with *Corral de Tierra*? Let me ask you, which Steinbecks have you read?"

After he'd read *Corral de Tierra,* Miss Babb had suggested Steinbeck's *The Red Pony,* which he loved, even though he cried when the pony Gabilan died. He'd read a lot more Steinbeck since then.

"Uh. *Red Pony, Long Valley.* Uh. *Cannery Row.* Oh. *Tortilla Flat.* And *Sweet Thursday,* too."

"You should read *The Pastures of Heaven,* then."

She pulled a green-and-white paperback from under the counter, one swift movement she seemed to have been practicing.

"It all takes place in the Corral. You'll love it."

"You never told me about this one."

"Some books are best for waiting. You're ready now."

She scanned the green-and-white paperback into the computer, and then she took out a chunky silver date-stamper from below the counter. *Ker-chunk, ker-chunk,* she stamped the return date in green ink on the cards in the backs of the books.

"Miss Babb," Travis said. "If you have a computer, why do you still use a date-stamper?"

"I only do this for special readers, Mr. Williams. Friends of the library. And I like the sound of it."

She opened the back cover of *The Pastures of Heaven.* *Ker-chunk.*

✦ ✦ ✦

The man who called himself Gitano was asleep under a bottlebrush tree. He was curled up against the mural of old Salinas, his back to Travis. In the lowering dusk he was hard to make out, nothing but a soft pile of blue-and-gray cloth. "I am Gitano and I have come back," the man had yelled. A strange thing to say; what did it mean? It was a familiar sentence, something Travis had read in a book. As the last light of day faded, Gitano seemed to sink back into the mural.

Travis swung into his backpack, the books thumping against him, and wheeled away from the library down San Luis, headed to Riker Street. When he'd left Bella Linda Terrace this afternoon, he didn't yet know he was going to visit his old house, it wasn't even an idea then. But the library and his old house were so connected, it now seemed the obvious thing to do. He really should be getting home—he certainly didn't want to get busted by his parents—but he'd hadn't been to the old house since the move. He was willing to take that chance.

The streets of the neighborhood were quiet, but he could hear, over on Main, traffic honking and barking.

The afternoon wind had died, and the air around him was fresh and clear, the heat fading quickly. He felt like he was breathing again for the first time in a long time.

He pulled up on the sidewalk in front of 137 Riker. At first, everything looked the same, all the lights were on, the shallow porch of the bungalow inviting. The bike lurched forward an inch or two, and Travis felt he could go right up the walk, into his old house and his old life.

The dining room curtains were open, the room bright and clean. A fancy table was set for dinner, two candles lit and flickering. The scene was perfect, and all quite wrong.

When Travis and his parents lived here, they ate at a small table in the kitchen. Back then, the dining room was his dad's music room. Keyboards and guitars and speakers lined the walls. Cords snaked everywhere. It was never neat.

The lawn in front of 137 had been completely resodded, and strange flowers grew out of the beds along the bottom of the porch. On the porch, an old-fashioned swing-chair sat waiting. A square flag with a giant pumpkin and the word AUTUMN rustled in the dying breeze. Definitely not his house anymore.

Just then a woman came into the dining room. She wore a white apron and carried a dish she held with oven mitts. Behind her followed a man and a little girl, a first or second grader. The family sat at the table, the mom and dad at each end, the little girl in the middle facing the street.

The girl waved at Travis, and her parents turned to see who was outside.

He stood on the pedals of his bike and pushed off, away from his old house, quite uncertain how to feel about what he'd just seen.

Travis coasted through the neighborhood past the dusky blue houses. He zagged over to Central, headed home, to Bella Linda Terrace, knowing he was probably late and headed for some kind of trouble. But the Steinbeck House was on the way.

132 Central was where Steinbeck had been born and raised, and where he had written *The Red Pony* and *Tortilla Flat* when he returned home to take care of his dying mother. After Travis started reading Steinbeck, his parents took him to the house for lunch. Volunteers from the Valley Guild served lunches there to help pay for the upkeep of the house and to provide scholarships for local students. Travis loved being in the old Victorian, knowing that the famous writer had lived in its rooms, which were done up in the style of the times, but he was a little disappointed that he couldn't go upstairs to Steinbeck's

boyhood bedroom. The manager told him that their insurance didn't allow it; the stairs were too steep. He'd always wanted to go back to the house, as if he could breathe in more of Steinbeck's world there, get closer to the books he loved.

Tonight, small spotlights showed the front of the house, but it was otherwise dark. Travis sat on his bike across the street. He tried to imagine what it would be like to be in the upstairs bedroom looking out, to be the writer creating his stories. He wondered if he'd ever sit in his own window and write his own stories.

A light came on in the two small attic windows above the front door. A shadow appeared, a person, who pulled aside the lace curtains and looked out one of the windows. A man. No, younger—a teenager. The boy sat down, his head still visible. He was looking at something that Travis couldn't see.

Travis crossed the street to get a better look, but as he approached the house, the line of sight grew too steep, and he couldn't see anything of the window. He crossed back to the other side.

The boy was still there, a silhouette against the warm yellow room. He stood up and walked out of sight, then crossed the back of the room, then out of sight again, then appeared before the window, staring down. The boy,

Travis saw, wore a white shirt with dark suspenders. He sat down again, quite still, his left hand holding his tilted head.

It didn't seem quite right. Not normal, for sure. Why would a teenage boy be in the house at night? But he wasn't doing anything. This was no burglar.

Travis stared at the figure in the window. The boy was concentrating. Reading, maybe, or writing. The rest of the house was completely dark inside. It didn't make any sense that someone would still be there at night.

The long, low whistle of a freight train broke the evening stillness. Travis looked east, past Oldtown. He could almost feel the train's rumble.

When he turned back to the Steinbeck House, the window was dark and the boy was gone.

Sweating bullets and pumping at full speed, Travis blew through the stone-walled entrance to Bella Linda Terrace—beautiful, beautiful place, ha!—and tore down the streets. His head was filled with sentences he kept trying out—where he had been, why he hadn't left a note, the seven different excuses why he was late, even the truth of it. The excuses and the truth all seemed lame to him. He wasn't sure he'd believe any of them himself.

No two doubts about it. He was in trouble.

But from the far end of Harbor Mist Way, Travis could see that his house was dark. His parents weren't even home yet.

When his parents finally did get home, a little before ten, he was already in bed and reading the first pages of *The Pastures of Heaven*. Maybe this book held some clue to what he'd seen in the window of the Steinbeck House.

THREE

ALL DAY FRIDAY AT SCHOOL TRAVIS STARED OUT THE WINDOW, BUT NO ONE SEEMED TO NOTICE. He couldn't stop thinking about the library, how good it was to be back there, and he was amazed at how those books seemed to fall into his lap. It was weird to realize, too, that the library seemed more of a home to him than his old house—there was a new family in that house, it wasn't his anymore. But the library still was.

In Mrs. Lamy's Spanish class, last period, Travis kept going back to the boy in the window at the Steinbeck House, for some reason the spookiest piece of yesterday's puzzle. Whenever the image of the boy came to him—a teenager in suspenders in front of the window—Travis got the strange sensation that the answer was too easy to miss. But it was just some teenager in a window, and it wasn't even that late at night—what was so weird about that?

At one point he thought, Oh, I know, I'm in some scary book now, and that's Steinbeck's ghost calling to me. Out loud—he actually did this out loud, he couldn't believe it—he made the spooky-movie ghost noise while everyone else was quietly studying irregular verbs, "Ooo-eee-ooo." Everyone turned to look at him as if he'd farted. Just great. He'd never make more friends if he kept this up.

That afternoon, Travis hung out at Hil's again. After last night, it would be a relief to play video games, knock off a few badgers—the badgers always gave him the fits, he could never nail them. But over sodas and cookies in the kitchen, Travis surprised himself by asking Hil if he'd ever read *A Wrinkle in Time*. Hil had; it was one of his favorites, all-time.

"Weird," Hil said, and now he made the spooky-movie ghost noise, the exact same one, "Ooo-eee-ooo. I just started reading it again last night. Went to the mall with my mom and bought a new copy. It's awesome."

So Travis dropped the word *Camazotz* on Hil and told him about Bella Linda Terrace being like Camazotz, and Hil totally got it. They talked about the name Bella Linda Terrace, and Travis showed him that it actually didn't mean anything at all, and Hil got that, too.

"The street names, dude," Hil said. "Talk about weird. You live on Harbor Mist, right? You see a harbor, you see mist? No. And Grand Junction and Merrimack. Too weird. The streets should have names like Lettuce and Artichoke and Kale, all the stuff that grows around here. And this street? Serendipity. What does that mean?"

"It means—" Travis said.

"I know what it means, it's like a coincidence or something. But what does it mean for a street name? You're right, man, this place is weird. Now you know why I stay inside so much. Thank God for the pool."

They took their sodas to the front porch and stared at the quiet, empty, and way-too-bright streets. It was hot again, and the afternoon wind was up and strong, but it felt good to be outside.

They spent the rest of the afternoon dreaming up a video game called Camazotz. In this world everything was gray and brown and blue, very dark, but perfect. The houses, the children, their games, all the same. Just like the book.

The heroes of the game, naturally, were two thirteen-year-old boys—each dressed in outrageous and colorful T-shirts and big goofy hats. They wandered through Camazotz with their Plink-Plunkers and Plink-Plunked the houses and children and balls, trying to locate hidden passages that led to cool and colorful and exciting worlds. There was a hidden world under every boring house.

They sketched five levels of the game—an underwater world, an inside-out world, a backward world, a world without gravity, and a world in which dogs were the masters—and they each shot soda out their nose countless times from laughing. They didn't play a single minute of a real video game. It was the best afternoon with Hil since school had started.

Travis's parents knew they'd screwed up. Big-time. When they came home at ten on Thursday night, Travis already in bed and reading, he could hear how sorry they were by the way they rushed up the stairs together, then opened his door slowly and quietly. They smiled big, fake, soft smiles. Travis stared at them.

"We're sorry, kiddo," his dad said. He sat on the edge of the bed and ruffled Travis's hair. "We should have called, we know, should have told you we'd be late. I know, totally unfair. But I was in this big emergency meeting, and your mom had this killer report to do, so she just stayed. And . . . well . . ."

"That's right, honey," his mom said. She leaned over his dad's shoulder. "We're really, really sorry."

It was like being in the hospital; his parents were doctors telling him he had an incurable disease.

"We know it's been crazy lately," his dad said, patting the bed. "And we haven't been around as much, and, well, and . . ."

"And?" Travis said. It was the meanest question he had ever asked anyone.

"And tomorrow," his mom said, "tomorrow everything's clear, the slate is clean. Your dad and I will be home by six, won't we? And we'll go to Sheila's for burgers, we haven't been there in ages. And this weekend we'll all hang out together. Hey, let's spend the day at the pool on Saturday. Won't that be great?"

"Okay," Travis said. He said this with a little sulk in his voice. He was enjoying making his parents pay, and he certainly wasn't going to tell them where he'd been while they were out. "But you promise. Sheila's, and the pool, too?"

"Absolutely," his father said. "That's my kiddo. Now, you get some sleep."

His parents said nothing about the library books scattered on the bed.

On Friday night, as promised, they went to Sheila's, a funky bar and restaurant in Oldtown, where Travis's dad had been a bartender before his new job. The burgers at Sheila's were the best, and the French fries were simply unexplainable they were so good—French fries from another planet.

Sheila, the owner, made Travis a Roy Rogers with five cherries on a plastic sword; "his usual," Sheila called it, and even though Travis thought it was a little kids' drink, he still loved it. Some things shouldn't change. Travis and his parents used to eat dinner here every Sunday night—always burgers and fries—and everyone at Sheila's was happy to see them.

Saturday at the pool started out great. It was warm, but not as hot as it had been that week. A thin layer of feathery clouds softened the sky, and the wind didn't come up in the afternoon. They took a picnic lunch and the newspaper and some books, almost like the old days at the library. But mostly they swam. And dived and slid down the slide. Maybe it was the clouds, but hardly anyone else was at the pool. Travis kept a lookout for Hil, but he never showed up. Which was okay, Travis decided. He was more than happy to hang out with his parents again, just the three of them.

But in the afternoon his parents began to drift away. His mother went back to the house to start dinner, and his father begged off more pool time and lay down under the big oak tree.

Travis swam and swam—he felt like he could live in the pool. At one point, for no real reason, he looked over at his father.

His father was sitting up and holding his BlackBerry, poking it with a tiny stylus.

Travis watched for a long time. While his father stared at the tiny computer, his face didn't move at all, and Travis couldn't tell what his father was feeling or thinking. He always used to be able to read his father, no matter what his mood. But right now his father didn't look happy or sad or angry or interested or bored. He just stared.

Before the new jobs and the new house, life had been different at home. It seemed like their house was always full. His dad was there, playing music or helping Travis with his homework or just goofing around. His mom, too, who always came home right after her day of teaching third grade. Mostly everyone was home together, doing "life stuff," which is what his family called the ordinary events of their lives.

His dad worked at Sheila's a few nights a week, and sometimes he had gigs with the Not Band on weekends, and his mom occasionally had meetings at night, but the house was never empty. Even after his parents went back to college a few years ago, they were still around all the time. They had their regular jobs *and* homework, but they were home. Everyone was together.

Then they finished their degrees, got new jobs at the same software company in Gilroy, and moved to Bella Linda Terrace. Travis was really starting to hate their new life; it confused him. All that work to get new jobs to make more money to buy a big house, and they were never in that new house.

His parents told Travis they knew these changes were hard on him, but he was a big kid now, they said, and could take care of himself. *He* knew he could take care of himself, but he didn't have to like it.

His father owned four guitars, two keyboards, a herd of harmonicas, and tambourines and other instruments to bang on—bongos, congas, egg shakers—as well as tape decks, speakers, microphones. All this equipment sat in the new garage, unpacked, pushed into one corner. Now there was only the BlackBerry; it had stolen his father's brain.

His father set down the BlackBerry and called Travis out of the pool, time to go.

The house was filled with the scent of his mom's spaghetti sauce and garlic bread, but she wasn't in the kitchen. Travis called out, but she didn't answer. She was in her office. He stood outside the office door and listened to the keys of her computer madly clacking.

✦ ✦ ✦

Sunday was okay. In the morning they went shopping at the big mall north of town. It was a Pants Expedition, one of the funny ways Travis's family shopped—one piece of clothing at a time, shirts or shoes or underwear. They'd shopped like this for years. Today it was pants, and for some reason they all found the word *pants*, even the very idea of pants, funny. They ate lunch at Rotten Roger's Crab Hut, a cheesy chain place, and they all thought that was pretty funny, too.

In the afternoon they went to the pool again, which was much more crowded today. Even Hil was there, and he and Travis played Camazotz zombies, stiff-armed and brick-stepping off the high dive. When Hil and his family left, Travis and his parents sat under the biggest of the scraggly oaks around the pool, and they all read quietly together. His parents were starting to look relaxed.

Through the branches of the oak, the sky was still feathery white clouds. Travis loved this tree, its gnarled, zigzaggy branches. If you could freeze lightning, he thought, it would look like this tree.

It was so comfortable there on the lawn under the

tree—pool splashes echoing, his parents pretending to read but dozing—that Travis almost told them everything.

"You know . . ." he said. He *wanted* to tell them everything, about Camazotz, about the old house, how he'd gone to Salinas on his bike, and the library and Gitano and the boy in the window. But he stopped himself. Maybe there were too many things to talk about any one of them. He shut, quietly, the part of him that wanted to talk about all of this. It felt like closing the cover of an opened book.

"Yes, Travis?" his mom said after a moment. "What were you going to say?"

"Uh, just, you know, that I really like this tree."

And then Monday was school, and school was school, and Hilario was Hil, and everything was the same. But Travis's problem today was having a little too much time to stare out the window, and every time he did, he was drawn back to everything that had happened since last Thursday. None of what had happened would let him go. Something important had changed, but that wasn't the end of the story. This story, whatever it was, was just beginning, and he was determined to follow it.

So when he woke up on Tuesday, he knew he was going back to Oldtown. He had to see the library again, and the Steinbeck House, wanted to look for Gitano. Too much had happened for Travis to ignore it; how could he possibly do his homework? He shouldn't leave the house, he knew that, and it did worry him that he was going to do it, but he went anyway.

Down Natividad over the highway into downtown, the afternoon wind up again under a clear, hot sky, pushing against him, as if trying to stop him.

Downtown he turned right instead of left and scooted through the parking lot of the National Steinbeck Center. It was a modern building, glass and rough brick. Travis always enjoyed the annual field trip. Yes, his class went every year, as every student in every class in Salinas went every year, but that didn't mean it wasn't cool. You'd think a museum devoted to a writer would be nothing but books and blank paper and a desk, maybe a pen. What else was there to a writer's life?

But the National Steinbeck Center wasn't so much about the man who wrote the books as about the books themselves. Steinbeck's best-known novels had been turned into rooms, big rooms with high, black ceilings, one room for each book. You stepped into the book—a lettuce-packed railcar from *East of Eden,* the rusted boiler used as an apartment in *Cannery Row* and *Sweet Thursday,* the ranch hands' bunkhouse in *Of Mice and Men.*

Travis had been many times, and the rooms were pretty much the same now as when he started in first grade, but it was always fun, walking into those books.

He kept on and pulled up in front of the Steinbeck House. An old woman in a long white apron was sweeping the front porch. Otherwise, everything at the house was still. Travis looked to the attic window. It was dark, there was no one there.

He lowered his bike and went up the walk.

"Excuse me, ma'am?" he said. "Are you open at night?"

The woman stopped sweeping and leaned against one of the porch's pillars. Under her apron she wore a red Victorian-era dress.

"No, I'm sorry. We only serve lunch. Close at three. No dinners."

"Oh, I see. Thank you." Travis stared at the front door.

"Anything else?" the woman asked.

"But someone stays here at night, right?"

"Lord, no. But funny you should ask. Just today I was thinking about a customer we had a few years back. Strange little man, wanted to spend the night here. Offered us quite a bit of money, too. Big Steinbeck fan. I had to say no. I told him—and this is the truth—no one's spent the night here in over thirty years. Since we opened the restaurant. Our insurance doesn't allow it. Told him we were pretty sure the house was haunted. Should have seen his face. White as a sheet."

The woman laughed and slapped her knee.

"Oh, okay. Well, um, thank you."

"You're welcome, young man. Come back for lunch soon."

Travis sped off to the library.

The man who called himself Gitano wasn't there. Travis felt that if he could see him again, he'd be able to figure out why Gitano seemed so real and yet so out of place at the same time.

He poked around in the trees by the mural of Old Salinas; maybe Gitano was sleeping back there. He stepped closer to the mural and leaned into it, squinting. In the background of the sepia-tone painting of Main Street a hundred years ago, among the tiny horses and carriages at the far end of the street, walked a figure in a serape and an old straw hat. The man in the straw hat was leading a horse, headed out of Salinas and into the hills. It could almost have been Gitano, but Travis was pretty sure Gitano didn't have a horse.

As he went into the library, he felt a pull of disappointment that the boy in the window and Gitano weren't around. But that didn't matter much; he was here. He had some questions for Miss Babb, questions he knew she could help him answer.

Over the weekend he'd been reading Steinbeck's *The Pastures of Heaven* and Ernest Oster's *Corral de Tierra*. He knew the two books were about the same place, the same hidden valley, and even though he'd read *Corral de Tierra* a gazillion times, he only had a general idea of where it was. He and his parents had gone there a few times when he was really small, but if he had any memory of those trips, they were overshadowed by the Corral in Oster's book. He knew it was off Highway 68, on the road to Monterey, and in his mind, he could see the stoplight at the intersection of Corral de Tierra Road. What he wanted to know was, could you get there on a bike?

Miss Babb was working on the floor of the picture book shelves in the kids' section, which looked as though Triumphant Weasel and his pals had come through the library, but it was probably just a preschool class.

Miss Babb stood up fast.

"Oh, Mr. Williams," she said, smoothing her long skirt. "I'm so glad you're here. I was hoping you'd come back."

Travis had to smile.

"Have you heard?" she asked him. She seemed excited, but not in a happy way. "We're closing."

"But it's not even five," he said, and the minute he said it, he knew he'd said the wrong thing.

"Oh no, Mr. Williams." Miss Babb put her hand on his shoulder. "We're open until nine tonight. No, the library is closing. Forever. For good."

Travis had no idea what to say. He had no idea if he could say anything.

"We found out today. The city announced it a few hours ago. We'll be closed by next March unless something happens."

Miss Babb stared past Travis, through the window, past anything that might actually be out there.

"But somebody has to do something," Travis said.

"Yes, somebody does."

"Good. Are they gonna do it?" he asked.

"I don't know, Mr. Williams. Are you?"

FOUR

MISS BABB EXPLAINED THAT THE CITY SIMPLY DIDN'T HAVE THE MONEY TO KEEP THE LIBRARY OPEN. The city council had already cut the budget of every city agency as deeply as they could. The library, they deemed, was disposable. There had been a special election last spring—didn't he remember?—for a measure that would raise a special tax, one that would replace the slashed funds—police and fire and roads—and keep the library open. But the voters said no.

Travis did remember the election; they'd discussed it in class. But the election campaign took place while Travis and his parents were getting ready to move. They'd been busy.

Travis and Miss Babb were standing in the kids' section, stone-still and face-to-face, while the world went on around them.

"You can help, Mr. Williams," Miss Babb kept saying.

"But I'm just a kid."

"We need everyone, Travis. Anyone who cares about the library."

She called him by his first name. He didn't know she knew his first name.

"But, I, well . . ."

"But nothing. Butts are for sitting on. Here."

She pulled an orange flyer from a hidden pocket in her skirt. On Thursday, there would be a meeting of the Save Our Library committee.

Travis folded the note and put it in his back pocket.

"I'll think about it."

"No, don't think," she said. "It's too late for thinking."

Travis was in bed reading *The Pastures of Heaven,* but he couldn't concentrate. The TV in his parents' room across the hall chattered and hummed, just loud enough to bother him. He was thinking about the library, tumbling over the fact that it was going to close. Forever.

He was staring at the book he held without reading the words. He was looking at the thing, the object, the pages and the typeface, the cover and the artwork. The glued-together spine. And the striped bar code and the paper sleeve and the renewal card. The black stamp on the edge of the pages, PROPERTY OF SALINAS PUBLIC LIBRARY.

The book's paper cover showed a color photograph of the Castle, an odd formation of rocks at the top of a steep mountain; it was a honeycomb of caves and pillars carved in pale yellow rock. Travis knew this place was called the Castle because a credit on the back of the book told him so. And he knew it, too, from Oster's *Corral de Tierra*; in Oster's book many of young Steinbeck's most exciting adventures had taken place on or near it.

On the inside of the front cover of the book someone had scribbled in ink in one corner. The scribble was a wild spiral, penny-sized. Part of the scribble, though, showed no ink, just rounded grooves in the cover's thick paper. Travis could feel the grooves with his fingertip. He guessed that someone reading the book had been taking notes, and the pen had stopped working, gotten clogged at the nib, and this person had tried to start the flow of ink by scribbling these circles.

This was something about library books that Travis loved, evidence of the other people who had read the same book. Dog-eared pages, old bookmarks, slips of torn paper, a stripe of colored marker on a page, coffee and food stains, every once in a while a booger. Sometimes people wrote notes in the margins, usually in pencil; one of his favorites he'd found in a bad science-fiction novel: OH PUH-LEEZE! Travis couldn't have agreed more; that part of the book was really boring.

Reading a library book wasn't something you did on your own. It was something you shared with everyone who had ever read that book. You read the book in private, yes, but other hands had been on it, had softened its pages and loosened its spine. With hardcovers, the clear shiny Bro-Dart, put on to protect the dust jacket, quickly got scuffed and crinkly, and sometimes you would find a thumbprint pressed into the plastic.

The book, when you were done with it, went back to the library, and from there to other hands. When you read a library book, you were connected to all these strangers.

And now the library was going to close. Totally not fair. He'd just found it again, found some way into his old life, a way into the person he was before Bella Linda Terrace. He'd gone to the library looking for a book, but he found so much more. And they were going to close it? Completely, totally not fair.

He could stay in his room and sulk, that was easy.

Maybe Miss Babb was right, though, maybe he could help save the library.

No, not maybe. He had to.

✦ ✦ ✦

The Paraiso Conference Room in the library basement was jammed with the oddest assortment of people Travis had ever seen in one place. There were quite a few grandparents, older people with gray and silver hair, and some moms, or they seemed like moms, and a couple of sets of parents, and one very serious-looking man in an important-looking suit. Travis counted eighteen people altogether; only two of the seats at the long table were empty. He was glad he'd come, but he was a little embarrassed to be the only kid.

"Thank you all for coming," Miss Babb said. "But before we get started, I want to make sure you all have something to drink and some cookies. Rule number one for saving the world: Always have cookies."

Travis sat directly across from Miss Babb. He looked down at the mountain of Oreos in front of him.

"We're still shy a couple of folks, but—oh, here they are. Constancia, Hilario, come on in; get some cookies."

Travis turned to find Hil and his mother, both a little out of breath.

He smiled at Hil, but tried to turn away, as if acknowledging Hil would make everyone else in the room aware that he was just a kid. Hil, however, would not put up with being ignored.

"Big T," he said. "My man, give me some." And he put out his hand for a Camazotz handshake. They'd invented the handshake that day on Hil's porch when they invented the Camazotz video game. It was a slow-motion, dead-faced, super-serious handshake that went on forever. Travis hoped no one was watching.

"Welcome, everyone," Miss Babb said. "To the first meeting of the Save Our Library committee."

There was a scattering of quiet applause, what Travis's dad called "tennis clapping."

"You all know why I've called you here," Miss Babb said. "But I'd like to hear from you why *you* came. Tell us why you want to save the library. Jack, let's start with you."

"Okay," an older man said, sitting up straight. He was bald with a silver goatee, and Travis recognized him from last week. He'd checked out books on hydrology, and Miss Babb had made a joke about wells and digging. "My name's Jack Ray, and I'm a biblioholic." Everyone laughed. A biblioholic, Travis knew, was someone addicted to books.

"Seriously," Jack said. "I love this library. Think about it—all these books and they're free. It's amazing. Now that I'm retired, I don't have much money to spend on books and I depend on the library to feed my reading habit. I'm worried that those of us in Salinas without the money to go to the mall, well, where will we get our books? Without books, I'll be even poorer. Much poorer."

Travis had never thought about the library that way. He knew that when they'd lived in Oldtown his parents didn't have much money, but he only knew that because now they had more money. When they used to go to the library, it was a fun family day, and he didn't think, back then, that they did it to save money. His parents bought him books from the mail-order catalogs his teachers handed out, occasionally they'd buy him a new book at a bookstore, and he always got at least one new book on his birthday and at Christmas. But the library, that's where books came from. And they were free.

Next was Olive Hamilton, one of the grandmotherly women. She was dressed all in purple.

"I agree with everything Jack said." Olive's eyes were pale gray but sparkly. "So let me add this. The Internet. Don't have a computer; ain't gonna get one. They're just too darn ugly. But I do need one now and then—to send e-mails to old friends, and all that. Especially for my family tree, learning about my ancestors. Do you have any idea how many people use the Internet for genealogical research? Without the library, I wouldn't have a place to surf."

Miss Babb went around the room. Everyone had something unique and important to say about the library. People loved the morning story hours for their younger children; so many children had learned to read here. Magazines and newspapers from all over helped people learn about events in the world that TV didn't show them. The librarians, someone said, were so good at helping people find the exact book they needed or wanted or would love; otherwise, it would take forever to go through the entire collection. The library hosted book clubs, cultural celebrations—Travis loved the Day of the Dead festivities in the fall and the Chinese New Year celebrations in February—and readings by authors, both published and unpublished, sometimes readings by local school kids.

When the man in the fancy suit spoke, he talked about the library as a quiet place, a bit of relief from the bustle of everyday life. Not simply, he said, because Miss Babb was always shushing him—Miss Babb blushed now—but because it wasn't about buying things. The library was quiet in a lot of ways, and the man in the suit appreciated that.

Miss Babb took notes the whole time.

Then it was Travis's turn. He thought everything that could be said about the library had been. He took a sip of fizzy water.

"I like the way the books feel," he said. He told the committee what he'd thought about while reading *The Pastures of Heaven*, how a library book connected you to strangers, not just the writer, but to all those people who had read the book before you.

He hadn't thought ahead; the words came to him when he spoke.

He also wanted to tell them about how coming to the library last week had been so important to him, how it made him feel at home again. But he stopped himself. This meeting was about the library, not about Travis, and those thoughts were personal anyway. He wanted to stay focused on what was best for the library, and then he was proud of himself for being so mature. He simply said thanks, and he was done.

"My name is Constancia Espinoza," Hil's mother said. "I was born in Salinas. My grandparents were farm-workers, my parents, too, and so was I for a long time. It was very hard for my family to keep us kids in school. So I learned to read at this library. I learned to read at the same time as my son." She turned to Hil, who was beaming. "Every day someone here is learning to read. The Resource Center helped me with career counseling, and because of that, I got a better job. And because of that, we now own our own home. There are so many of us in this valley—mostly we speak Spanish, but some who spoke English first, too—who want to learn how to read, to make better lives for our families. That's why we have to save the library. Gracias."

There were a few tears in the corners of her eyes when she finished.

Hil was the last to go. He talked about his mom a little bit, telling everyone that learning to read at the same time as his mom wasn't only about a better job. It was a lot of fun, too.

And then he told everyone about *A Wrinkle in Time*. He told them all about Bella Linda Terrace, and how it was like Camazotz. It was Travis's idea, he said, but he would never have known that about where he lived if it weren't for that book. He told them about the afternoon on the porch when he and Travis invented the Camazotz video game and handshake. He wanted everyone to know that books weren't just about wasting time, or because some teacher made you read. "Books," Hil said, "help you see the world better."

At first Travis was surprised that Hil had spilled their

big secret, but while he was talking, Travis saw that everyone there was nodding and laughing—Hil was always funny, he couldn't be unfunny—and Travis figured the library was the best place of all to talk about Camazotz.

Everyone at the table, absolutely everyone, had read and loved *A Wrinkle in Time*. Some had read the book when they were kids, and some had read it as adults. Travis's father and mother often read his books when he was finished with them, but he always assumed that was just his parents being weird; he loved the idea of other grown-ups reading kids' books. Soon the whole room was talking about Madeleine L'Engle and what a great writer she was. Jack Ray made Hil and Travis stand up and show them the handshake. Everyone laughed.

"And with that," Miss Babb said. "Let's take a break. We've got an awful lot of cookies to eat."

After the break, Miss Babb took over. She explained the library's predicament as clearly as she could; it cost the city more than eight million dollars a year to fund the library, and there was no longer any money for that. Travis could tell by all the head-nodding and long sighs around the table that everyone knew what was going on. And they were obviously not pleased.

Miss Babb changed gears quickly. Yes, the outlook was grim, but there was no time to dwell on that, that would get them nowhere. There was work to be done.

First, she told them, they had to raise money, anything they could get to keep the library open, even if only for an extra day. Every day the library was open meant it wasn't closed. And second, they had to raise awareness, had to let everyone in Salinas, and all over the world, know about the impending doom. Publicity was key.

Travis was nodding now, his frustration falling away as a sense of hope for the library came into Miss Babb's voice. Of course, Travis thought, if everyone everywhere knew, they would not let the library close. He was amazed that his feelings could swing so quickly, and simply because of words.

"I have two words for you," Miss Babb said. "John Steinbeck. This is, after all, the John Steinbeck Library. We cannot overlook that. With that name behind us, people have to pay attention. We're very lucky about that." There was more nodding and jotting on pads of paper. "Readers around the world love his books. Clearly, *his* library—by which I mean ours—cannot be closed."

Travis thought of all the tourists who tramped through Salinas looking for Steinbeck's places and characters. If everyone who'd ever read a Steinbeck book would just send in one dollar, Salinas could build a library as big as a football stadium. It was a crazy idea, he knew, but just maybe . . . He started to put up his hand. No, it really was a crazy idea.

Miss Babb wanted them all to know that the Save Our Library committee was not alone, that it was only one of many committees getting to work on the problem. The library's director and administration were working hard with the city to find a solution—cutting hours, cutting staff and services, anything to stay open. Rally Salinas, which Miss Babb called an "umbrella organization," would coordinate the different committees and spearhead the publicity drive. The National Steinbeck Center would help, too. Travis imagined all the other people at all the other tables around town, everyone nodding and sighing and being frustrated and hopeful.

"But you all," she said, "you are the people who actually use the library, so it's important that your voices be heard. The voices of the readers."

"What do we do first?" Travis asked. He hadn't really meant to say anything, but now seemed a good time, and he felt that if he didn't say something, his head was going to explode.

"You always ask the right question, Mr. Williams. I count on you for that." Miss Babb smiled at him.

She handed out flyers with all the news on them, along with the phone numbers and e-mail addresses of the mayor and the city council. Committee members should pass out flyers to anyone who would take them and urge people to contact the city government. This was the first wave of publicity, but it was only the beginning.

What about money? Couldn't they raise money? A bake sale, a book sale, a garage sale? The questions were flying.

"Absolutely," Miss Babb said. "Who's going to volunteer?"

Hil's hand shot up.

"Me and T," he said. "We can do a car wash. Three bucks a pop."

Travis did the math. Or close enough.

"But we'd have to wash three million cars."

"Fine, five bucks," Hil said. "And that's not the point. No way we can raise that much money. But we go out on the corner, and some people stop and get their cars washed. That can't hurt. *And* everybody sees us. *And* our ginormous Save Our Library banner."

"Okay," Travis said. "I'm in."

"And by the way," Hil said. "The banner should have a giant sun on it, don't you think? The flyers should, too."

Miss Babb looked at Hil, her head tilted.

"Well, it's S-O-L, isn't it, Save Our Library?" Hil said. He looked around, but no one answered. "Sol? It's Spanish for the sun."

"Oh, that's perfect, Hilario," Miss Babb said. "Can anyone draw a sun?"

To Travis's surprise, the man in the important-looking suit raised his hand.

"Now, what's next?" Miss Babb said.

By the end of the meeting, five different projects were planned and the responsibilities divvied up, and the next meeting of the committee was scheduled. The city council would meet in a few weeks to make its final decision, and the committee had to be ready.

"We're done saving the world for today," Miss Babb said. "See you next week. Are there any cookies left?"

Not one crumb.

On the way out, Travis picked up a copy of *The Long Valley* from the long shelves of Steinbeck's work near the main checkout counter. The book was displayed on top, face out, on a one-book wire stand. He wasn't finished with the books he'd checked out last week, but there was something about the library that always made him want more books. Sometimes when he was with his parents—before the move—he'd take more books than he could possibly read in the three weeks he was allowed to have them. And today, the urge to take another book was even stronger, as if he had to stock up before the library closed.

Besides, he was already done with *The Pastures of Heaven*—and halfway through a second time—and something about that book was calling him to read more Steinbeck. In *The Pastures of Heaven,* nothing and no one were quite what they seemed. The man who told everyone he was rich had very little money. The deformed Tularecito was thought by most people to be a freak, but he turned out to be an amazingly talented artist. And the place itself, the Corral de Tierra, was imagined as a paradise, yet it was dangerous and mysterious. Maybe Steinbeck had more to tell him about those things that weren't what they seemed; maybe Travis could learn something from Steinbeck about his own world. Couldn't hurt to take one more book.

Outside the evening was beautiful, deep purple and hushed. The heat had dropped again, and there was a hint of real autumn around the edges of Indian summer. Travis could smell the new season in the air—baked soil and dead leaves waiting for the first rains. There was no wind, only a gentle breeze.

Hil's mom and Miss Babb were talking and laughing

together. Miss Babb tapped Travis on the shoulder as he went by, and smiled her thank-you smile. Hil was waiting for him.

"Dude, Hil," Travis said. "Great idea about the car wash. And the sun, too. Sol, I get it. I had no idea you were so into the library, I mean—"

"I know, T," he said. "I know what you thought. I know you're tired of playing video games, I get it. You're thinkin', ol' Hil, he's just a vidiot, glued to the tube, sits there—"

"No, no," Travis said. "It's just that I, I mean, we, well, until—"

"Camazotz day. I know. It's cool, T, I didn't know either. But it doesn't matter. We're here now."

"Yeah."

Travis put out a robotic hand, and they executed a lengthy Camazotz handshake.

"Travis, would you like a ride home?" Hil's mom asked.

He was dying to go by the Steinbeck House again, but wasn't quite ready to tell Hil about what he'd seen there. It was probably just some teenager sneaking around, but why would a sneaky teenager break into a house to sit in the window? No, it was more than that, he just wasn't sure what. He wanted to check into it.

He begged off, told Hil and his mom he had an errand to run—what it might be, he'd never be able to say. He made plans with Hil to meet the next day and work out the car wash details, then fetched his bike.

Deep into the alley, Travis spotted a small fire under a willow tree. Gitano was sitting before the fire, and perched on the fire was an open tin can. Gitano stirred it slowly with a stick. The scent of pork and beans rose up to Travis.

Travis wasn't sure if he was happy to see Gitano. He kept wanting to see him, wanted to ask him questions. He couldn't shake the idea that Gitano and the boy in the window, all of it, everything that had started with his return to the library, were all connected somehow. But what would you say to this tired old man? Hello, can you tell me about Camazotz?

Gitano looked at him and smiled, then gulped down a heap of beans from a wooden spoon.

He wanted to ride past the Steinbeck House. And then again, he didn't. So he rode the blocks around it for a while. But that was crazy, too. The boy in the window was just a boy in the window, as Gitano was just an old man down on his luck and eating beans in an alley. What else could it be? If the boy wasn't in the window, that would be fine with Travis, he'd have his answer. And that answer was that the world was still the same old world.

Travis stopped in front of the house. The light was on in the attic window; the boy was at the desk, his head down, not looking up. He was concentrating.

Night was coming on. It was much darker than the last time Travis was here—man, he was going to be so late—and because of that, because the night outside was darker, the lights inside brighter, and the contrast between the two sharper, he could see the attic in more detail. It was clear that the boy was writing something. Every once in a while, he'd bring the pen to his face, tapping the end of it against his cheek; he was thinking. Then the pen would disappear, return to the paper.

The boy's head was moving back and forth now, slowly, following the trail of words he left on the page. Occasionally, he'd look up at the ceiling; occasionally, he'd look out the window. Travis waved once when he did this, but the boy didn't respond. Then, as the image of the boy came into sharper focus, Travis saw, quite clearly, that this boy had large ears, ears that stuck way out. Just like Steinbeck.

Travis actually felt a chill down his spine. And then he said out loud the words he'd been dying to say out loud, "It *is* Steinbeck's ghost." The words rang in the air, and the world stayed pretty much the same. The words sounded true, and there was no denying them.

Travis did a little dance on the sidewalk, a sort of goofy, Hilario kind of dance, to see if that would rouse the figure in the window. But no, the boy kept writing. Travis was sure of this: The boy in the window was writing something. A police car came around the corner a block away, and Travis jumped on his bike and headed off. He wasn't doing anything wrong, he knew that, but it was a good excuse to get away, get on home.

The ride home was a snap, no traffic, no wind, a great night for a bike ride, and Travis thought that perhaps he'd never ridden his bike any faster. He was racing home, trying to get there before his parents had time to invent new punishments for him. But he was also way too excited to ride any other way.

So much had happened in the last few days—the library, Gitano, and yes, that really was Steinbeck's ghost—but he didn't know what to do with it all. He wasn't afraid of what was happening, and was pretty sure zombies and ghouls weren't suddenly going to be chasing him down the street. He knew these things were all connected—but how, and why? What did this mean? His brain was an enormous hamster wheel with hundreds of hamsters spinning around and around. So he pedaled to keep up with the hamsters, pedaled and panted and flew all the way home.

He shot off Natividad and was zooming down Boronda, about to glide through the gates of Bella Linda Terrace, when he saw them.

On the ridge of the Gabilan foothills closest to Bella Linda Terrace, three black silhouettes stood looking over the valley, toward the Santa Lucia Mountains, toward Corral de Tierra. The figures were as still as stone, but they were definitely human. No movement at all, just watching.

He skidded the bike to a stop.

All the not-thinking he'd done on the bike ride, all the not-thinking he'd pedaled into himself, vanished. He knew who these figures were, and he knew it immediately. There was a Steinbeck story, "Flight," where a man was being chased by sheriff's deputies through the Santa Lucia Mountains near Big Sur, and all during the chase, whenever the man looked up, he found three black figures standing on ridge tops high above him. The man knew they were not chasing him, they were simply watching him.

Travis knew that the figures on the ridge below Fremont Peak were Steinbeck's Watchers. And that story, "Flight," was in *The Long Valley,* which he had in his backpack.

He gazed up at the Watchers. They were not looking at him. They were looking far away, into the west. Then they turned in unison and disappeared from the ridge, as if they'd been waiting for Travis to arrive.

Travis knew what he had to do, if he could just get his feet to cooperate. He was going to go home, turn on all the lights, and watch some mindless television until he fell asleep. Maybe even beg his parents for a Gamebox.

His parents!

He pumped all the way home and, just as he was about to cruise into the driveway, heard a car honking behind him. Travis tore into the house before his parents could say anything, grabbed the note he'd left for them off the kitchen table, and slammed into the bathroom.

The note had said he was at Hil's, and that wouldn't work anymore. He had to think of something else—he was just out riding around Bella Linda Terrace. That'd do. His parents believed him, but they weren't happy he had been out after dark. They gave him the "better be more careful" lecture. Standing there in the kitchen with them, he really wanted to be angry, but he couldn't. It was a lie, a stupid lie at that, and he had to stick to it.

After a late dinner, Travis and his parents watched a silly cop show together, but he couldn't relax, couldn't get everything out of his head. He kept wanting to talk to his parents, tell them everything that had happened. But just like over the weekend, he kept his mouth shut. How did you even begin to tell your parents about ghosts and Watchers? So he watched some cops shoot at guys and drink coffee and drive recklessly: TV.

Later, in his room, he sat at his desk for a long time and looked out at Salinas, a pearl-string of lights along the highway, and at the barely visible outline of the Santa Lucias, to where the Watchers had been watching.

He got into bed, cracked open *The Long Valley,* and turned to the story called "Flight."

FIVE

AFTER SCHOOL ON FRIDAY, HIL AND TRAVIS COMPLETELY SCOPED OUT THE CAR WASH SCHEME. Hil was an excellent planner, and between the two of them, they had, they imagined, everything covered. Hil would contact the Old Stage shopping center, two blocks from the entrance to Bella Linda Terrace, and get permission to use the corner of their parking lot at the intersection of Natividad and Boronda. He would arrange to have a banner made and, with his father, figure out a way to raise it: Car Wash—Save Our Library—$5.00, and the big sun. Travis would collect the other materials, the towels and hoses and soap. He figured his parents would help with this.

When they were done planning, they walked around Bella Linda Terrace and hit every house with a flyer. Travis noticed something he'd not seen before. Every house in Bella Linda Terrace had a satellite dish—including his own—and every dish pointed to the same spot in the sky. The houses looked as if they were scanning the galaxy for news from the Mother Planet. Travis pointed this out to Hil.

"Yeah," he said. "You know, the more we talk about it, the weirder this place gets. I'm gonna blame you, T. You started it. Because of you, I know I live on this really strange planet. Before you, I was perfectly happy here."

They agreed, though, that it was better to travel this weird planet together. With every block, Hil and Travis expanded their ideas for the Camazotz video game, imagining the unexpected worlds behind the dull facade of each neighbor's house.

Travis and his parents ate at Sheila's again that weekend. Halfway through their burgers and fries, Travis brought up the library closing. He knew he had to be careful.

"You hear about the library?" he asked them.

That seemed safe enough.

"I know," his dad said. "It's horrible. I love that place."

"Do you remember," his mom said, "how we used to go there every Saturday?"

"Of course I remember," he said. She talked about

the library as if it were an extinct dinosaur. "The last time we went was only a few months ago. *Before* we moved."

"Maybe we could go again," his dad said. "That'd be nice."

"It's just so stupid," Travis said. "How could they close the library? I mean, it's the library. People need to have free access to all that information."

His mom looked at him with really big eyes.

"That's true," his dad said. "But you know, the taxes are already so high. There's just not enough money."

"But that's not the whole picture," Travis said. "The state's cut off so much money we used to get from them for things like fire and police. And libraries. The state's making us pay for their poor planning."

His mom's eyes got a lot smaller then; Travis couldn't see into them. His dad looked at his mom, but she only looked at Travis.

"Good point. I guess," his dad said. "But you have to understand, Travis." This was a bad sign. If his dad used his name, and started with "you have to understand," he was obviously going to say something Travis did not want to understand.

"The world's changing," his dad went on, "and there's just not that kind of money anymore. At least not around here. We pay taxes, and they're killing us. I'll miss the library, too; I wish we could save it. But I'm sorry to say, I don't think we can. It's a different world nowadays, Travis. I don't like it either."

His dad looked out at Main Street. Travis looked, too. The world, at least here in Oldtown, looked pretty much the same.

"But we have to do something," Travis said. He felt himself rising up in his chair. "I mean, we have to try. We love the library."

"Well, yes, we do. I know that." His dad turned to him. "But what?"

"We can have a car wash."

Travis's mom and dad looked at each other, a weird surprise on their faces, as if Travis had just sprouted ears and a tail.

"Ooooo-kaaaay," they cooed.

Travis spelled it out for them, the car wash plan. He made sure they knew it wasn't only about the money, but publicity, too.

Instantly his dad got into it, and Travis felt the old spark he used to see in his dad, *before* the new job. On one of the restaurant's paper place mats they sketched out everything.

"She," his dad called, and Sheila, the owner and his dad's old boss, came out from behind the long wooden bar. Travis had always loved the bar here, not just for the cherries and olives his dad used to give him, but because it looked old enough to belong in a Wild West saloon.

"What's up, Don, Lyndsay? And Travis, my handsome man. You look like you need a favor. Don't ask for your job back, though. I got enough trouble."

She put a glass of olives and cherries in front of Travis. Sheila was pretty and funny and smart, and she always treated Travis like a friend.

"Towels, She," his dad said. "We need lots of towels."

Sheila agreed to rent more towels from her supplier—the bar used about three hundred a week. His dad offered to pay, but Sheila refused. It was a noble cause, she said. She loved the library, too.

While Travis and his dad were working on the car wash plan, his mom grew quieter and quieter, and sat back with her arms folded. She was onto him, Travis knew. She was going to sit back and wait until Travis slipped up. Then she'd pounce. Travis clearly knew way too much about the library.

"Who else is gonna help with the car wash?" his dad asked.

His mom leaned forward, her arms still crossed. He was the bird in the birdbath, she was the cat. He was doomed.

So he gave up.

"The committee," he said. "The Save Our Library committee." He pulled a folded flyer from his back pocket and handed it to his mom.

"So," she said. "Tell me about this committee."

There was a tiny smile hiding in her face. Maybe it wouldn't be that bad.

His parents were pretty mad. About him riding his bike to the library, sure, but mostly mad that he hadn't told them. He had lied to them, and he knew it and they knew it.

Still, during the excruciatingly long and quiet drive home, they didn't go ballistic. The word "punishment" had yet to surface. They were being calm—angry but calm.

So Travis played it the same way. He wanted to yell at them, yell that they had stranded him on Camazotz and it wasn't fair and he was bored out of his gourd and at least they got to go to work and the library was something he cared about, but they wouldn't know about that, would they, they were always at work. The words rose up in him, but he didn't let them out.

He would let his parents be right—they *were* right,

on one level—and not insist on his being right—oh, *he* was right, too. He had played this game before, waiting, and it felt good to be bigger than his anger. He let his parents do most of the talking.

At home, around the dining room table, the deal was made. His parents knew the library was important to him, and they were beginning to see that they had to give him more freedom, too.

So. He could ride his bike to the library, when it was daylight—by daylight they meant the sun was still visible—and when it wasn't raining. If it was raining, he had to take the bus. But coming back, especially in the dark, yes, in the evening, too, was another thing. He would have to get a ride back, with Hil's mom, or maybe Miss Babb, or one of the other committee members. Or he could wait for his parents to come get him.

Agreed? Deal. Pinkie swears all around.

Not bad, Travis thought. Not bad at all.

The next meeting of the Save Our Library committee was held in a larger conference room, the Ricketts Room, named for Doc Ricketts, Steinbeck's best friend. This room was more like a theater, all chairs and no long table, but still too small for the turnout that night. Miss Babb stood at a lectern, and every speaker had to stand to be heard. The original committee members had brought friends, and some new members came because of the flyers. They were thirty-seven altogether.

Travis drove in with Hil and his mom. To go over the car wash with him, and to make his parents happy.

Each of the five subcommittees gave their reports and doled out responsibilities to new volunteers. Over the coming weekend there would be a bake sale in front of the Maya Cinema, a used book sale in front of the library, a tamale sale in the Alisal neighborhood, and an information table in front of the National Steinbeck Center for out-of-town visitors. And the car wash.

Nine people, including Miss Babb, signed up to help with the car wash.

Travis signed up for a new subcommittee, the mailing committee, which would stuff envelopes and mail out flyers to every address in Salinas, and to magazines, newspapers, and libraries and library associations around the world.

Miss Babb had never looked so excited. She seemed to be glowing. At the end of the meeting she hugged Travis and thanked him about a hundred times.

Travis had Hil's mom drive past the old house on Riker, said he wanted Hil to see it. But honestly, it was because he knew this route would take them past the Steinbeck House. They were going pretty fast down Central, but Travis saw, if only briefly, that the light was on, and the dark shape of the writer sat in the window.

Steinbeck's ghost. It had to be.

The day was ideal for a car wash. It was the first of October, and Indian summer was hanging on, bright and crisp and dry. The sky was a smooth blue plate.

Hil's father, a round bald man with tattoos up and down his arms, helped put up the banner. He'd planted two tetherball poles in old car tires he'd filled with concrete, and the three of them stretched the banner across the shopping center's main corner. The banner was professionally made; it was huge and no one could miss it. The sun design, all yellow and smiling and reading an open book, made Travis happy just looking at it. Theodore, the man in the important-looking suit, had done a great job.

The car wash was all set up by ten, but by ten thirty they hadn't washed a single car. Travis kept stacking and restacking the towels, checking the soapy water.

Then Hil—leave it to Hil—had an idea. Hil's father pulled his enormous gold truck into the car wash's orangeconed lane, and Travis began washing it. Hil stood on the sidewalk close to the stoplights and did a crazy dance, pointing all the while to the banner. Once he even dropped to his knees, his hands clasped, a frightful beggar.

A minute later the first car pulled in. When the first committee members arrived—Jack Ray and Theodore, both in shorts and T-shirts—seven cars were waiting in line.

The line never ended. All day long the cars kept coming, and so did the volunteers. A circus, Travis thought, a real riot. The cars got washed and dried—vacuumed for two bucks extra—but not without a lot of fun.

It was Miss Babb who started the water fights. Late in the afternoon, she came up to Travis, who was taking a break, and asked him if he was hot and tired and needed some refreshment. When he said, "Oh yeah," she lifted one of the hoses and let him have it full blast, right in the chest. Travis shook his hands and looked down at his shirt. Then slowly, very slowly, he leaned over, picked a soapy rag out of a bucket and threw it right at her, bull's-eye. At that moment, Travis felt water stinging him from behind. It was his dad brandishing one of the other hoses, and Travis ran after him with fistfuls of soapy rags. Within minutes, every volunteer, and several customers, were drenched and bubbly.

All day long there was music and food and talk talk talk. And laughter. They took turns passing out flyers in front of the Safeway and the Colonel Foxworthy's Coffee Emporium and the Mango Tango juice bar. Everyone they talked to seemed concerned about the library, almost angry. More than five hundred flyers were passed out.

Near the end of the day, Travis was sitting alone under the banner, tired and wet, when he realized that it was still noisy at the car wash. The talking wouldn't stop. Hil's dad and Travis's mom stood talking with Miss Babb, and everyone's hands were flying everywhere, and Travis knew they were talking about the library. Hil and Jack Ray were looking at one of the flyers and pointing to it, obviously coming up with better information and designs for the next one.

When he'd first heard about the library closing, Travis had felt completely alone. Now, he knew, he was part of something huge, and he figured that, with everyone working together, the library might stand a chance of winning. He'd played soccer when he was in third and fourth grade, and the coaches were always talking about teamwork. For the first time he felt like he knew what a team really was: each person working toward the same goal.

The last car was dried and buffed a little after six. An

enormous moon, bursting orange, rose from behind the lime quarry against the mountains. When they counted the money in the cigar box, and added the money from the tip jar—Travis's idea—it came to $578.44. That was a long way from eight million dollars, but it hardly seemed to matter.

✦ ✦ ✦

After the car wash, Travis and his parents went to Hil's house for pizza with his family. It was the first time the two families had gotten together, and the talking just continued, about everything under the sun. It almost felt, Travis thought, like the old days. And on Sunday, both families hung out at the pool—wet again—a great day made a little bigger by the glow of the car wash's success.

But when dinner was over on Sunday and Travis went up to his room to catch up on homework—he was really behind—suddenly all the excitement was gone. His room was just his room, nothing more. He walked around it and looked at all his stuff, as if he were seeing it for the first time. His room and his life looked absolutely normal to him, and that's what was weird about it.

He had continued to live his normal life—going to school, watching TV, listening to music—but he had this other life now, and it felt more important than his normal life. It—Camazotz, the library, the books, Gitano, Steinbeck's ghost—felt like his real life now. Hil was somewhere in the middle, sometimes a part of his normal life and sometimes a part of his real life. Travis didn't know yet where Hil would end up.

Yes, those were the right words, *normal* and *real*. They could have meant the same thing, those words, but there was a big difference, Travis felt. Normal was the everyday life, the dum-dee-dum-dum kind of life, the walking down the street but not paying too much attention life, the life the whole world lived. The real life was the wide-awake, eyes-open, noticing-every-rock-and-every-shift-of-wind life, the life each person lived when they were most alive.

In his Sunday-quiet bedroom, Travis stood suspended for a moment between his normal life and his real one. Which one should he follow? He didn't have a choice, really. He'd have to follow both lives, live in both worlds.

He looked around his room. Yes, his normal life was still there—there was his computer, there was his CD player, his basketball. He would wake up in the morning, and his normal life would continue.

He looked at the stacks of books on his desk. These were his new life, his real life. *A Wrinkle in Time* led him to the library. Which led him to *Corral de Tierra*, which led him to *The Pastures of Heaven,* which led him to *The Long Valley.* And these books had led him to the other mysteries that surrounded him—Gitano and the Watchers and Steinbeck's ghost—led him deeper into a world he'd never suspected.

Books could do that to you. When you read, the world really did change. He understood this now. You saw parts of the world you never knew existed. Books were in the world; the world was in books.

He sat at his desk and stared out at the Santa Lucias in the west. Tomorrow he would resume his normal life. Tonight he would read.

He flipped through his library copy of *The Pastures of Heaven,* reading the first paragraph of each story, to remind him of what happened in it.

Travis didn't understand everything that happened in *The Pastures of Heaven,* but he knew enough. There was something dark in the stories, some kind of curse. Every family that moved into the Corral expected to find paradise. But they never found it, and often their lives were ruined—they lost their money and their farms, their honor, sometimes their lives. They had all wished too hard for a perfect world. He couldn't help but think of Bella Linda Terrace, and he wondered if his parents had made the same mistake.

When he looked out the window at the Santa Lucias, he didn't only see the silhouette of the mountains. He saw into the past, saw all the people who had ever lived in the Corral, and all the stories about them. He also saw more deeply into his own world, his own life.

After a while he got into bed and opened *The Long Valley*. He'd read "Flight" a few days before, and there he found the Watchers he'd seen on the ridge behind his house. Tonight he started *The Red Pony*, the novella in the back of *The Long Valley*. It was all he could do to keep from crying when Jody's foal Gabilan died, even though he knew that part was coming.

He continued to the second section of *The Red Pony*, "The Great Mountains," and found it was all new to him. He'd forgotten this part, about Jody and the mountains that obsessed him, which Travis now knew were the Santa Lucias. Jody was always looking off toward these mountains, the same view Travis had from his bedroom window.

Then the book almost leaped out of Travis's hands when an old stranger arrived on Jody's father's ranch. The stranger was an old "paisano," half Mexican and half Indian, and he claimed that he had once worked on the ranch. The first thing the old paisano said in the story was, "I am Gitano, and I have come back."

Travis dug himself deeper under the covers and kept reading.

✦ ✦ ✦

In *The Red Pony* Gitano spent much of his time looking at the Great Mountains, the Santa Lucias. When Jody asked him if he'd ever been there, Gitano told him that, yes, he had been there, once. But it was a long time ago, when he was a child. Had he ever been back? Jody wanted to know. No. What had he seen there, in the Great Mountains? Gitano refused to talk about what he'd seen.

A noise broke Travis's reading. But from where?

Travis sat up, looked around his room. The noise—whatever it was, a snapping twig, a door clicking shut—could have come from anywhere. In the fresh silence, Travis heard the echo of the noise. It might've come from the front yard or from inside the house. It might have come out of the book.

He floated through the house. Not a whit of noise, not even his father's incredibly loud snoring.

The memory of the noise, the echo of it, called him outside.

He put on shorts and sandals, went down to the garage, and slipped out the side gate on his bike. Like most kids, Travis knew how to sneak around at night undetected.

The houses of Bella Linda Terrace were bone-white in the harsh glow of the orange streetlights and the white cloud of almost-full moonlight. Tonight every house seemed even more like its neighbor than before.

He shot through the front gate of Bella Linda Terrace and crossed Boronda Road. He pulled up in front of the barbed wire fence that bordered the neighboring foothills. He stared into the world in the night. He wanted to move past the fence, but couldn't.

Were the Watchers at the top of the ridge again? He couldn't tell. Something was up there, shapes moving across the blue-green hills.

He turned to go home. There was Bella Linda Terrace, Camazotz, waiting for him. He had a sudden thought. Did the high stone wall around Bella Linda Terrace keep people out, or keep people in? It was hard to know. Everything looked different under the sodium lights.

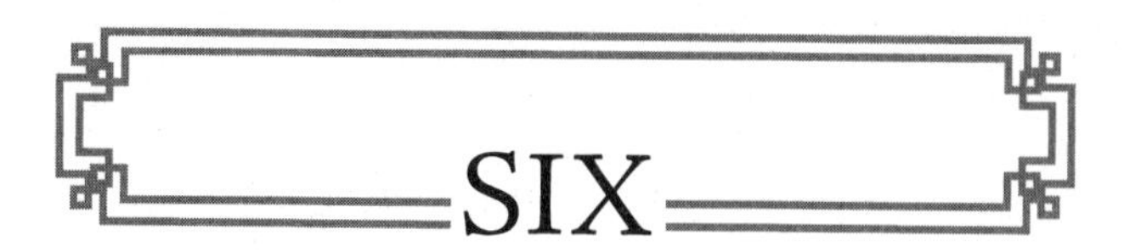

SIX

TRAVIS COULDN'T WAIT TO GET TO THE LIBRARY AND SEE MISS BABB. At school that day, he'd come up with a great idea for the committee to consider.

He was staring at a poster of famous writers behind Miss Galbraith's desk in third-period English, when it struck him. He didn't know who all these writers were, but it was the photos of the writers that inspired his truly simple thought: Writers were real people. At least before they were dead. He knew this thought was connected to Steinbeck's ghost. Seeing Steinbeck's ghost in the attic window had made him realize that writers had been kids once, had grown up somewhere, and were only writers when they sat down to write. They didn't just live in photos on the backs of books.

And if writers didn't care about libraries, then who would? Travis thought the committee should invite famous writers to put on a benefit reading for the library. There had to be famous writers living around here. The committee could sell tickets and raise money, and the more famous the writers, the more publicity for the library.

At lunch he went to the computer lab and surfed the Net, where he found several writers he recognized who lived nearby. Laurence Yep, who wrote *Dragonwings,* lived in Pacific Grove, and Beverly Cleary, who wrote all the Henry Huggins and Ramona and Beezus books, she lived in Carmel. Travis loved both these writers. The one writer he couldn't find was Ernest Oster. It was weird; there wasn't a single mention of Oster or *Corral de Tierra* anywhere on the Internet. He assumed Oster lived near Salinas somewhere, if he was still alive.

Travis wanted to fly into the library and heroically slap the list of writers in front of Miss Babb—he'd imagined this all day—but when he saw her, he knew the time wasn't right. She looked like she'd been punched in the stomach.

The mailing committee was scheduled to work in the library's A/V room, a small office off the back corner of the main collection. One side of the room was stuffed with DVD players, CD players, reel-to-reel tape decks, and a bulky, old-fashioned 16mm film projector. The walls were crowded with shelves of DVDs, CDs, even record albums, the big black vinyl discs his parents used to listen to.

Miss Babb was sitting at a small table, surrounded by boxes of envelopes, stacks of bright green flyers, pages of mailing labels. The other chairs were empty.

"Oh, Travis," Miss Babb said, looking up and forcing a smile. "Bad news. We've canceled the meeting. I tried calling, but you'd left already. I'm sorry."

The other four members of the mailing committee had called earlier that day. Everyone had a good "excuse." Miss Babb said the word *excuse* as if it tasted sour.

"You might as well get on home," she told him. "We'll reschedule, work up some new flyers."

"But I'm here. Can't we just do it anyway? I mean, we have to, the big council meeting is right around the corner."

"That's sweet, Travis. But we'll never get through all these on our own. I think we'll be okay without these flyers. Maybe I'm just too worked up about it all."

"No," he said. "We have to do it. I know we can. Every little bit, right? It might take all night, but we can do it." There was a huge difference between Travis's normal life—school and home and all that—and his new, improved, and much weirder life—the library and everything around it. In this new, improved, and much weirder life, he had endless energy to work on anything. At home, his mom had to beg to get him to load the dishwasher or take out the trash. But at the library, he couldn't wait to get started.

"I can't ask you to stay that late."

"You can ask my parents."

Travis called his mom at work. He always started with his mom. She was the stricter of his parents, and it sometimes seemed easiest going straight to the heart of it. He hated getting permission for something from his father, only to have his mom take it back.

Miss Babb explained everything, promised to give Travis a ride home, ten o'clock at the very latest. Travis swore he'd done his homework already. And this was true, he'd done it at lunch, but he would have lied if he hadn't. The library could not wait. Homework was important, sure. But the library, that needed to be taken care of now.

"Okay, then," Miss Babb said. "Dig in."

She thumbed one flyer from the stack, folded it into three parts, slid it into an envelope, licked the flap and sealed it, then peeled off a mailing label and attached it.

Travis stood over her.

"I bet we can do them all, every single one," he said. "I've got a system."

"Oh, yeah?" she said. "What do you bet?"

"Take-out sushi for dinner. You pay."

"Sushi?" she said, her head cocked to one side.

"Heck, yes. I've been eating sushi since I was born. I mean, we're only a few miles from the ocean. Please tell me you like sushi."

Miss Babb looked from the stacks of envelopes and flyers to Travis, back again.

"You're on," she said.

Travis showed her what to do. One of them would take the envelopes out of the boxes, and stack them so that the flaps were open and tiered like escalator steps. The other would take small stacks of flyers, five or ten, and fold them into threes, but not too creased. The top flyer would slip off easily enough, then it could be zipped into the top envelope. Wet paper towels from the rest room were faster for sealing the envelopes, and no one ended up with the dreaded "mint-glue mouth." When a stack of envelopes was done, Travis would flatten it, putting in the final creases, and when all of the envelopes were done, they would add the mailing labels.

Travis set up two stations to run his system.

"Piece of cake," Miss Babb said. She was obviously delighted, relieved.

"Piece of sushi, you mean."

"I give. You win. Sushi it is."

The flyers flew and the envelopes enveloped, and Travis and Miss Babb talked about, well, about everything—the library and the weather and new movies and old movies. Pretty soon they were deep into the mailing.

While they ate—California rolls with crab and avocado, and unagi nigiri, Travis's favorite, broiled eel on a piece of sticky rice and wrapped with a seaweed belt—Travis spelled out his idea for the benefit reading.

"Funny you should mention it," Miss Babb said. "I was just thinking the same thing today. Now I know it's a good idea. If you had it, too, it's gotta be good."

He showed her the list of writers he'd drawn up. There were twenty-three so far, all of whom lived between Salinas and San Francisco. He figured at least four or five of them would come to their aid.

"We may think alike," she said. "But you actually do the work. This is great, Travis."

"The only one I couldn't find," he said, munching his last piece of unagi, "is Ernest Oster. I'd love to invite him, he'd be perfect. I mean his book is all about Steinbeck and everything, and he'd be great, I just know it. But I can't find anything."

"Yes, that is a shame."

✦ ✦ ✦

The library closed at eight on Tuesdays, and tonight was emptied and locked up by 8:05. Only Travis and Miss Babb remained. It was cool being in the library alone in the dark. Creepy, but cool.

In the fourth grade Travis's favorite book was *From the Mixed-up Files of Mrs. Basil E. Frankweiler* by E. L. Konigsburg. He read it at least five times and did a huge book report on it, including a diorama that showed James and Claudia sleeping in the Metropolitan Museum of Art in New York City. James and Claudia had sneaked into the museum, having run away from their home in Connecticut in search of adventure—Claudia's idea—and hid out in the museum for an entire week, sleeping in a four-hundred-year-old bed that probably belonged to a king. For baths, they splashed around in a big fountain, then scooped up all the coins museum-goers had thrown into it for luck.

Even though nothing too exciting happened in the book—the paintings did not come to life, there were no ghosts or zombies—Travis loved it. He used to dream about being alone in a big museum at night. Being here in the library now was pretty close; he felt sneaky, adventurous.

"Okay," Miss Babb said. "It's time to have some fun."

She hauled out a beige, cloth-covered suitcase and opened it. Inside was a turntable; Travis recognized it from his father's old record albums. Miss Babb was always busy, always doing something, but now that the library had closed and they were alone, she seemed both more relaxed and more full of energy somehow. She was practically dancing as she set everything up.

"This is a record player," she said. "A little bit of the old magic. And this," she said, slipping a big black plate from a cardboard sleeve, "is a record album, thirty-three and a third r.p.m. It's from a time before"—she paused for dramatic effect—"computers ruled the world."

At first they listened to recordings of old radio shows, from way before television—*Fibber McGee & Molly, The Lone Ranger,* Charlie McCarthy, W. C. Fields. Travis was amazed at the vivid pictures that sprang up in his head when he listened to these old shows. He was stuffing and sealing envelopes, but he saw everything those characters did.

Then Miss Babb put on a record of poets reading their own poems, really old recordings, with scratches and pops and hisses. Travis didn't "get" the poems, but it wasn't about "getting" them, Miss Babb said, it was about the words the poets used, about those words sinking into your body. It was about the pleasure of that.

But the best was last.

"Now, Travis," Miss Babb said. "You have to understand that what I'm about to play is a bit risqué. That is, it's totally inappropriate. For anyone. And that's why it's so funny. I give you *Monty Python and the Holy Grail.*"

Travis had watched Monty Python reruns on TV with his dad. Monty Python was a group of comedians from England, perhaps the silliest people who had ever lived. Listening to them in the bright room in the dark library, they were even funnier.

Miss Babb actually fell out of her chair once, she was laughing so hard, and at one point Travis thought he might never breathe again. All Miss Babb had to say was, "She turned me into a newt," and Travis would start laughing all over again.

They finished the very last envelope at ten minutes to ten. Travis called his mom and told her he was on his way home, and he and Miss Babb scrunched his bike into the back of her Volvo. Travis didn't ask her to drive by the Steinbeck House. He knew the window would be lit, the writer at his desk.

All the way home, he and Miss Babb sang Python's "Finland, Finland, Finland, country that I love," and repeated, word for word, the "How Do You Know She Is a Witch?" sketch. He could not get enough of "She turned me into a newt."

Miss Babb parked in front of Travis's house, but before he could get out, she put her hand on his wrist. She'd turned serious on a dime.

"Travis, I have to tell you something. I actually know Ernest Oster. He's a very nice man. But I can't tell you where to find him. I made him a promise years ago. I promised not to tell anyone where he is. He's a very private person, and I can't break that promise."

Miss Babb looked at Travis, right at him, as if she were testing him. It made him a little uncomfortable, but he knew this was a big moment, so he kept his eyes steady, did not look down or away.

"But," she said, "you have a great idea. And the time might be right for Ernest to come out of hiding. Don't ask me any more questions about him, okay? I already feel like I'm cheating. Just listen. You can find him. And it's easy. Everything you need to know is in the library. And that's all I can say. Deal?"

They shook on it.

✦ ✦ ✦

Travis and his parents had to park blocks away from City Hall. Normally Oldtown Salinas was deserted at night, the streets and sidewalks empty, most of the businesses closed. Tonight, though, the place was jumping, streams of people headed in the same direction. The city council's only agenda item tonight was the library, and Travis couldn't believe all these people were here to save it. Just awesome, he thought.

The city council's chamber was a squat, glass-walled building—Travis thought it looked like a bottle cap—right next to the sidewalk on Lincoln Street, but tonight it was impossible to see. News vans, their white antennae aimed at the sky, blocked the view. There were news crews from all over: local stations, San Francisco stations, national stations, even one painted with what looked like Swedish words.

Between the vans and the building, the sidewalk was filled with people milling about and talking in small clusters. In the dusky blue evening, the crowd looked to Travis like a school of sardines, hundreds of individuals moving as one.

Spots of intense white light punctuated the little plaza, where reporters interviewed citizens.

Hubbub, Travis thought. It's a hubbub, a brouhaha. He loved these words; they sounded like what they were.

He spotted the Save Our Library banner and pulled his parents toward it. Miss Babb, Hil and his parents, Jack, and all the others were there.

Miss Babb, of course, had a plan. She'd applied for a slot on the agenda for the Save Our Library committee. Three of its members would be allowed to speak for two minutes each. There were so many people who wanted to speak tonight, the time limit was absolute.

"I just found this out now," Miss Babb said. Everyone huddled around her and her clipboard as if this were the big game and there was only time to draw up one last trick play. "As committee chair, I've made an executive decision. I'm hoping that the following members will speak on our behalf. I'm just another whiny librarian, so I'm leaving myself out. I want *readers* to speak. Jack, will you briefly describe the committee, what we've done, how much money? Constancia, will you speak about the literacy program and career counseling?"

Miss Babb looked up from her notes. She looked at Travis.

If this were a book, Travis thought, he would have said, "Gulp."

"And Travis, I'd like you to talk about the library's books and how they make you feel connected. What you said at the first meeting. But be brief, okay?"

Gulp.

Miss Babb looked around the huddle.

"Any objections?" No one spoke. "Any seconds?"

"Second," Hil yelled.

"The motion is carried. Excellent, everyone."

Travis expected silence then, but another sound reached him, low at first, moving up through his legs and into his chest. He felt it before he heard it. It grew louder with every pulse, moving in from around him, closing in on him.

"Save our library, save our library, save our library . . ." The chant grew louder and louder, and soon took over the plaza. The reporters stopped yakking to watch.

"Save our library . . ."

It was a sound—not the words or their meanings, but the volume and breath of it—that Travis had never heard before. This wasn't the sound of a hundred people chanting. This was the sound of a strange animal's roar. Everyone here was one small part of a bigger creature, and that creature was growling and singing at the same time.

"Save our library . . ."

Travis was chanting, too, they were all chanting. The sound came from inside him, and from outside him, and it flowed through him.

Everyone smiled while they chanted.

A few sharp, staticky words from portable loudspeakers outside the chamber doors shattered the chant. The chant drifted off in waves, like the tide going out.

". . . in an orderly fashion, please. Slowly, please. The first two rows are reserved for tonight's speakers. Orderly, please, don't push, please . . ." And slowly, because there was no other way to fit this many people into the squat, round building, they all squeezed in.

On the far side of the chamber, nine men and women sat behind a curved table, each with a glass of water and a microphone in front of them. They talked in whispers to one another, occasionally waving to someone in the audience. Travis half expected the council members—a silly thought, he knew—to be dressed like British judges, in black robes and powdered wigs. But these were just people. Citizens of Salinas, like everyone else.

The room was filled to overflowing, and the fire marshall, the only one there in uniform, escorted handfuls of people away from the crowded exits. He assured them that they'd be able to hear from outside; loudspeakers had been set up. News camera lights heated the chamber, but the open doors allowed a breeze.

Travis shut his eyes and listened to the babble of voices. There was no meaning in any of the words, just sound bouncing off the walls. Argle-bargle.

It required much pounding of the mayor's gavel to quiet the assembly.

Travis had forgotten to be nervous until everyone

was quiet and the meeting started. He made up, rather quickly, for his forgotten nerves. What on earth was he going to say?

He turned from his front row seat to the back of the room. His parents and Miss Babb and Hil all waved at the same moment, and when Travis saw them his breath caught. He didn't know whether to laugh or cry, so he just went ahead and laughed.

The Save Our Library committee was second on the agenda, after three speakers from the library's administration, each of whom received substantial applause.

Jack followed, describing the Save Our Library committee. When he announced how much they'd raised so far, over ten thousand dollars, and how they raised it, there was an immense crash of clapping and whooping and shouting.

After Hil's mom spoke, several people in the audience were wiping tears from their eyes.

Travis stood before the microphone. He feared he would never utter another word as long as he lived. But then . . .

"I once," he said slowly, "got a book from the library that had green marker all over the pages, and I loved that."

And he talked, talked about the green marker and thinking about who had scribbled in the book and who else had read it before he had. He talked about feeling connected.

Or at least he thought he talked about those things. He didn't really hear himself speaking. For a long time after the meeting he tried and tried to remember what he had said, but couldn't. He couldn't remember the faces of the city council members, couldn't see or hear the crowd around him. All a big blank.

His turn at the microphone must have gone okay, though, because people were applauding—he heard Hil whistle through his fingers—and he was sitting down and felt instantly relaxed and exhausted.

The parade of speakers continued for an hour and a half. Everyone was in favor of saving the library, of course. Travis realized you'd have to be an idiot to show up tonight and say, "Gee, I think they should close the library, libraries are stupid."

The cheering only got louder as the night moved on.

There was a brief recess. The council, the mayor said, would convene, then return with their decision on the matter before them. "The matter before them" was whether or not the city council would call for an election on a sales-tax increase in support of the library.

The chamber was hot and stuffy, airless; the evening breeze that trickled into the room only proved how hot and stuffy the chamber was. But no one left during the recess, and Travis understood why. He felt that he, too, had to stay, wanted to stay, because if he left, something bad might happen, some trick might get pulled. No, he was in it for as long as it took.

Miss Babb wriggled her way to Travis and Jack and Constancia, thanked them all. She grabbed Travis by both shoulders.

"You," she said. "You were great. You know why I picked you. Because you *get* it. You *know* how important this is."

The intense chatter of the room stopped when the city council filed into the chamber. The silence in the chamber, Travis saw on their faces, terrified them. They looked like white mice dropped into a box of snakes.

The mayor, Kara Schleunes, was a tall, elegant woman, about Miss Babb's age—Travis could only guess this, he still couldn't tell with adults. She wore a prim gray business suit, a flowing emerald scarf, and she seemed to be holding her face perfectly still, determined not to give away any emotion.

"Thank you, everyone," the mayor was saying into her microphone. "Please be seated. Please take your seats."

No one sat down.

"Very well," she said. "Before the council records the votes, I'd like to say a few things. It's a privilege to have so many of you here tonight, and to know that so many of *us*"—she hit that word hard, paused, looked about—"care so deeply about our library. I only wish we lived in a different world."

If this were a book, Travis thought, he would have to write that his heart sank.

The voting proceeded from left to right.

The first vote was cast by council member Hidalgo.

"Council member Hidalgo votes a resounding yes," she said, loud and proud, with no hesitation.

The chamber erupted with yelling, whistles, hooting, stamping. The mayor's gavel restored order.

Before his vote, council member Tristes spoke briefly.

"In light of the city's fiscal crisis, and given that a similar measure was declined by the voters last March, a second election seems unlikely to succeed. Given that such an election would cost the city even more money it does not have, I must regretfully vote no."

Travis had never heard booing like this before. The gavel pounded and pounded against the booing.

The voting continued, more quickly now.

No, yes, no, yes, no, no. Mayor Schleunes was the last to vote, and she voted no, as Travis expected she would, but she seemed to say no with a good deal of regret in her voice.

The vote was official, six to three against the library.

The booing was loud, but the gavel was louder.

"Pursuant to the council's recommendations"—the mayor stayed seated, but did look at the crowd—"it is with great sorrow that our final decision has been made. The library will close March first of next year. Thank you for your time, ladies and gentlemen. This meeting is adjourned."

The booing and hissing rose like a wave and crashed against the walls of the chamber. Travis sat stunned within the great noise, stunned and emptied, everything sucked out of him, unable to move or think at all. The noise rose and rose, overflowing the room, overwhelming the last shreds of silence. Travis thought the noise was so loud it might drown him and everyone else in the chamber.

The fire marshall appeared in front of the city council's table, flanked on either side by two policemen. He carried a bullhorn that squeaked and popped when he turned it on.

"By order of the fire marshall," the bullhorn squawked, "I order this crowd to disperse. Please, exit the building at once, in an orderly fashion."

He kept repeating these words, and he and the policemen moved forward into the crowd, herding them into the cool night.

Travis allowed himself to be pushed away from Jack and Constancia, pushed away from where he'd seen Miss Babb and Hil and his parents get pushed to. He didn't know where he wanted to go, but he knew he wanted to be alone. If he was alone he might be able to do what he really wanted to do, which was get down on his knees and pound really hard against the sidewalk. He wanted to break something. All he could do was pound on his leg with his fist.

The booing stopped, but the talk could not be stopped. He would be okay, Travis knew that, he just needed a little time to himself, to gather himself. He drifted toward one of the news vans in the street.

"Why so glum, chum?"

Miss Babb was standing right behind him. Travis turned; he knew his face showed nothing but confusion.

"We lost," he said.

And he pounded on his leg again with his fist, as hard as he could, and looked away from Miss Babb. He thought for a second he might cry he was so frustrated, so he took a big gulp of air. When he finally looked back at Miss Babb, he found she was smiling.

"But we lost," he said, his hands shaking in front of him.

"Who says?"

"They did. They voted," he said.

Didn't she get it?

"Okay," she said. "*They* say we lost. But this is just the beginning. We're probably going to lose a whole bunch more before it's over. But we will win. The only way we can lose is if we stop trying. That's how you lose. Look, we're all ready to go. More mailings, more publicity, all set up. More meetings, more walking our feet off. And the reading, too. We've got a plan, Stan, ain't no time for mopin'."

Miss Babb turned and looked over the crowd.

It seemed to Travis that the crowd was listening to her. The first despair seemed to have left the people-thronged plaza. The voice of the crowd—all those voices making the one voice of the crowd-creature—had changed. It was no longer hushed and low, the crowd voice, it was high and sharp. It was alive again.

"Besides," Miss Babb said. "How can you say we lost?

Look at all these people. Did you see the city council? They were scared. I'm sorry to disappoint you. I know it would be easier to accept a loss and go home. But we didn't lose."

"You're right," he said. And she was. He knew it.

"Good, we've got a lot of work to do. We've got a reading to put together. And you've still got to find Ernest. Oster, I mean. You know he can help us."

They walked into the crowd. Travis could see Hil entertaining the committee members. Whatever he was telling them, they were laughing.

"You know what's wrong with city government?" Miss Babb said. "No cookies. I mean, jeez."

The next day Travis went straight to the library after school, and after an hour on the Internet, he'd come up with contact information for six of the possible readers on his list. But when he looked again for Ernest Oster, he still found nothing. All he found were five listings for copies of *Corral de Tierra* for sale. The cheapest copy was ninety-eight cents, the most expensive thirty-five dollars. That was all he found. Did Ernest Oster even exist?

Miss Babb was busy at the front counter, so Travis asked Mrs. Paonessa, one of the reference librarians, for help. She showed him a number of thick volumes on contemporary American authors, and some other guides to American literature, but there was nothing about Oster. It was as if he'd written one book and completely disappeared. Not one word anywhere.

But Travis knew he had to find him. It was too important. Oster and the library and Steinbeck, all these threads were braided together in Travis's life now. Maybe meeting Oster—or finding him at least—could pull the threads of the braid together. Oster was such an expert on Steinbeck, he might be able to really help the library's cause, maybe people would listen to him. And maybe, just maybe, he could help Travis figure out what was going on with Steinbeck's ghost and the Watchers and Gitano. Maybe Oster was the missing piece. The trouble with any missing piece, though, was exactly that. It was missing.

Travis was sitting on the floor in front of the reference stacks, staring into what he thought was space. But the space came into focus, a white-and-black spine with the word SALINAS in nondescript type.

It couldn't be, that would be too easy. He pulled the phone book's white pages from the shelf and opened it to O.

Oster, Ernest. Spreckels. 989-1648.

Oh.

II
THE WRITER

SEVEN

TRAVIS SAT AT THE KITCHEN TABLE AND STARED AT THE PHONE. He knew he was going to pick it up, knew he was going to call Ernest Oster. But then what?

Walking home from school, Hil asked Travis if he was going to come over, maybe they could work some more on the Camazotz game. Hil had finished *A Wrinkle in Time* and had new ideas for some of the hidden worlds. He seemed particularly interested in an Ice World. But Travis begged off. He had promised Miss Babb, he told Hil, that he'd do some research for the benefit reading. Hil volunteered to help, but no, Travis told him, that was okay, it was nothing much really. He'd be over in an hour or so. Cool, Hil said.

Travis continued to stare at the phone. In the backyard the afternoon wind hummed low, rattled the leaves of the young birch trees. He picked up the phone, put it back in its cradle.

He had no idea what to expect of Ernest Oster, or any other writer, for that matter. Before this—this thing, this mystery, this new, or was it renewed, life of his—Travis hadn't given much thought to writers. Books had been books, things unto themselves. Even the photos of writers on their books seemed almost fake somehow, like the generic photos in department store picture frames. The writer didn't seem to Travis any more important to the existence of a book than the threads that sewed the pages together or the glue that fastened them to the spine. The one writer he had always had a clear idea of—before all this—was Steinbeck, and that idea was based on a bronze statue, not a living, breathing person.

The phone just sat there. Travis punched in Oster's number, but without lifting the receiver. A practice run.

Travis knew precisely three things about Oster: He published his first book in 1972; he was living in Salinas at the time the book was published; he currently lived in the small town of Spreckels a few miles outside of Salinas.

There sat the phone, dull black plastic around a bunch of wires and chips. Just sitting there. Travis wished the phone could make the call for him.

Okay, four facts. Miss Babb talked about Oster as if he were a spy or something. But what else did Travis know? It was the unknowing that made the call so hard to place. Oh, he also had no idea what he would say.

He picked up the phone and punched the numbers.

"Hello," a man's voice said softly, a little surprised.

"Hello," Travis said. "May I speak with Ernest Oster, please?" Suddenly he was so polite. His parents would be glad to know that.

"Speaking." The voice was wary, as if asking a question.

"*The* Ernest Oster," Travis asked, "author of *Corral de Tierra*?" Nothing was coming out right. Travis knew he sounded like a bad actor playing a lawyer on TV.

"Ye-es?" The voice drew the word out, put a great big question mark on it. Travis could almost hear Oster moving away from the phone.

"Hi, I love your book and my name's Travis Williams and I live in Salinas and I was, well, we were, I mean, the committee, the Save Our Library committee, I mean, I was wondering . . ." And the words kept pouring forth, and Travis had no idea what he was saying. But he was afraid to stop talking.

When he paused at a double um—"um, um"—Oster jumped in.

"Travis, is it? I've heard about the library. Terrible shame, truly. But I'm not sure how I can be of help."

"Well, the thing is," Travis said, "we thought that because your book is all about Steinbeck and the library's named after him, well, we thought you could help. See, we're putting together this benefit reading. And I was wondering if you would be one of the readers? It'd be great. Everyone loves your book."

"Well, I'm not sure everyone loves it," Oster said. "But it's kind of you to say that. However, I really don't think so. The book never did very well, you see, not even around here. I haven't been a writer for a very long time. But thanks for thinking of me."

No, no, Travis had to say something. If Oster hung up the phone, that was the end of it, Travis just knew. What did he mean, he wasn't a writer anymore? That was crazy. Travis had read his book and knew Oster was a writer. You couldn't just quit being a writer, could you?

"Oh, please, Mr. Oster," Travis said. He couldn't decide if he should turn up the whine in his voice or turn it down. You could never tell how adults would react to one's whine-level. He turned it down, just to be safe. "See, the thing is, the library's so important to our community. And as a writer, you know how important the library can be." There was a tiny silence that needed to be bridged, so Travis jumped. "Maybe I could come out there and talk to you about it in person? Paint the big picture?"

Travis said this before he knew what he was doing. Good thing, too. What was he thinking? He waited for his answer.

Oster started a sentence, a disappointing sentence. "Well, this week is . . ." and then that sentence stopped. Travis listened to the silence that followed; it was like the pause between gears shifting on a bike. "Sure, why not? I really don't think I can help you with the reading, but you're right, the library is important. Maybe I can help you in some other way."

"Great"—Travis couldn't hesitate—"how about tomorrow afternoon, after school?"

"Sure. If you think you can get here all right? You know how to find me?"

"Piece of cake. Third Street, right? Around four thirty?"

"That's fine. I'll make some lemonade. See you then."

Lemonade?

There it was, that easy. You just picked up the phone.

✦ ✦ ✦

The town of Spreckels sat tucked up against the western edge of the Salinas Valley, at the base of the sharp, black Santa Lucias. Corral de Tierra, which Steinbeck called the Pastures of Heaven, was just over the first ridge of mountains that rose up behind the town and the Spreckels sugar beet factory. It would take about an hour to get to Spreckels on his bike.

As soon as school let out, Travis zipped from Bella Linda Terrace into Oldtown, then down Main Street, which he followed out of town, where it turned into Highway 68, the road that led to Monterey and the ocean. As soon as he cleared the last houses and shops, the vast flat Salinas Valley spread out before him, a hundred miles south, nothing but acres of corporate farmland. The land was so fertile and its produce so abundant, Steinbeck called it "the valley of the world." The strong scents of soil and manure were a cloud around Travis as he rode. In one of the fields, giant wooden farmworkers, painted in bright colors and shown at their tasks, stood guard. Behind them, real farmworkers, identical to their oversize wooden counterparts, worked up and down rows of iceberg lettuce.

The wooden cutouts of the farmworkers seemed like an insult to the real workers; the wooden figures were all smiling, and Travis was certain that the real farmworkers behind them were not.

Travis thought of Hil's mom, who for most of her life had been a farmworker, sweating in the sun for very little money so other people with more money could have lettuce in their salads and tacos.

Travis's grandfather and great-grandfather had both been farmworkers, too, arriving with the great Okie migration to California in the 1930s. Steinbeck had written about this migration in his most famous book, *The Grapes of Wrath*. Travis had tried to read it last year, really wanted to, but after a few chapters gave up. It wasn't that the language was too complex, but he felt that the world it described was somehow too big for his brain. He hadn't been ready then, but maybe he was now. Not only had he grown up a lot in the last year, but since he'd gone back to the library, he felt he'd changed several years' worth in only a few weeks.

Coming up on a little rise, Travis saw Spreckels tucked up against the mountains. The blow-back from mammoth trucks shook his bike.

Spreckels was two things. First, it was the enormous sugar factory that seemed as old as the valley itself. The factory was a gated compound of smaller buildings, in the middle of which stood an enormous galvanized steel barn as big as an airplane hangar, and two bunches of even taller white silos. The enormity of the factory, especially seen against the flat farmland nearby, made it seem like one of the wonders of the world, like the pyramids of Egypt.

Second, Spreckels was a town. A company town, it

had been built by the sugar company in the 1920s for its employees. The town was only three blocks wide and five blocks deep, and it was right across from the main entrance to Spreckels Sugar. It had one small store, a post office, a nice little park, and a school, and the rest of the town was houses. Spreckels was surrounded on three sides by endless acres of sugar beets and lettuce.

Travis had once been to the town of Spreckels on a field trip, and it had felt almost like a ghost town or a deserted island. Is that why Oster lived here now? To be away from everyone and everything?

He glided off 68 onto Spreckels Boulevard and, sheltered from the wind by a tunnel of towering sycamores, coasted down a long slope toward the factory. Was everything here called Spreckels? Maybe the school's soccer team was the Spreckels Spreckels.

He stopped in front of the factory's main gate. The factory had been closed for several years, but a few cars and trucks still motored about behind its chain-link fence. Up close, the grand structures of the factory seemed much smaller than when he'd first seen them from far away. The Santa Lucias behind the factory turned it into a more ordinary place.

Travis cut into the town, speeding past stucco bungalows and weathered Victorians, all with wide porches.

222 Third Street was practically hidden. Pale green juniper hedges blocked the view of the porch, continuing around the sides of the house and covering all the windows. It was a blue-gray house with white trim. That was about all you could say about it: a house. It didn't look like a writer's house, for some reason.

Travis circled in the middle of the street for a while, unsure why he was so hesitant. He was meeting a stranger, yes, that could always make you nervous. Maybe Oster was one of those weird recluses—*recluse,* that was the word—who had holed up in his house for decades, hoarding old newspapers and used aluminum foil. But Miss Babb knew him, and she would have told Travis if he needed to be careful.

No, what troubled Travis was that Oster wasn't really a stranger. He was the author of one of his favorite books, one he'd read a gazillion times. Travis felt as if he'd spent years crawling around in Oster's brain. He knew how Oster felt about the world—the trees and the hills, the weather and the sunsets, the crazy and wonderful and sometimes cruel things people did to one another. Oster, through his writing, had helped Travis to become who Travis was. Oster was no stranger. And yet.

The wind crisped through the leaves of the sycamores that crowded the streets. A chill crept around the edges of the afternoon, the shadows longer today. Autumn was here.

Travis hitched his bike to the white fence of number 222.

✦ ✦ ✦

Ernest Oster, the writer, had indeed made fresh lemonade. With real lemon wedges floating in it. Travis could smell, and then taste, summer in it, high summer, the first week of August. When he took a sip, he could not help but close his eyes.

The lemonade was the only brightness in an otherwise dark living room. Two table lamps only seemed to make the shadows in the corners of the room more shadowy. It was a quiet house; it reminded Travis of his grandmother's house in Santa Maria, everything old and perfectly in place.

They sat in two green overstuffed chairs that half faced each other.

Oster was a smallish man, not much taller than Travis, and he seemed like his voice sounded: quiet, guarded. He wore dark blue slacks, polyester, and a light blue short-sleeved shirt, also polyester, with a white T-shirt underneath. His shoes were black and wanted to look like dress shoes, but they had tennis shoe soles.

Short, white socks. His hair was gray, trimmed close. Square, silver glasses shrunk his blue eyes; he seemed to be squinting all the time. He would have made a good math teacher, Travis thought. A math teacher for the air force.

Oster didn't look anything like a writer. Travis supposed he'd expected him to look something like Steinbeck, or like the photo of Hemingway in Miss Galbraith's class, on safari, holding a rifle, one boot propped on a wild boar.

"So," Oster said. "I suppose Charlene has sent you. Come to roust out the old recluse, have you?" That word.

"No, sir," Travis said. "She, uh, wouldn't tell me where you lived. Said it was a secret. I found you myself."

"You don't say. Let me guess. You looked in the phone book."

"Uh, actually, I did."

"Good for you, young man. No one ever thinks about the phone book anymore."

"Yes, sir." Travis was happy to have the lemonade—it gave him something to do.

"Well, then," Oster said. "About this benefit reading. Wonderful idea, by the way. I've given it a lot of thought, but I'm afraid I'm still going to have to say no."

Oster looked away, to a window covered by heavy drapes.

"Why not?" Travis's politeness, it seemed, was staring out the window, too.

"I'm flattered that you like my little book so much, Travis. I really am. But you see, that was a long time ago. And no one paid much attention, I'm afraid. Went out of print almost instantly. I'm surprised the library still has a copy. I haven't thought about it in ages, and I certainly don't consider myself a writer any longer. A lark of my youth, if you will. And no one—except you and maybe Charlene—would even know my name. I wouldn't be much help."

"But—"

"No, really, I must say no."

"Okay." That's all Travis could say. He just knew that Oster said no to the reading for some reason he was not revealing. When Oster spoke, he didn't look at Travis, but spoke to the draped window, as if someone he knew were behind it.

"But"—now he did look at Travis—"I will help out. I love the library, too, and I do need to get out more. This house is too dark. Tell you what. When's the next committee meeting? I'll be there. Whatever I can do."

"Oh, that's great," Travis said. He felt silly. If this were a book, he probably would have said, Gee whiz. "There's a meeting next Tuesday after school. I mean, four o'clock. Stuffing envelopes and stuff. We're raising awareness."

"Count me in. I am a highly trained envelope stuffer. Runs in the family. My father was a stuffer of envelopes, and his father before him."

They both laughed.

Oster wanted to know more about the committee and the work being done for the library, so Travis went into great detail. He was trying to hook Oster into the library. One thing he was fairly certain of when it came to adults: When you met their greatest resistance, it was best not to attack directly. Sneak up slowly, from behind, all flowers and candy and thank you. Oster had said no to the reading, but not to the library. Whether Oster knew it or not, there was still a chance to get him to agree to the reading. This wasn't the big no, just a little one, and a smart kid could always find a way around the little no.

"Well, then," Oster finally said. "It must be time for you to be getting on. But I'll see you Tuesday, four o'clock. I'm glad you came by, Travis. I need to shake up these old bones."

Oster led the way out of the living room, but Travis

stopped in front of a short glass-fronted bookcase. There was a bookcase just like it at home; a lawyer's bookcase, his parents called it. Oster's bookcase was filled with hardcover editions of Steinbeck's books, every one of them, it seemed, and old editions, too. In the bottom corner of the lowest shelf, almost hidden, was a single copy of *Corral de Tierra*.

"Oh, yes," Oster said. "My Steinbecks. You said you were a Steinbeck fan, too, didn't you?"

"Yes, sir, I'm just reading *The Pastures of Heaven* right now; it's awesome. It's all about Corral de Tierra, you know? Which you wrote about." Travis thought this was perhaps the stupidest, most obvious thing he'd ever said.

Oster smiled and nodded.

"Here," Oster said. He opened the case and slipped out a hardcover without its jacket. "This is a first edition of *Pastures*. It's one of my treasures. And rather valuable these days, though I'd never sell it."

Travis was almost afraid to touch it, afraid he might ruin it somehow. But he took it. He opened the pages, scanned the type. It was an ordinary-looking old book, but when he opened it, a rich smell came up to Travis, the scent of old paper, yes, but something deeper, too, richer. It smelled of the earth, of the soil, as if the book had been buried for a long time.

"Oh, and this, of course." Oster lifted a plain picture frame from the top of the shelf. He took the first edition from Travis and handed him the picture frame. It was a letter, under glass, cramped blue writing on a long sheet of lined paper. "This, this is my most prized possession. A letter from Steinbeck himself. Look at that writing. I mean, his penmanship."

The writing on the letter was tiny, incredibly tiny. But precise, almost like the "handwritten" font of a word processor. The ink was blue, not a smudge on the tan, lined paper. Travis could make out the words, and he clearly saw the greeting at the top, "Dear Ernest Oster."

"Wow," was all he could say.

"Steinbeck had amazing penmanship," Oster said. "He could fill one page with over a thousand words, which is something like four pages of a printed book. And you could read them all. But check out the signature."

The signature at the bottom was a series of slashing blue lines that may or may not have spelled real words.

"He loved to write longhand. Wrote all of his books that way, had other people type up the pages for him. He liked the mechanics of it, pens and paper and fancy ledgers, and especially pencils. He once had to stop working on a novel for over a month because he couldn't find the right pencils. Can't imagine what he'd think of computers; probably hate 'em."

Travis had never met a writer before today. But here he was, talking to one of his favorite writers and holding the actual writing of one of his other favorites, and the two were connected. Travis could almost feel the connection stretching all the way to himself, from Steinbeck to Oster to Travis. His brain was pretty much one big wow.

"Um," he said, pushing through the fog of wow. "How did you, I mean, when was . . . I mean . . ."

"Good story. Here, sit down again, I'll get you some more lemonade. Go ahead, read it. It's okay."

It was still light out, plenty of time to get home, so Travis sat down and began to read.

Every word was startlingly clear. The letter was dated 1956, almost fifty years ago, older than his parents. How old did that make Oster? Travis couldn't tell.

The first part of the letter was all advice about writing. Steinbeck told Oster to read a lot, everything he could get his hands on. "Never use a typewriter, they're too noisy, you won't be able to hear your sentences, and that's urgent business, how the sentences sound." Steinbeck found, he wrote, that number 2.5 pencils offered the best line. Be poor, if possible, he recommended; it wasn't comfortable, but it helped get the work done: "Being rich makes you lazy." And Oster shouldn't try to prove how smart he was, but get out of the way of the story, and let it tell itself. Oster needed to be as clear as he could be. "Only a fool," Steinbeck wrote, "is willfully obscure."

When Oster returned with the lemonade, Travis was halfway through the letter. What he read stunned him. Oster was talking now, but Travis heard nothing. He was reading.

"To your question about the Watchers in 'Flight,'" Steinbeck wrote. "Yes, they do exist. Everyone who lives in or around the Santa Lucias has seen them. The legend is as old as the hills themselves. What do they mean, you ask. Well, you'll have to ask them that question yourself. I'm not sure they mean anything. They just are, they simply exist.

"Now, about Corral de Tierra. There was a town there, and everything I wrote about the town is true. But that is all I will say. I can never reveal the location of the town, it's good that it's dead and buried, it should stay that way. What happened there—what I did NOT write about—was so awful, I cannot imagine sharing it with anyone. Yrs."

The signature was illegible.

Travis looked up. "What?" he said. "I'm sorry, I wasn't paying attention."

"I was telling you about the letter," Oster said. "When I was a junior in high school, I wrote an essay about Steinbeck, and somehow got up the nerve to write to him. I was so surprised when he wrote back. I never expected that."

The connections—everywhere Travis went these days, every piece of paper he picked up, it all seemed connected, as if his return to the library had brought him to this man's house for the purpose of reading this letter. Was this the end of the thread, was this where it all stopped?

Oster took the letter gently from Travis, but not to take it back, to read it again.

"He didn't really answer your questions. Kind of mysterious about it all," Travis said.

"Oh, I know. This letter," Oster said, "is part of the reason I came out here. I grew up in Illinois, you know. I wanted to find the answers."

"Did you ever find them?"

"Not really. I spent a lot of time in the Corral when I got here. Hiked up and down it. Saw the Watchers once or twice. Found lots of ruins, abandoned houses and barns, old foundations, artifacts. But never found the town. You're reading *Pastures,* you know about it. I hounded that valley until I knew every square inch. Then I stopped going there."

"What happened?"

"I got scared off," Oster said. "I wasn't wanted there. Some locals took a few potshots at me. Warning shots. I got scared."

Travis tried to peer into Oster's eyes, see what he was seeing.

"You ever go back?" he said.

"No. Not once."

"Why not?"

"There's something in that valley I don't quite understand. It was too much of a mystery for me, at least back then. Haven't thought about it in ages."

Oster stood up and went to the bookshelf and put the framed letter back. In the dim, slanted light of the two lamps, Travis saw that the top of the bookshelf was clean, not a speck of dust. A little too clean for someone who'd not thought about this in ages.

"Well," Oster said, "glad you got to see that. Always exciting, I think, to get that close to a writer one loves. And so, next Tuesday, four o'clock. Ready to stuff those envelopes."

Travis knew their meeting was over, knew that the

thousand questions bouncing around in his head would have to stay there for now, bouncing around all the way home.

"I'll walk you out," Oster said.

✦ ✦ ✦

Before heading back to Highway 68, Travis stopped in front of the Spreckels factory gates again. Behind the factory, the Santa Lucias were black in the soft golden light of the afternoon.

On the high ridge stood the three Watchers, motionless. Gulp, Travis thought, gulp, gulp, gulp, and gulp. The connections were endless, it seemed to him, and a little frightening.

In Steinbeck's "Flight," the Watchers appeared here in the Santa Lucias, not in the Gabilans on the east side of the valley near Bella Linda Terrace where he'd first seen them. Were they going home?

When he'd first seen them, the Watchers frightened Travis, as if they were stalking him. Today they seemed to be leading him. But where?

Now look, Travis, he said, trying to get serious with himself. How is it possible that characters from a book, imaginary characters from an imagined book at that, could suddenly appear in the real world? That—along with pretty much everything else that was happening these days—was just crazy talk. He remembered, without trying to, the Ice Men in Virginia Hamilton's *M. C. Higgins the Great*. M. C. Higgins grew up hearing about the Ice Men, but had never seen them, until one sweltering Appalachian day, there they were, trudging through the thick forested trails, with pale pale skin, leaves tied around their feet and hands, and the enormous blocks of ice on their backs, a whole line of Ice Men coming through his front yard. M. C. Higgins wasn't prepared to believe in the Ice Men, until they left a block of ice for him on the porch, cool but melting.

Okay: Travis made a deal with himself. If he could get the Watchers to see him, acknowledge him, then he would believe they were real.

He raised one hand high and waved to the Watchers, swinging his arm back and forth over his head.

The Watchers kept watching for a moment, then each of them turned and moved off the ridge, away from Travis, down the far side and into the Corral.

Was that the signal Travis was looking for?

EIGHT

ALL THAT WEEK TRAVIS BURIED HIMSELF IN HIS ROOM. In his real life, that is, or what he thought of as his real life now. He read parts of Steinbeck over and over. He concentrated on *The Pastures of Heaven,* finished it a second time, and read the beginning again and again. What had Steinbeck written to Oster, something about not telling anyone what had *really* happened there, that it was good the town was now lost? And Oster. Why had Oster decided not to go back to the Corral? He had moved, he told Travis, to California in part because of the letter and that mystery, and then he'd written an entire book about the Corral, but then let some riled-up rancher scare him off with a couple of what he called "potshots." That didn't add up, not at all. Maybe there were clues in the book.

As much as he read, though, as much as he came to understand from the book that there was something not quite right about the Corral, there were no "aha" clues that jumped out at him. Whatever the mystery was, it was, well, pretty mysterious.

And he reread "Flight" to see what else he could pick up about the Watchers, and he reread the Gitano portion of *The Red Pony*. But there were no obvious clues there either. The more he read, the more he found himself entrenched in the stories and the more certain he was that everything in his "real life" was truly connected. He just couldn't find the map that would lead him to the simple solution he craved, the how and why of these sudden connections.

In his other life, his non-real life, as he was coming to think of it, everything went on pretty much as normal, school and homework, and going back and forth from one to the other.

Hil was still around, but he had just started soccer practice—he was a terrific player—and he really threw himself into it.

Travis's parents, he had to admit, were being great; they weren't working quite as much, and took him to Sheila's again and the pool, and that was the realest part of his non-real life.

But still, he waited for any chance to slip out of the non-real life, and get back to the real life. And finally, the next Tuesday came, and it was time for the committee meeting.

There were only three members present: Miss Babb, Travis, and Ernest Oster. Everyone else, according to Miss Babb, sent along their regrets.

"That's one more thing about saving the world," she said. "It can get kind of lonely."

But hearing her say this made Travis feel less lonely. At least they were in it together. And besides, he'd have a better chance to talk to Oster.

Miss Babb had decided that information was the library's best defense. And offense, too.

"We are, after all," she said to the two of them as if speaking to a crowded room, "a library. Duh! Information is all we have."

The first order of business that day was a vote on "appropriations." Should the committee set aside some of its money for mailing costs—paper, printing, postage?

They agreed to one thousand dollars for these costs; the remaining nine thousand dollars was to be sent to Rally Salinas. That money would be used to keep the library open as long as possible.

When Travis showed up in the A/V room that day, Miss Babb and Oster were already there, chatting close to each other, smiling and laughing. If he hadn't known it already, Travis would have guessed that these were two long-lost friends reunited. They were flat-out happy.

Miss Babb had composed a new flyer to be sent out to the mailing list. The flyer was an update on the city council meeting, but it stressed the point that the fight was far from over: They still needed money and volunteers. There was a quote from Travis at the bottom of the flyer: "Libraries connect us to other human beings—Travis Williams, age 13." Travis thought it was really cool, although he tried to pretend he hadn't noticed.

There was a second flyer as well, a press release to be sent to newspapers, magazines, radio and television stations, and other libraries around the world. During recess and lunch at school Travis had spent hours on the Internet gathering addresses for Miss Babb. It was important, she said, that the world know that Steinbeck's library was closing.

Miss Babb went off to her office to add new entries to the mailing lists, and left Travis and Oster to fold and stuff.

They stuffed and folded and talked about Miss Babb, what a great person she was. And then there was silence. A really uncomfortable silence.

The one notion that had been dogging Travis since

he'd met Oster was hanging around and just wouldn't go away, like a pesky little dog. Why, Travis was dying to know, had Oster stopped writing, why had he never written another book?

Given that his head was filled with a million other questions, and that Oster was sitting right across from him, and they were alone, Travis tucked his politeness away and broke the really uncomfortable silence. How much more uncomfortable could it get?

"I want to ask you a question," Travis said.

"Okay," Oster said. He set aside the stack of flyers he was folding. He seemed to know this would be a big question. "Shoot."

Go ahead, Big T, Travis could almost hear Hil egging him on.

"Why did you stop writing?" he asked, looking away, suddenly very interested in the engineering of letter-sized envelopes. "Why didn't you write another book?"

Phew. He said it.

Oster pushed back in his chair and sighed. He swiveled his head on his neck, as if sore. He sighed again.

"I'm sorry," Travis said. "It's just—"

Oster put up his hand.

"No, Travis. It's a good question. Do me a favor. Let

me answer it for you. You'd be doing me a favor, honestly."

Oster picked up the short stack of flyers and began to fold them again.

"I didn't quit," Oster said. "Not at first. Only later. Travis, I'm going to tell you something I've only told one other person outside my family—and that person was Charlene. It's not a huge secret, gosh, no. No one cares about the writing career of Ernest Oster, so, no, it's not a secret. It's just embarrassing, is all."

Oster stopped folding. He was looking through the wall across from him.

"I *did* write a second book. Wrote it after I finished *Corral,* but before that was published. It was called *Steinbeck's Ghost.*"

Travis was unaccountably giddy at these words. Maybe Oster had a copy, maybe he'd loan it to him. A new Ernest Oster book, how cool was that?

"But where is it? How come I've never seen it? It's not on the Internet."

"Very few people have. It was never published."

Oster paused, looked straight at Travis.

"This is the difficult part. For me. My publisher, the same one who published *Corral,* he rejected the second book. Sent me a one-sentence letter. I can still remember it exactly. Sorry, it said, but this is just a typical ghost story. And that was that. *Corral* didn't sell much at all, and I knew when I got that letter that I was a one-book writer. Some writers only have one real book in them. So I put the second one away. I won't lie to you; that was a very hard thing for me to accept."

A cloud of questions flew from Travis: Why didn't? Wasn't there? How about?

"No, you're right," Oster said. "I could have kept going. Probably should have, now that I think about it. But I quit. Can you understand? I had two children by then, and I didn't have a choice. I gave up writing and went to work for Spreckels. I did what I had to. I stuffed envelopes, in a manner of speaking. I pushed a load of paper at Spreckels. For my family."

Spreckels. The high fences and bland concrete buildings rose up in Travis's mind. Spreckels looked like a prison.

"I don't care," Travis said, "what anyone says. *Corral de Tierra* is a great book, and I really wish you'd written more. Your publisher was wrong."

Travis wanted to look away, but he didn't.

"Thank you, Travis. You have no idea how much that means to me."

"Tell me more," Travis said.

"More?"

"About you. I've never met a writer before."

The afternoon flowed on. Travis listened. It wasn't until he was back home that night that he was able to put the whole story together.

Ernest Oster was born in 1940 in Waukegan, Illinois. It was, all in all, a terrific place to grow up, a typically American small town. Long, slow summers playing outside till all hours, diving and swimming in creeks and ponds, brass bands in the town square. In the winter, snow and ice—skating and snow forts and neighborhood snowball battles. An old stone-built downtown, wide-porched brick and wood Victorian homes. Waukegan was a picture postcard of an America that only existed in movies and books anymore.

Oster had lived a remarkably normal childhood there. His father was a loan officer at a bank, his mother a hardworking housekeeper and wonderful cook. Oster had an older brother and a younger sister, each two years on either side of him, and they got on, and fought, too, as brothers and sisters will. Oster went to school, had best friends, rode a bike, joined the scouts. Nothing out of the ordinary, and maybe that was the most extraordinary thing of all.

If you wanted to know what it was like growing up in Waukegan, you had to read some of Ray Bradbury's books, especially *Something Wicked This Way Comes* and *The Halloween Tree*. Take out the spooky bits, and that was Waukegan. Bradbury, Oster had said, was born in Waukegan and lived there until he was a teenager.

Travis had read both *Something Wicked This Way Comes* and *The Halloween Tree*. What he loved most about Bradbury was—and in this way he was a lot like Steinbeck—you really felt, when you were reading him, that you were there in those places. Travis could smell the burning leaves of a Bradbury autumn.

"Did you know Bradbury?" Travis asked. "Was he a friend of yours?"

"I did meet him," Oster said. "But he's twenty years older than me. I met him later, when I was a teenager. But I'll get to that story."

Suffice to say—Oster used this phrase several times—it was a happy childhood, everything a kid could ask for.

Suffice to say, Oster should have been happy to live in Waukegan his entire life, follow his father into banking, marry and have kids there, die a happy man. All in Waukegan.

Then something happened. When he was fourteen.

A small thing, it might seem from the outside, but a powerful thing nonetheless. Oster wasn't kidnapped by aliens or forced into servitude by an evil landlord. He didn't discover that he was a wizard. Nothing that dramatic. But equally potent.

He checked out a book from the library.

Oster had always been a reader, though not particularly voracious. And most of his books came from the public library, the same library Bradbury had once frequented.

He read all the typical stuff a boy would read—adventure. The Western shoot-'em-ups of Zane Grey, the bizarre science fiction of Edgar Rice Burroughs's Tarzan novels, stories of war and sports and mystery. He liked to read, but he liked to do other things, too. Reading was simply one part of his happy childhood.

Then, when he was fourteen, in 1954, he asked his favorite librarian, Mrs. French, for something new. He'd grown weary of adventure. He wanted, he told Mrs. French, a book about the real world.

"Well," she said. "That's easy." She took two steps, slipped a book from its shelf, and put it in Oster's hands before he could read the title or see the cover. "You look like you're ready for this."

"Kind of like Miss Babb has done for me," Travis

said. "She's great at that." Travis remembered, vividly, the first time Miss Babb gave him *The Red Pony*. He could still feel the threads in the cloth on the cover of the book.

"It's what librarians do," Oster said. "And it's almost a kind of magic."

Oster told Travis he would never forget that moment—what Mrs. French said, the grace with which she moved, the bright spring sunlight bouncing on the library's stone floor.

That book was *The Grapes of Wrath* by John Steinbeck. Oster's first thought was, oh no, this book was much too long. But because he liked Mrs. French so much, no, *admired* her, he checked it out.

That night in his bedroom, in the attic of a perfectly ordinary home, Oster cracked open *The Grapes of Wrath* and read the first sentence: "To the red country and part of the gray country of Oklahoma, the last rains came gently, and they did not cut the scarred earth."

It's hard to say how a quiet moment like that can have so much impact on one's life, Oster said, the silent reading of a few bits of prose. But such moments—at least Oster liked to believe—can change your entire life. You just have to be ready.

After reading those words and the book that followed, Oster never saw the world in the same way again. He knew almost immediately that there was a big world outside of Waukegan, that it was real, that the people there were real people, and that he needed to know more about the world, needed, absolutely needed, to go out there.

And he never saw Waukegan in the same way after that either. His hometown was no longer a cozy background for his childhood games. It was a real city filled with real people, whose lives he had only begun to fathom.

With the reading of some words on a page, the world popped from two dimensions into three. Three? No, four. Time, too, counted. There was depth and time in the world, and he suddenly understood this fact.

In this briefest of moments—"How long does it take to read a sentence?" he said—there was one other sweeping change, the biggest of all for Oster.

Before that sentence, he'd just been a kid. After it, he was a writer, and he knew, at least then, that he always would be a writer.

"You can't unring the bell," Oster said.

Was that what had happened when Travis remembered the word *Camazotz,* he'd rung some bell that had changed the world? He didn't want to unring the bell.

"What was the first thing you wrote?"

That night, after reading the first two chapters of Steinbeck, Oster started his own short story. This was not something it had ever occurred to him to do before.

The story was about a young boy, obviously Oster himself, who, while swimming in a local pond one day, is almost drowned. The hand of some dark, deep-dwelling creature tried to pull him under. When he tries to explain this to the adults—his parents, the fireman, the police chief—they all laugh it off as impossible. But the boy knows what has happened; death came looking for him, and he barely escaped.

That story was exceedingly melodramatic, horribly written. As it should be for a first story. The adults are all idiots; the boy is heroic and misunderstood. A train wreck of a story. But a story, and he finished it.

After that night, after Oster's world cracked open, he continued to write stories, and he continued to read Steinbeck. In six months he read everything Steinbeck had published up to that point, and he wrote countless stories—all of them horrible.

Every night Oster sat at a makeshift desk in front of the window of his attic bedroom, from where he watched the other kids riding bikes and playing tag and acting as if nothing had changed.

Travis didn't see the A/V room at all anymore. He was in the attic bedroom in Waukegan, looking out the window, west toward California and Salinas. And at the same time he was in the window in the attic in the Steinbeck House, and he was Steinbeck looking out at Corral de Tierra. And he was also in his own bedroom, looking west toward Salinas at the Steinbeck House. The connection between the three of them—Steinbeck and Oster and Travis—was suddenly clear to him. Maybe that's what it took to be a writer: You had to sit and stare out the window for a long time until you started to write stories. Maybe, if he sat in his own window long enough, Travis would write his own stories.

"What then? Is that when you moved to Salinas?" Travis asked.

No, not for some time yet. When he was done with reading Steinbeck, Oster read anything else Mrs. French put in his hands—Hemingway, Faulkner, Ellison—any book about the real world.

Oster wrote and read and made plans to leave Waukegan.

"But when did you meet Bradbury?"

He was a senior in high school, and it was practically an accident.

Bradbury was an established, much published writer

by then, and during a visit to Waukegan, he was asked to speak to some of the English classes at Oster's high school. Afterward, he ate lunch with a select group of seniors. Oster's favorite teacher, Mrs. Weinberg, invited Ernest. The lunch was nice, everyone asked all the right questions, but as soon as the last lunch bell rang, the other students went back to their classes and their ordinary lives.

Oster didn't leave; he still had a raft of questions. Bradbury, a short, smiling, laughing, easy-to-read fellow, had a few hours to kill. Bradbury didn't drive, never had, only ever took the train, and the next one didn't leave for several hours. Would Oster care to join him for a cold soda? Oster skipped his classes for the afternoon.

"You played hooky with Ray Bradbury?" Travis was too delighted by this—what an idea!

"It was great, one of the best things that ever happened to me," Oster said.

They ended up in a nearby park, on a broad lawn next to a shallow lake pocked with ducks. They drank their sodas and talked. Oster mostly listened. The afternoon seemed to go on forever.

Oster could no longer remember everything Bradbury told him that day. But a few things had always stayed with him.

Writers, Bradbury told him, should only eat sandwiches for lunch; that way they could eat and read at the same time. Oster should take a typing class; that would save him lots of grief and money. A writer had to read anything and everything, and make up his own mind about what he read. College was fun, but it had nothing to do with being a writer. Life, that was for writers.

Bradbury talked, and Oster soaked it in. What struck Oster today, more than forty years later, was that Bradbury had taken his wish to be a writer with seriousness and respect. And he'd been uncommonly generous; he didn't hold anything back. If Oster had any doubts about becoming a writer, Bradbury dispelled them that day.

"Is that when you came to Salinas?" Travis asked.

No, Oster went to college, not far from Waukegan, where he studied chemistry—he'd always loved science—and where he met Eve. They were married in 1962 and had two children, Kristen and Nicole, who both lived now in San Francisco. Eve had died two years ago, of breast cancer. Oster still missed her every waking moment.

Just after Kristen was born, they up and moved to Salinas. Back in Waukegan, Oster had been writing the whole time, nights while he worked as a chemist during the day, but he and his wife decided to take a chance. They saved up as much money as they could and moved to Salinas in 1968. He was going to write his first novel.

"But why did you come here?" Travis said. "I'm not sure I'd move here if I was from someplace else."

Travis had such a strong image of Bradbury and Oster's world in his head, he couldn't imagine anyone leaving it behind.

"Steinbeck," Oster said. "That simple." He knew what book he wanted to write, *Corral de Tierra,* and he knew he could only write in California, knew he needed to see and feel and smell this landscape to write it.

Travis knew the rest, Oster told him. *Corral* was published, the second book was rejected, he had a family to take care of. End of story.

It was dark when they finished. All the envelopes had been stuffed, sealed, and labeled. Miss Babb had ordered in Thai food for them, and empty Styrofoam and plastic cluttered the table.

"Did you ever meet him?" Travis asked. "Steinbeck?"

"I'm afraid not. I had hoped to, but no. He was living in New York then, had been for a long time. Still, I kind of hoped he would come back to Salinas at some point. I arrived in the summer of 1968. He died in December that year."

Oh, Steinbeck came back after that, Travis thought.

I can't prove it, but I've seen him, just a few blocks from the library.

"I think I would have liked to meet him," Travis said.

"Really, now?" Oster smiled, a tight, sly smile. "I can get you close. Have you ever been to the aquarium?"

"Tons."

"How'd you like to go again? There's someone I want you to meet."

NINE

OSTER WOULD PICK UP TRAVIS IN BELLA LINDA TERRACE LATE SATURDAY AFTERNOON. Afternoons were the best time at the Monterey Bay Aquarium, Oster claimed. That's when all the tired tourist families gave up and went in search of sugary snacks to revive them. In the afternoon, he said, you had the place all to yourself, could really see the fish.

Miss Babb called Travis's parents to set up the outing with Oster, and she assured them that Oster was a good friend of hers and completely reliable.

So they were ready to go on that front, but first there had to be a family meeting. That Thursday night, in the immaculate living room, his parents—they were speaking as "your parents," a unit of one—wanted to go over some things with him. They were thrilled, they told him, that he was so involved with the library and that he had shown so much responsibility and initiative and overall maturity. They had faith in Oster, based on Miss Babb's word, and thought the trip to the aquarium would be a "wonderful experience" for him.

And they wanted him to know that they had full confidence in Travis. They wanted him to know that they trusted him and knew he would act responsibly, and that they weren't worried at all. Which was, of course, their way of saying that they were worried, weren't really that confident, and had some grave doubts about the whole enterprise. So Travis waited for the "but."

"But," they said. They actually said it simultaneously, as if they'd been rehearsing. Then they looked at each other and laughed a little.

"But," his mom said, "we'd feel safer if you took this with you."

Travis half expected his mom to pull a shiny revolver from her purse, but it was only a cell phone.

"Just in case," his dad said. "And it's not for yakking to all your friends, okay? It's so you can call us anytime, for any reason whatsoever."

A year ago Travis had hounded his parents for a cell phone—a lot of kids at school were getting them—but they'd refused. No matter how many strains of "please, please, please" Travis sang, no phone appeared. Rather than being thrilled with the appearance of the phone now, however, Travis was a little disappointed. It just wasn't the same to be given a phone for security reasons. It made the phone feel like homework instead of a cool new gadget. The phone was shiny and red, and Travis wished he was more excited about it.

"Deal?" his mom asked.

"Deal."

Just then the phone rang, and Travis nearly jumped up, but it wasn't the cell phone, it was the house phone. He and his parents waited, letting the machine pick up; they'd always been a let's-see-who-it-is sort of family.

"Hey, dude, it's Hil. Call me tonight, I want to ask you something."

"Can I call him back on *this?*" Travis asked, pasting on his biggest, fakest, oh-please grin. "I mean, I have to try it out. Just to be safe."

"This once," his mom said.

He went up to his room and punched the numbers.

"Yo, Hil, guess what I got," Travis said, and then they talked about the phone for a long time. Travis was apparently more excited about it than he'd thought. It was a pretty cool thing. Hil was jealous; he was *dying* for a cell phone, but thought Travis's phone might be good for his own cause. The more his friends got phones, he figured, the closer he was to getting one of his own.

"So, anyway, Alexander Graham Bell," Hil said. "The reason I called was to ask if you wanted to come to my soccer game on Saturday. It's the first game of the season, and we're playing the Strikers, and I hate that team, and we need all the help we can get. It'll be cool. My dad's gonna take us all out for ice cream after. Marianne's Ice Cream, which, as you know, is the creamiest ice cream in town. Root Beer? Pumpkin? Licorice? C'mon, you know you like it."

Oh. He really wanted to see Hil play. Hil was small but fast, very fast, perhaps the sneakiest player on the field, cutting through clumps of other players and emerging with the ball.

"Oh, man," Travis said. "I can't. I, uh, I'm going down to King City with my parents to see my aunt and uncle all day. Bummer. Maybe next week?"

"Sure," Hil said. "That's cool. Next week. Okay, gotta book. See you tomorrow."

Travis didn't even have an aunt and uncle in King City. Why had he lied to his best friend? The lie just sort of leaped out of his mouth, and what was worse, he knew he'd see Hil tomorrow at school, and he'd have to repeat the lie at least one more time—to his face.

Maybe it was the cell phone's fault, maybe he wasn't used to talking on it, and so he . . . no, he knew what was wrong.

Suddenly Travis realized what it was. He didn't want Hil to know what he was doing. It was important to Travis, at least for now, to keep Oster all to himself. But he didn't like the feeling at all.

He closed the new phone and dumped it into his backpack.

✦ ✦ ✦

When Oster pulled up in his dusty Dodge Dart, a car much older than Travis, almost as old as his parents, his parents invited him in, gave him a glass of iced tea, chatted with him in the kitchen. They were "vetting" him, his father's word.

It was strange to watch Oster and his parents together at the breakfast bar. He knew so much about Oster, knew of his inner world and his imagination. He had spent hours wandering through his book, and now he knew about his past and his writing career, even his wife's death. And yet here was Oster, chatting with his parents about the weather and the library and Spreckels and Bella Linda Terrace.

When it was time to go, his dad tried to push some money into Oster's hand.

"No, not at all," Oster said. "Today's special admission. A free behind-the-scenes tour from my friend Mike.

Mike McKenzie. Then Mike's gonna show us a rare piece of . . . let's call it Steinbeckiana. Something very few people get to see. Turns out, me and Travis are both big Steinbeck fans."

But Oster wouldn't say more, didn't want to spoil the surprise.

"Got your phone?" his mom asked, and they were out the door.

When they got in the car, Oster, looking straight ahead, said, "I see what you mean about Bella Linda Terrace, Travis. This is a very strange place. It's like a movie set; you could open the front door, and there'd be nothing behind it. Like you said: totally Camazotz."

Highway 68 was a two-lane road that followed an old river course between the Salinas Valley and the Monterey Peninsula. Valley oak and sweet grasses lined the road. To the north, out Travis's window, the low mesas of Laguna Seca faded into a hazy sky. To the south, steep folded hillsides hid the Corral de Tierra. There were no Watchers today.

Travis's mind was—once again—bursting with a million questions. He wanted to know about Oster and this place, the Corral, everything he'd seen there. But he held the questions back. He was watching Oster to see how he reacted to driving by the Corral. Travis still couldn't understand why Oster had never returned to a place he had spent so much time thinking about.

They stopped at a traffic light at Corral de Tierra Road. Both of them looked down the narrow, oak-shrouded lane that curved into the valley.

"Well, there she is, Travis. You ever been up there?"

"It's hard to say. I think so, a long time ago, probably with my folks. I don't think I've been, though, since I read your book."

"Maybe you and me'll go up there someday. I might be ready to go back."

The light changed to green. The weekend traffic crawled to the ocean.

Cannery Row was all noise and smells. They walked past T-shirt shops, jewelry stores, fancy restaurants and hotels, a cigar store with a ceiling of whirling fans, ice-cream parlors. Giant cranes in one vacant lot were hard at work on a Saturday. Tourists, like flocks of shorebirds, skittered about, gift-shop bags in tow.

Beyond the Row, Monterey Bay was quietly beautiful, broad and blue and calm. The bay, Travis knew, would still be this way, long after the last saltwater taffy machine stopped pulling.

Seagulls cawed, laughing, mocking.

"He'd roll over in his grave," Oster said.

"Steinbeck?"

"You bet. He was here again in sixty-two. Hated what had happened to it."

"Was it like this then?"

"Heavens, no. Back then, and later, when I first came here, it was just tacky souvenir shops, a few artist studios. But nothing like the old Row. All the factories had long been closed, no more sardines. And all his old friends were dead and gone. But now . . ."

"Now?"

"I love the aquarium. You do, too, we all do. And it's great for the city. But all the rest, the ritzy hotels and such. Not his style at all. A little too Disney for him. He'd hate himself."

"Hate himself?"

"Yes. It's all his fault. His books made this place famous. People all over the world know about Cannery Row. Without Steinbeck, this is just a bunch of old sardine canneries. But he'd laugh, too."

"Laugh?" Travis asked. They were passing a vacant lot that would soon be another hotel. Through the empty frame of the building, he could see the bright blue and dark blue speckled bay. He spied an otter floating on its back, cracking open a sea urchin on its belly.

"He'd laugh out loud. You see, the people around here, in Salinas and Monterey, the ones with money at least, they hated Steinbeck. Drove him out of Salinas. He told the truth about life, about the cruel and foolish things people do. And nobody likes to see the truth about themselves. Even when I first moved here, and for years after, people wouldn't talk about him, still got angry whenever his name came up. Even after he was dead."

"But now," Travis joined in, "they love him. He makes them lots and lots of money."

"Truckloads. You've got it, young man. That's the truth. Look over there. See that little park?"

Between two buildings, a neat little park rose on terraced stairs toward the top of a hill. Three tiny white houses filled one side of the park.

"Now those houses," Oster said. "Those are the kinds of shacks that used to cover this whole area, back when the canneries were open. Where the workers lived."

Travis had seen these before, on a field trip. It just wasn't a school year without a field trip to the aquarium.

"Those are the ones Steinbeck wrote about in *Tortilla Flat*, right?" Travis asked.

"Exactly. And they're the real thing. Imagine that.

Danny and Pilon and the gang might have actually lived in one of those shacks. If they'd been real people, that is. But look, over there. See that tree?"

A giant black cypress tree shaded one half of the park. Under it, a homeless man slept with his arms over his face.

"That tree," Oster said. "That exact tree is in both *Cannery Row* and *Sweet Thursday*. It's where Hazel or Mack, or any of the boys, used to go to think about things. And to sleep. Whaddya think? Is that Hazel asleep there?"

And it might have been Hazel, or any one of the Row's "denizens," as Steinbeck called them. There was a man in overalls, with a big bushy beard, and a grease-stained cap asleep under the cypress, a backpack for a pillow. Travis could swear there was a smile on his face.

"When I first came here," Oster said, "this was all a vacant lot. As it was back in Steinbeck's day. And you know what? The rusting boiler they lived in in the books, you know, the old boiler from the sardine cannery? The one with no windows but curtains inside? That was still here. The same one. Can you believe it?"

They stopped in front of a weathered wooden shack on the bay side of the street. Cracked narrow stairs led to a plain, unmarked door. The windows wore blinds. Although the shack seemed abandoned, it was the only building on the Row that looked like it belonged here.

"Doc's lab," Travis said.

"The Pacific Biological Laboratory. Steinbeck called it 'Western Biological' in the books. Never figured out why he did that."

Doc was Edward "Doc" Ricketts, Steinbeck's closest friend, a marine biologist. He collected and prepared samples of local marine life for study in schools and colleges.

Doc's lab was a stop on every aquarium field trip. The school group always stood outside the lab, while a docent told them about it. But the windows were always blinded, and the kids never got to go inside. Last year, after he'd read *Cannery Row,* Travis hung back when the field-trip herd moved on. He snuck down the sloping driveway and peered through a crack in the garage door. He saw jars and jars of pale white sea creatures suspended in clear liquid. Then he scurried up the stairs to the front door and peered sideways into the window. A saggy couch, glasses on a coffee table, an old record player. It was easy to imagine Doc and Steinbeck listening to classical music together and drinking Old Tennis Shoes whiskey. And talking, talking, talking.

A metal-gray seven-gill shark broke the surface of the deep, wide tank and snapped the pink chunk of salmon into its gullet. Splash and snap; silence. The shark swerved back down into the tank, threading through hundreds of other fish.

Travis and Oster were standing at the top of the giant kelp forest, looking down into it. Like a real kelp forest, the water here pulsed and surged with the bay's tide. It was harder to see the fish from the surface, behind the scenes and above it all, but the view captivated Travis. All around them, pumps and pipes hissed and throbbed and gurgled.

Mike McKenzie tossed a last chunk of salmon into the tank. Seconds later, another seven-gill located the salmon and finished it off.

Mike was an old friend of Oster's. They'd met just after he moved to Salinas and was beginning to research Steinbeck and *Corral de Tierra*. They became instant friends. Mike had been a volunteer at the Monterey Bay Aquarium since it opened in 1984.

Mike was one of those gruff adults—he spoke sharp and loud—who was just too nice to be truly gruff. In his khaki work clothes and knee-high black rubber boots, his hands on his hips, he could have been an army sergeant. But when he spoke—"a good snack-sized boy, this one, Ernest"—nothing could hide the smile in his eyes, the softness underneath the gruff exterior.

"Come here, Travis," Mike said. Gruffly. He was squatting next to the edge of the tank. "Just put your first two fingers in the water and splash around a bit."

Travis leaned forward to do so, but Mike grabbed his hand and pulled it back.

"They've already eaten. I forgot," Mike said. All three of them laughed.

Travis stared down into the tank. The view from here was incredible.

The great kelp forest was a twenty-eight-foot-tall tank with three sixteen-foot-tall windows, an enormous viewing bay that surrounded aquarium visitors and towered above them. Travis always loved standing in front of this tank, watching the rockfish, the sea anemones, the sharks, the starfish, the abundance of sea life that lived in the real bay outside the aquarium walls. Standing in front of the tank, it was obvious why this ecosystem was called a "forest." Long strands of seaweed, huddled together, rose from the rocky bottom of the seabed like the great redwood trees that towered over the earth.

The view from the glass side of the tank, the visitors' side, was absolutely clear; it was easy to watch the forest at work. But standing at the top of the tank and looking down into it, the surface dipping and slapping, Travis realized that the view from the visitors' side of the tank was more like a TV or a movie than the real, true-life ocean. From up here, Travis could, if he wanted, dive into the water, swim with the fish, be a part of the great flow of it all. This tank, like all the tanks in the aquarium, was connected to the ocean through a sophisticated pumping and filtration system. Travis imagined jumping into the tank and making his way through the pipeworks to the bay, and from there to the open ocean. This was no TV; this was the entrance to the real world.

"Okay, Mike," Oster said. "Thanks for that part of the tour. We still on for the second half?"

The three of them were standing in front of a T-shirt shop that seemed to sell nothing but Hairy Otter shirts. The otters on the shirts wore round spectacles and had golden, lightning-shaped scars on their foreheads.

"Perfect timing," Mike said. "I think we could all use a little refreshment, don't you, Travis?"

He nodded. He had no idea what they were talking about.

"Excellent," Mike said. "Gentlemen. To the lab."

As they climbed the creaky stairs to Doc's lab, Mike explained himself. When he was a kid, near the end of World War Two, he had worked for Doc Ricketts. He scoured the local tide pools for whatever creatures Doc needed—scallop, chiton, limpet, decorator crab. Doc paid him by the piece. It was a great job. When Doc died in 1946, the lab fell into disrepair, but an odd group of Row denizens came to possess the lab. It's not clear how that happened, it just did; that was Cannery Row for you.

Mike continued to hang around the Row, worked in the canneries until they closed, and pretty soon—again, it just happened—he became a member of the Old Tennis Shoes Club.

The Old Tennis Shoes Club was a social club, if you will. They got together now and then at the lab, listened to music, talked about the world and everything in it, had a little nip of Old Tennis Shoes.

Travis knew about Old Tennis Shoes. In *Cannery Row,* that's what the "denizens" drank. They bought endless bottles of it from Lee Chong's grocery. Lee Chong's was still on the Row, at least the building was; now it sold key chains. Old Tennis Shoes, according to Steinbeck, was a horrible whiskey, but it was cheap.

Mike had been a member of the club since, well, it must be forever because he couldn't remember. The main goal of the club was to preserve the lab as it had been when Doc lived there.

"Did you ever meet Steinbeck?" Travis asked.

A fire was already going in an old woodstove. Travis and Oster sat on an ancient sprung-spring sofa. Mike brought in a tray of drinks for them—grape Nehi for Travis, shot glasses of Old Tennis Shoes for himself and Oster.

"Oh, a few times," Mike said. He lowered himself into a ragged easy chair, took a sip of Old Tennis Shoes, and sighed loudly. "Heckuva nice guy. Snuck in here a couple of times before Doc passed. Snuck in a few times after, too. Still wasn't welcome here back then. I remember one time he fixed the broken gear on my bike—with a cork and a safety pin. Forget his novels, that man could fix anything."

Even though it was a fairly warm day outside, the wooden shack, built on pilings above the bay's shore, was chilly. Waves lapped under the floorboards.

Mike got up and stoked the woodstove, then went over to an old-fashioned record player. It actually said Victrola on it, it was that old. He snapped on a green-glass-shaded lamp.

"Bach's 'Art of the Fugue,' one of their favorite pieces of music. Him and Doc would put this on, light up their pipes, and just talk. I never knew what they were talking about, but I sure did like the sound of it. It sounded important. I was just a kid then, but kids know what's important, if you ask me."

There was a knock on the door just as it swung open, and two men entered noisily.

"Chuy, Gil, c'mon in." Mike did not stand, but raised his glass to them. "You know Ernest. And this young man is Travis. A special friend of the club."

There were handshakes all around. Travis watched and nodded. It was clear what good friends these men were to one another, how long they'd been coming here, how they fit into the furniture. More shot glasses of Old Tennis Shoes were produced, and the stove was fed.

Travis knew he was sitting perfectly still, as calm as could be. But he also knew he shouldn't be calm. He was inside Doc's lab, sitting where Steinbeck himself had once sat, listening to men who had actually known the writer. But it was just a normal day at the lab. And the fact that everyone was matter-of-fact about it all made being here even that much more exciting. Travis smiled and listened, tried to be cool.

After a while Oster looked at Travis and tilted his head toward the door. It was time to leave, but Travis wanted to stay forever.

"Well, Mike," Oster said. "It's about time we got going. Still got time for a tour, though."

"Absolutely," Mike said. "But Ernest, you know the way. Why don't you squire Master Travis? Old Tennis Shoes has some official business to conduct."

Everyone laughed. Travis was pretty sure he knew why they were laughing—it had something to do with Old Tennis Shoes, the whiskey, not the club. So he laughed, too.

When he first came in, Travis had seen the open stairway door in the back corner, and immediately wanted to go there. The doorway, which led down to the basement, was one of those irresistible black caverns that seemed to pull you into it. All during the visit, he wanted to ask if he could go down there, but thought that would make him sound like a little kid. Can I, can I, can I, huh?

Now Oster was headed into the blackness, beckoning Travis to follow.

"Careful," Oster whispered. "It's dark."

Not as dark as all that, though. Light from the late afternoon filtered into the basement. It was blue-gray down here, like being underwater.

The basement was a cement-floored workroom filled with high, narrow tables. Wooden shelves lined the walls, and on every surface of the tables and shelves, spectral shapes, as pale and luminous as the moon, floated in glass jars.

"This," said Oster, "is the real lab. Where work actually got done. Go ahead, look around."

Squid, starfish, shrimp, sea urchin—all the creatures Travis had just seen alive in the tank of the great kelp forest. Here they were, dead but preserved. Each specimen bore a typed label, the words faded to faint brown traces of ink. The specimens had to be at least sixty years old. There was a giant squid in a jar that was as tall as Travis. As dead as it was, it looked eerily alive. Travis got that horror-movie chill down his spine. He waited for the squid's huge, open eye to wink at him.

The sound of the lapping waves was louder down here, and Travis realized that the back of the basement, which sloped sharply, was open to the bay. The water could come right in. It was like a garage for a world where the ocean was the street, something fantastic and almost unbelievable, something from his and Hil's Camazotz video game. But this wasn't a video game, it was a real building, solid and undeniable. Nearby, Travis heard the sound of a small outboard motor.

Oster showed Travis around the equipment—embalming tubes, a microscope, stainless-steel gutters for disposing of "waste," a set of immaculate scalpels.

"Some of the specimens were shipped whole, then students would dissect them. And sometimes they were dissected here, used for their smaller parts. It looks rather brutal, I know," Oster said. "But think of the good these specimens did. They helped train the scientists who are working to save the oceans today. And I'm serious. Progress is always a little ugly."

"Oh, I know," Travis said. "Steinbeck and Doc, they both loved the ocean. They thought we were ruining it and didn't even know it. It's where life came from, they thought."

The sound of the outboard motor grew nearer, just outside the lab, and in an instant, the lab reverberated with the thock-thock rhythm of the motor and the sharp tang of gasoline exhaust.

Travis and Oster stared at each other, then they both stared at the opening to the bay. Neither of them moved, as if moving would make the noise noisier and the smell smellier.

The motor cut out, and Travis heard what he knew was the sound of a boat scraping up on the beach. In the silence that followed, there was a faint thud.

He looked at Oster, who was still staring out at the bay.

He didn't know if he was running because the outboard had started up again, or if the outboard started up again because he was running toward it. They happened at the same time. He wound his way around the pilings that supported the lab, and suddenly he was outside on a cramped beach. The day's light was awfully bright. A small red-and-white dinghy traced a steep arc of wake out into the bay, its two occupants dark against the horizon. In seconds the dinghy had rounded the corner of the aquarium and was gone.

At Travis's feet, a burlap sack squirmed, reeking of the ocean. Oster came running up.

They opened the sack, carefully, their faces turned away as if it might explode. Inside was a writhing mass of fish, crustaceans, shellfish, seaweed.

When they fetched Mike and the boys down to the beach, all anybody could say was, "Wow." Mike and the boys guessed the sack belonged to a party fishing without permits.

"They probably got spooked by the Harbor Patrol and dumped it here," Mike said.

"Did you see that?" Oster asked.

"Yes," Travis said.

They looked at each other. The expression on Oster's face told Travis that he knew what Travis was thinking. But they just held on to the look for a second without a word. It was Steinbeck and Doc in that boat, Travis was thinking. He was ready now to be convinced, no more doubts. Everywhere he turned, it seemed, Steinbeck's world was coming to life.

"Look at these beauties," Mike said. "The bounty of the ocean, my friends. We're gonna have us a barbecue tonight."

TEN

IT WAS A QUIET RIDE HOME. Travis was thinking about the boat and Steinbeck and Doc, and he got the very strong feeling that Oster was, too. There was so much to say, and yet silence seemed the only appropriate response. The sun setting at his back, Travis watched the hills of the Santa Lucias turn orange and pink and blue.

Halfway to Salinas, Oster pulled into the parking lot of a small general store. He got out of the car and walked to the back of the lot where weeds choked a fence. He stared out into the valley that opened on either side of the narrow road. He was looking far into the Corral.

Travis sat in the car, watching him, knowing that what Oster saw was completely different than what he saw. Looking into the Corral, Travis saw the unknown; Oster saw his past.

Travis got out and followed him. The silence had passed now, and he just had to talk.

"This is weird, I know," Travis said. "You're probably going to think I'm crazy. But back there, at the lab, for just a minute, I thought it was Doc and Steinbeck in the boat. I mean . . . I don't know what I mean."

Oster didn't move, he just stared.

"I thought the exact same thing," he said. "And yes, it is weird."

"Can I tell you something else?" Travis said. He stared into the valley, too.

"Shoot."

"Sometimes, lately, it's like . . ."

Travis had no idea how to say what he wanted to say. Could he really tell Oster about Steinbeck's ghost, about Gitano, the Watchers? Camazotz was one thing, but the rest, that was just crazy.

"Go ahead," Oster said.

"Okay. It's like this. It's like all the books I've been reading, they're coming to life or something. I mean, the more I read Steinbeck—and your book, too—" He paused for a long time. Oster waited. "What I mean is, the more I read, the more the world changes. Actually changes."

"Books do that."

If anybody else had said this, it would have made Travis feel like a little kid. As if they were saying to him, it's okay, children have such "vivid" imaginations. But

Oster said it with seriousness, with confidence. With respect. Travis knew that Oster understood.

On a nearby ridge line the Watchers appeared, black against the sky.

Travis lurched forward, started to speak. Held back. Spoke.

"Do you see them?" Travis asked.

"The Watchers? Yes. Yes, I do. I haven't seen them in years, since I was last here, but there they are."

They stood watching until the Watchers retreated from the ridge, moving deeper into the Corral.

"There's something in the Corral," Travis said. "And it's pulling me there. Something I need to know. I want to learn more about this place."

"I think we can arrange that."

If he was truly losing his mind, Travis no longer cared. At least he wasn't alone.

The days went on as before, going to school and hanging out with Hil when Hil wasn't at soccer. He saw his parents in the mornings and late at night, but they were starting to work more again, starting to come home later and later. When they were at home, they were tired. Travis had never seen them watch so much TV.

The rest of the time, he read. He read during lunch at school, during free period, and at home. He scurried through his homework to get to his reading. He continued to reread *The Pastures of Heaven,* and went through *The Long Valley* a second time. Travis had always loved to read, but now it was something bordering on obsession. Books, he knew, had led him to the mysteries that surrounded him; perhaps books would offer up the answers he was seeking.

He became fascinated with two of the odder characters from these books—Johnny Bear, the powerful but dim-witted giant who could remember and mimic perfectly every conversation he had ever heard; and Tularecito, the little frog, a dwarfish man who believed that gnomes lived underground, and who could draw and sculpt perfect renditions of the living world. In the stories about them, Johnny Bear in *The Long Valley,* and Tularecito in *Pastures,* they were shunned by everyone because of their special gifts. No one understood the things they saw and did.

He wanted to know as much as he could about these places and these characters before he saw Oster again. There was another stuff-n-fold session at the end of the week.

Until then, the rest of his life was reading. He took

some ribbing from the other kids—"Hey, bookworm," "Earth calling Travis." Even Hil got in on it, started calling him Shakespeare all the time, and one day that week Hil made a paper mask of Travis's face that he attached to the front cover of *The Pastures of Heaven*. "So I can remember what you look like," he said.

But Travis didn't care what the other kids thought. He couldn't help himself. The kind of reading he was doing wasn't about escaping from the real world. His reading had unlocked a door, and was leading him into a mystery about the real world. A *real* mystery about the *real* world.

Every book, Travis knew, had a mystery at its heart. In most books, though, the mysteries were easy to solve. Who had killed the school gardener? Where was the lost crystal? Could a vampire be repelled with garlic? These were mysteries with straight answers. The math teacher killed the gardener in a fit of jealousy and was sent to jail. The lost crystal was hidden in the cave of Inum Ortem, and once it was put back in the Mask of Trat'Ottrat with the five other crystals, the kingdom of Yrruc would be saved from the forces of darkness. Contrary to popular belief, garlic did not repel vampires, and everyone in the old mansion was eaten. Easy-peasy mysteries. Simple. Done.

Travis had read a lot of books like this. But the books he was reading now were opening up deeper mysteries. Mysteries that couldn't be solved, mysteries that didn't end, that continued long after the last page was turned.

At the end of *A Wrinkle in Time,* Meg and Charles Wallace found their father in another dimension and returned with him to their own. But they still didn't know what "IT" was, and knew even less about the shape of the universe, even though they'd traveled through it and arrived safely back to their own world. Meg and Charles Wallace had only one choice after their unsettling journey, a journey whose mystery seemed unfathomable: they had to leave the safety of what they knew and return to the perils of the unknown. So they did.

In Steinbeck's own books, there were mysteries that could never be solved. Who were the Watchers? Had Gitano really worked on the ranch when he was a boy, and why did he steal the horse at the end and where did he go? How did Johnny Bear and Tularecito come into their powers, and what did those powers mean? Every story in Steinbeck carried an unfathomable mystery, and Steinbeck wasn't the kind of writer who offered simple answers to difficult mysteries. Steinbeck's mysteries lingered.

But the one mystery that would not let him go, the

reason Travis kept reading *The Pastures of Heaven*: Where was this place? Steinbeck called it the Pastures of Heaven, or Las Pasturas del Cielo, sometimes Happy Valley; everyone else called it the Corral. It was a real place, Travis knew, and there had once been a town there, but there was not a single record of that town anywhere. Travis had looked online: nothing. However, he'd spent a long time looking for Oster and found nothing at first, and still, there was Oster, a real person.

And at the heart of the *Pastures* mystery was another one, possibly even bigger: What was the curse that shadowed the Corral? Why had everyone who moved there lost everything they most wanted?

The great thing about an unsolvable mystery was just that, it was unsolvable. It was as if the book never ended.

So Travis read. He took to reading at his desk at night, looking west across Salinas toward the Corral. As he read from the book, he looked up occasionally and wondered about the real world out there.

Oster and Miss Babb were already in the A/V room, folding and stuffing, when Travis got there. Miss Babb was dressed to kill, Travis thought, way too fancy for the library.

"Oh, Travis, good, you're here," she said. She seemed a little out of breath. "I've got great news. I've just met with some wealthy library patrons, and guess what? I collected almost thirty thousand dollars. Eek!"

And she screamed a little and clapped her hands, and stood up and took Travis's hand and twirled him around, and they were both laughing, and Oster was applauding.

"Thirty thousand dollars," she said. "Can you believe it? And all I had to do was talk and eat some fancy-schmancy hors d'oeuvres. The mushrooms stuffed with bacon were amazing."

"That is so awesome."

"Yes, yes," she said. "I am so awesome, aren't I? Look upon me, ye mighty rich ones and despair for your wallets."

"That's our Charlene," Oster said. "Saving the world one check at a time."

The first order of business was dinner. They decided on Indian food, delivered from The Clay Oven. Travis was psyched; he loved naan bread.

They stuffed and folded while they waited.

"So, you guys," Miss Babb said. "How was the aquarium?"

Travis and Oster looked at each other. Both looked as if they'd just seen a tap-dancing spider.

"What?" Miss Babb said. "What is it?"

"It was awesome," Travis said. And together they told her about the aquarium tour and going to Doc's lab.

"It was really informative," Travis said, wrapping it up.

"But?" Miss Babb said.

"But what?" Oster said. He looked over at Travis. "We went. We had a nice time."

"Nice? Informative?" Miss Babb said. "I don't think so. You guys are holding back something, I can tell. C'mon. Dish."

Travis looked over at Oster and shrugged his shoulders. Oster shrugged, too.

"Okay," Travis said. "But you'll be sorry you asked."

Together they spilled the beans—about Steinbeck and Doc, and the Watchers that night on the edge of the Corral.

"What I'm thinking," Travis said, "is that I've stuffed too many envelopes or something. What I'm thinking is that I'm a little crazy."

"But," Oster said, "it's better saying it out loud. No, Travis is not crazy, and neither am I. We saw what we saw, and no matter how I try to explain it away, it's too obvious to ignore. Something is going on. And I'd swear the Watchers want us to follow them. Don't quote me on that. I have to confess, I'm a little freaked out, too."

Miss Babb was staring at the wall across from her, staring into the space between Oster and Travis. She had her hand on her chin, the classic thinking pose. She was shaking her head back and forth just a little bit.

"Honestly, men," she said, looking up now, as if stepping back into the room again. "If I didn't know you guys any better, I would say you were crazy. But I do know you. And I must confess, I've seen the Watchers myself. Many times. Like you, I don't know who they are or what they mean. But I know this, they're there. And you can't ignore them. So. When are you going back? Into the Corral, I mean."

"How's Saturday?" Travis asked.

"Sounds good, I suppose," Oster said. "Saturday seems like a good day for hieing off into the mysterious world at our peril."

"Peril?" Travis said. "I'm ready for peril. Definitely ready."

"It's a deal then," Miss Babb said. "You guys be careful, okay? How I wish I could go with you, but my family and all, just no time. You've got to promise to give me the end of this story."

Just then, the naan bread and curry arrived.

III
THE WORLD

ELEVEN

SATURDAY MORNING CAME EARLY AND BRIGHT, AND STRETCHED ITSELF OVER THE VALLEY. Travis could tell already that the day would be warm, but not hot. Indian summer was still in the air, but it seemed to be taking it easy today, a weekend day. Thin streams of high clouds rode up from the bottom of the valley.

Travis was dying to get to the Corral, see it, explore whatever mystery was there for him, or as close as he could get. And he also needed to get away from Bella Linda Terrace, that was certain. Even though he was anxious to get going, he was disappointed that his parents had left for work early—on a Saturday!—and that things were so uneasy between him and Hil, had been growing more so all week. They only saw each other at school now, and their conversations there were reduced to grunts and forced smiles. At first Travis wanted to believe that this was all Hil's fault—he was so into soccer—but he realized it was mostly his fault. Travis was just too distracted to be a good friend.

And then Hil had called on Friday night, wanting to make sure Travis was coming to his soccer game. Travis forgot that he'd promised him that he would go. Much to his surprise, Travis lied again. He told Hil he was driving up to San Jose with his folks, some kind of museum thingie he'd forgotten about.

But what else could Travis say that would make any sense? That he was going off into the hills in search of a lost town? That he was going with some old guy who once wrote a book thirty years ago? That the Watchers were leading him there? That this all had something to do with the library, but not really? That he was on a journey he needed to follow on his own, without Hil? At least for now. None of it made any sense, not even to Travis.

So he lied again. And Hil didn't even ask him to come to next week's game.

And his parents? Aargghh! They both had "killer" deadlines on Monday. They needed to "fortify" their "positions," had to "ambush" the competition, find new "strategies." Travis couldn't tell if they were going to work or going to war.

When his parents got involved in the library campaign—the meetings, the car wash, going to Sheila's, all that—Travis hoped they had finally returned to their senses. But it was like one of those happy dreams that, when you wake up, leaves you feeling sadder because it was, after all, only a dream.

When he went down to breakfast that morning, there was a note on the kitchen table and an overstuffed picnic basket. Have a great time with Ernest, the note said, and be careful up there. Call them on the cell if he was going to be later than seven.

Travis ate a bowl of Lucky Charms the size of a basketball, and watched cartoons until his eyes began to vibrate. At eleven he went out to the front porch to wait for Oster. Time to get out of Camazotz.

When he and Oster stopped at the main gate of Bella Linda Terrace, Hil's family pulled up next to the Dart on the passenger side. Travis didn't see them at first, but Hil called out, "Hey, Big T," and when he turned, Hil was waving and making his usual goofy faces. Then Hil's face stopped, shut down, and he looked at the floor of the car. Travis knew what had happened. Hil had seen the lie he'd been told. Travis wasn't going anywhere with his family.

Travis was waving, trying to get Hil's attention, when

the light changed, and the two cars headed off in opposite directions.

✦ ✦ ✦

"So, Travis. Tell me more about you," Oster said. "I'm afraid we've talked too much about myself. I know you like to read."

Facts. Travis started with facts. When he was born and where. Where he'd grown up, where he lived now. Where he went to school, then and now. His favorite movies, TV shows, games. His friends, the old gang from Salinas, and Hil, of course, his best friend. If they were still friends.

The more he talked, the more confused the facts became. One fact led into another, and these facts had to have other facts to explain them. And suddenly the facts weren't just facts anymore, they were stories. But no one story ended and offered the chance for a new story to begin. They all connected. A never-ending story.

Pretty soon Travis was talking about his parents. Not where they came from or what they did, but how complicated everything was, how much he missed their old life.

"And," he heard himself saying, "it was great downtown. My mom was a teacher, and my dad was a bartender and he played in a band, and we all hung out all the time. Then they went back to college, and they got new jobs, and we got this great new house, and everything's *supposed* to be perfect."

He stopped talking. He was afraid he might start yelling.

"*Supposed* to be perfect?" Oster asked. He was driving, looking straight ahead, but he raised one eyebrow: a big question, a complicated one.

"I hate it," Travis said. "I hate it all. I hate the new house, and the new jobs, and I just hate it all."

Silence again. They were driving past the Salinas Valley Vegetable Exchange. Trucks, two trailers long and heaped with lettuce, were creeping out the front gate onto Highway 68, headed east. By tomorrow this lettuce would be halfway around the world.

"I don't blame you," Oster said. "Not at all. Life is short, Travis. You're learning that now, and that's important. Maybe you always knew it. Most people don't learn that until it's too late. You know what's important. You, your parents, your family. The library. You want to have it now. You don't want to wait until everything is *supposed* to be perfect."

Oster's voice was different when he said this—slower, deeper, more . . . what was it? More intense. He remembered Oster's story about Ray Bradbury, that important afternoon they'd shared together in Waukegan, the things Bradbury had told him about writing and life. And Travis thought, This is one of those moments: important. Travis knew he should be paying attention with all his might, and he was.

"When did you know? You know," Travis said.

"Well, I suppose I'm like you a little bit. I've probably always known it. Some people are different that way. You and me, we're different. Not better, mind you: different. And it doesn't help us much either. I've always known life is short—that one day the things you love can disappear. But I've had to learn the same lesson over and over."

"I don't get it," Travis said.

"It is *very* complicated. And I don't mean too complicated for a kid. It's complicated for the smartest people."

They were passing the Spreckels turnoff now. Oster nodded that way.

"See," Oster said. "Two years ago, my wife died. Eve. We'd been together forever. Like you and your family. In that whole time—longer than you can imagine right now—there wasn't one day that passed I didn't know how lucky I was. My wife, my daughters, all of us together. I knew it. But when she died, I was filled with regret. I kept thinking of all the stupid things I'd done that kept me away from my family. Like working. I worked too much. And for what? She was still dead. All that working didn't change anything."

Oster drove without looking at Travis, who was watching him closely. He wanted to understand what Oster was saying. He felt very close to understanding it.

"But my parents, I mean . . ."

Silence filled the car again.

"It'll be okay, I think," Oster said. "I've met your parents, I've heard you talk about them. They get it, Travis, they do. Your parents know what's important. Most likely, you get it from them. They're just confused right now. They're lost a little bit. We all get that way now and then. They'll figure it out."

Rows of valley oak flashed by the window.

His parents *were* a little confused right now. Travis never imagined he would think this about his own parents, but there it was.

"How can I help them get unconfused?" he asked.

"Simple. Talk to them. Tell them what you just told me. It's hard, I know. But it's all you can do. How can they know if you won't tell them?"

At the turnoff to Corral de Tierra Road, they pulled into a vacant lot on the other side of the street from the general store. A billboard planted in the middle of the lot shouted COMING SOON! with a painting of a proposed shopping center, El Paso de Corral de Tierra.

The developers, smaller writing said, were PLEASED TO ANNOUNCE THE ARRIVAL OF A STATE-OF-THE-ART SHOPPING CENTER, A DEVELOPMENT THAT WILL PROVIDE TWENTY-FIRST-CENTURY SERVICES TO THE PEOPLE OF THE HIGHWAY 68 CORRIDOR, AS WELL AS ATTRACT TOURISTIC SUPPORT TO THE AREA, ALL DESIGNED TO REFLECT THE SPIRIT AND AESTHETICS OF THE LUMINOUS WORLD OF JOHN STEINBECK.

"Gobbledygook," Travis said. "What does it even mean? I mean, 'touristic'? Is that a real word?"

"It means they're gonna build some stores here. Whether we like it or not."

The billboard painting showed rows of shops that looked like every other shopping center in the world.

"But it's ugly," Travis said. "And what does it have to do with Steinbeck? It's stupid."

"It's stupid, all right."

"Why can't we use this money for the library?"

Oster started to speak, but Travis cut him off.

"Because libraries are free," Travis said. "Can't make any money off of them."

"Exactly."

"You know," Travis said. "I've read a lot of Steinbeck. There's no place in Steinbeck that ever looked like this"—the buildings were angular and modern, painted purple and green—"and I don't remember a single Mango Tango franchise in any of his books."

"Good thing we came today. Might all be a postcard tomorrow."

Behind the empty lot, dark groves of oak marched up steep hills into the Corral. Despite the vivid painting, Travis could not imagine the reality of an ugly shopping center in such a beautiful place.

They got back in the Dart and headed up into—where were they going? All those names for it. And all those different versions of it. There was Corral de Tierra the valley, as well as Corral de Tierra the town that no longer existed. There was Steinbeck's fictional town, Oster's fictional version of Steinbeck's fictional town. Was this a hunting ground for California Indians, the stumbled-upon Eden of a Spanish conquistador, the dark lure of the Watchers, Travis's deep imagining of all these? Or the site of a new shopping center?

It was hard to say which was which; one place and all places. Travis had looked at many maps of the area—topographical maps at the library, satellite maps and photographs online, road maps in the glove compartment of his dad's car. But no map gave him the sense of the place he got from reading, or from what he saw now in front of him.

They drove along a narrow curving road, up and over a slight rise. Gates and mailboxes hinted at houses behind the thick stands of old trees—sycamore, willow, eucalyptus, birch.

Travis and Oster scanned it all. Oster was smiling.

"My, my," was all he said.

They passed the entrance to the Corral de Tierra Country Club. A parking lot, clubhouse, and tennis courts looked down on the road.

"My, my," Oster said again.

Travis remembered something in the last chapter of *The Pastures of Heaven,* and he was trying to put the memory into words when Oster veered off the road onto the shoulder.

"There it is," Oster said, pointing out the driver's window. "Right there, beyond the tennis courts. It's the Castle."

Far away, on the highest peak, a sand-colored bluff broke the reign of black-green manzanita scrub. The bluff was hard to make out from this vantage, more of a smudge than a castle. But he knew what it looked like; he'd seen the photo on his library copy of *The Pastures of Heaven.*

For a second he realized his library books were probably overdue. Not that it would matter, he thought, if the library was closing. And then he had a horrible thought: What would happen to all those books if the library did close? Would they just put them out on the sidewalk, or worse, keep them locked up and unread in the empty building?

"Let's go check it out," Oster said.

He spun the car around and headed back to the country club, passing through the iron gate. At the far end of the parking lot, they got out of the car. The Castle, still far away, seemed much closer than it could be. If this were a book, Travis thought, you would say it dominated the horizon. You would say it was awe-inspiring.

"Corral de Tierra, a fence of earth," Oster said. "That's what it means, literally. My god, it's beautiful."

The Castle was a corrugated rock face on the steep side of a mountaintop. The rock face must have been several hundred feet tall, several hundred wide. The corrugations in the rock face looked like enormous pillars, and the top edge of the bluff was harshly geometrical. No wonder it was called the Castle. It looked as if human hands had created it.

"What's it made of?" Travis asked. "How did it happen?"

"It's sandstone. Very soft, porous. All the hills up and down the coast have sandstone running through them, from when this area was ocean bottom. When the ground cover falls away—like here, it's too steep for plants and trees—the rain and wind erode it, cut it into these shapes. There are hundreds of little cliffs like that back in these hills. But this is the granddaddy."

The sky and its now gathering clouds leaped over the Castle.

"My, my," Oster said. Travis knew from the tone of this "my, my" that it was said with some irritation. "Look, look there, just below it. That house."

At the foot of the Castle sat an enormous house, at least three stories. It was done up in the style of an English mansion.

"How dare they?" Oster said. "Right in front of it."

There was a darkness in Oster's voice Travis had not heard before.

"It's butt ugly," Travis said.

"Got that right." Oster spit on the ground.

"I was just remembering," Travis said. "At the end of *Pastures*—he kind of jumps into the future in the last chapter? And he predicts that one day the valley will be all golf courses and big houses with big gates around them."

As if the world needed to make this point clear, a golfer on the fairway below them shouted, "Fore."

"You're right," Oster said. "I'd forgotten that. Well, Steinbeck was a pretty sharp guy."

There was someone behind them, coming their way. They turned to greet him, a young man in khaki shorts and a green polo shirt. On the shirt's breast was the embroidered logo of the country club.

"Good morning, gentlemen," he said. "How can I help you today?"

"Oh, no thanks," Oster said. "Just enjoying the view."

Travis watched the young man's eyes. He couldn't see anything there.

"And you are club members?" When he said this, the young man glanced at Oster's car.

"No, not members," Oster said. "Just enjoying the view. I hope—"

"I'm sorry, then, gentlemen, I'll have to ask you to leave. This is private property. Members only."

Oster put up a hand and started to speak. He dropped his hand. It was clear, Travis saw, that this young man was official and serious.

"Well, good day, then," Oster said.

They got into the car and drove off. The man in the

green shirt watched after them until they were back on the main road.

"Fine. If we're not wanted here, that's okay. Anyhow, we got more important business. Now, let's go look for that town," Oster said. "I'll show you where I think it was. *If* I can find it. Who-ee, it's been ages."

✦ ✦ ✦

They drove farther into the valley, and the road straightened itself across a plain. Trees crowded the narrow way. On either side, broad paths, guarded by rail fences, showed an occasional jogger or horse and rider.

Then they were following a large creek, and the road twisted and swerved and cut back on itself. The creek was low, barely a trickle in the rain-dry autumn. Travis knew that in the spring this creek would be a tumbling, green-and-white monster, swift and treacherous.

The road here was a tunnel; they could see nothing of the surrounding hillsides, nothing of the nearby homes.

Without warning, the road began to rise, and the car was splashed with bright sun. They rose up and up, clinging to the side of an exposed hill. Patches of prickly pear cacti barricaded the sides of the road. And just as suddenly, the road plunged down again and around a curve, and the world opened up into a spectacular view.

Before them was a broad valley, surrounded on three sides by sinuous hills. Here and there, pods of horses munched on grass, lazy in the warm day. At the far end of the valley, a red-tailed hawk glided close above the final ridge.

Oster pulled the car onto the shoulder.

"Well," he said. "This is it. Easy to see why he called it heaven. And this is only the half of it."

It was just like Travis remembered. Remembered? No, read. He had read the words on the page, black on white, and it was as if he had made this place spring to life, as if his reading had created the world.

"Go ahead," Oster said. "Say it."

"Say what?"

"Wow."

"Wow!"

They continued through the valley. The fields on either side of the road were brilliant green, as green as emeralds, a green obviously inspired by heavy irrigation. The fields were fenced all the way to the road. Large houses and outbuildings rested against the feet of the bordering hills. Horses, a few cows, some goats.

They drove up the valley, rising again on another

twisting road. Travis was afraid they were leaving it already, but the road ended at a yellow sign, DEAD END. Oster parked, got out, and stretched. Travis got out and turned around, not ready for what he saw.

They had entered the valley, not at one end of it, but from the side, and stretching out in front of him now, southward, the valley ran far away, rising and falling over gentle slopes until, miles in the distance, it ended at another ridge of the Santa Lucias. This view he had never imagined, had not read out of a book. The world surprised him.

✦ ✦ ✦

They ate lunch by the side of the road. Travis was anxious to get going, follow wherever Oster led him, learn what he could about this town, this valley. But he could wait.

They saw no one else the entire time, except for a school bus that came up to the end of the road, laboriously turned around, and drove away without so much as a wave. It was Saturday, and the bus was empty of children. It made no sense at all.

While they ate, Oster explained all he knew of the Corral. He started by telling Travis many things Travis already knew. He spoke slowly, his eyes focused far away. Travis knew that Oster had to walk around in the story for a while, get used to it. Travis let him wander. Stories had to be told from the beginning.

Oster told him again about coming to Salinas to write a novel, and traipsing around the valley, and getting scared off.

Then he backed up from there and retraced his steps. The town, he'd been looking for the town of Corral de Tierra. No one else in Salinas would admit to its ever having been here, but Oster knew better. He'd read Steinbeck's book.

The town Steinbeck described wasn't much of one—a general store, a short string of two-story houses, a blacksmith. The tiniest Western-movie town imaginable, bleak wooden buildings on a muddy road. Travis looked into the near section of valley and could almost see it, where the road broke sharply.

"Right there," Oster said. "Right where the road breaks. That's as close as I got. But it had to be there. Back then, there were several old foundations, all clustered together, like you'd find in a town. But now, just look at it, it's all been plowed up, plowed under."

"I can see it," Travis said. "Right where you're pointing, a perfect place for a town. It had to be there." At least, he wanted it to be there.

From the day Oster had received Steinbeck's letter,

he needed to find the town. Something awful had happened here, and he had been determined to find out what it was.

Travis was having a hard time imagining something awful happening in a place so beautiful.

Oster never did find out what had happened, though. And he found no proof of the town's existence. He spent weeks in the records department of Salinas's City Hall, but no piece of paper anywhere mentioned it.

He came to the Corral frequently while he was writing the book. He hiked all over, looking for some kind of evidence, any kind of relic. Even trash heaps, there were a lot of those. Trash heaps were always good evidence for how and where any group of humans lived. What we threw away said much about what we valued.

He stopped in at farmhouses, barns, anywhere he could find people. He asked a thousand questions. No one knew anything. Perhaps, he began to feel, the town had only ever existed in Steinbeck's imagination.

Then one day—must have been spring; the air was crisp, the hills lime-green—he came upon an old campsite in a narrow ravine. There wasn't much to it, a fire pit, broken bottles, sharpened sticks. He was digging through the ashes when a rifle shot screamed down at him. He actually saw and felt the pop of dust in the hillside next to him before he heard the shot. Then he heard the sound of its resounding echoes.

He froze, put his hands in the air. Silence. He started to speak, to apologize for trespassing, but all he got out was, "Hey, there," when he heard the snap and crack of the rifle's breech, then another shot—puff and boom.

The rifle's breech cracked open again.

Oster turned and carefully walked away from the fire pit, down the hill. His body shook the whole way. But he could see his car.

That's when the third shot cried past him, over his shoulder. It was too precise a shot to be a miss; it was a warning.

A dire warning is what they call it in books, Travis thought.

Oster never went back to the Corral. He sensed that he'd asked too many questions, gotten too close to something that was being kept hidden. He was frightened. Today was the first time he'd been back.

Travis's hand was shaking. Oster stared out over the valley.

"Look," Oster said. "It's a scary story, you don't have to tell me. If you're afraid, we can go. I'm pretty sure we won't get shot at today. But if you want . . ."

"No, no," Travis said. And he wasn't afraid for himself,

he discovered. It was just Oster's story; he was more afraid for Oster, Oster from a long time ago.

"Now what?" Travis asked. "Are we going to go look for the town?"

"I hadn't expected all these houses and farms out here. Look at all those fences. The whole place, it's owned. I don't see how we can even get close."

"But we've got to keep looking, don't you think?" Travis said. "For something. If we're right, well, if I'm right, coming up here is something I'm supposed to do. It ain't no picnic."

"Well," Oster said. "What do you say to a little hike? If I remember correctly, up at the top of this mountain, or pretty close by, around here somewhere, there's one of the sandstone bluffs. You still game?"

"We've come this far," Travis said.

Travis ate all three of his sandwiches. Real fast.

TWELVE

IT HADN'T RAINED SINCE LAST SPRING. That was the way it worked in California. The rains started in late October or early November, and continued through April. After that, no rain at all. It was almost time for the first rains again.

Travis smelled the dust with every step he took. The leaves and grass and branches crackled and broke underfoot, and every step brought the dust to his nose. The earth was quiet, dormant. Waiting. That smell, Travis thought, that's the smell of Salinas, of California. The smell of waiting for rain.

He didn't know if he loved the smell because of the smell itself, or because it meant the rains would soon come.

Two months from now these hills would be such a bright green that it would hurt to look at them. The hills, and the life that depended on them, would be refreshed.

Vibrant, that was the word. Or *verdant,* another good word. And then, only a few months after the rains had soaked the hills, the green would fade. By June the hills would be the color of gold, as intensely yellow as the intense green of spring. All through the summer, the grass would fade from gold, duller and duller as summer marched to autumn. And then the hills would be this color again, brown almost. No, not brown. The grass would be so dead it was transparent, invisible, and the brown of the hills would show through. Then the rains would come again.

Travis followed Oster up one steep ravine after another. Every time they got to the top, another ravine rose above them. Oster would stop and turn, look with a question at Travis. Travis would nod and they would continue.

After some time they came to a grove of oak on a flat terrace. They sat on a fallen oak trunk, and Oster pulled some water bottles from his knapsack—"before backpacks we had knapsacks, same thing," he said. They gulped down the water. Even this high up, they could not see the broad valley. The trees were dense here.

They both turned at the same time. The clopping sound had come from above. At first there was nothing but the careful clop-clop, then a shuddering of scrub brush, and then, behind the brush, a reddish shape appeared. When the pony stuck its head out of the brush, Travis almost laughed.

The pony stepped forward. Its front legs poked out of the scrub.

Stillness invaded the terrace.

The pony nodded and nickered. Its mane was black and stiff and short. It nodded again.

Travis held out his water bottle and splashed some into the dust.

The pony leaned forward, about to take a step, then pulled back. It stepped forward again, removing itself from the scrub. It inched toward them and the water, its nose close to the ground. Travis heard sharp bursts of air from its nostrils.

When the pony reached the muddy pit where Travis had poured the water, it sniffed at it and licked tenderly. It nickered and snorted and stomped one hoof.

Travis cupped his hand and poured water into it, held it out to the pony. Travis could smell the clean, cool water.

The pony inched forward and slurped the water in Travis's hand.

The pony stomped his hoof again, and Travis refilled his offering. The pony drank like this for several minutes.

"Gabilan." He was dying to say the name aloud, so he

did. He knew he might scare off the pony, but he had to say it. Gabilan, Jody's colt in *The Red Pony*. The two animals were identical—red coat, black mane and tail, white forelegs like little socks, white blaze between black glittering eyes.

The pony pulled back, tilted its head sideways. He was looking at Travis with one wild eye. They measured each other for a long time.

Gabilan—Travis could think of it no other way—pony-hopped in place on his front legs, then seemed to collapse, cutting away from Travis, spooked, climbing fast into the scrubby hillside.

Travis looked at Oster, whose hand was poised in midair, as if he'd been turned to stone. They were both too stunned for a moment to say anything, as if saying anything would break the spell of what had just happened. Silence. Then Oster spoke.

"Gabilan," he said. "You may be right. No, you have to be right. The mystery's here, Travis."

Perhaps the shouting had reached the pony's sensitive ears first—why it had run off—but it was only now that Travis and Oster heard it. A man's voice, but far away, not the next ravine, maybe the one beyond that.

"I am Gitano, and I have come back." Later, both Travis and Oster would agree this is what they heard.

But now they stood quietly, putting on their packs, and together raced after the voice. They crossed several ravines before they heard the voice again. It was farther away now, up the hill, moving up and away.

"I am Gitano, and I have come back."

Breathless, the both of them, they looked to each other, locked eyes, and with no outward sign, agreed to follow the voice.

The voice stayed well ahead of them. Travis knew they would never catch up, that the voice was in control of this chase. He also knew who belonged to the voice. Gitano, the man outside the library, the character from *The Red Pony*. It seemed impossible. Not impossible that such a man existed—Travis had seen him, he believed in him—but impossible that he should be up here.

By the time they broke out of the oak grove into the open air, the voice had dissolved. Travis sensed that the voice would not return. Which did not matter at all. Oster was right, the mystery was here, and they were following it.

Oster, breathing heavy, his hands on his knees, simply pointed. There it was.

It wasn't the Castle, but close enough. The sandstone bluff was enormous, as wide and as high as the school's gymnasium. The bright rock, almost white against the dark manzanita forest, seemed to pulse, vibrate. It was rock, Travis knew, inanimate, but it certainly seemed alive.

Since they'd been in the oak grove, making their way up the steep ravines—how long had they been climbing?—the thin clouds had continued to thicken and gather. The air was warm, but the sky was gray.

Travis and Oster were doing what they seemed to be doing a lot lately—they stared.

"May I saw wow again?" Travis said to the air.

"Please do."

"Wow," he said.

The face of the bluff had been carved into rounded columns, like bowling pins. The entire surface of the bluff was beaded with small holes. Travis could almost hear the rain beating against the rock, creating the holes. He could almost see the gushing water cascading over the top of the bluff, how it shaped and shaved the columns.

In the center of the bluff, at its base, was a dark opening.

"A cave." Travis said the word as if he'd invented it.

"Let's go. Who can resist a cave? And besides, I don't think we're here by mistake."

Oster was right; they'd been brought here—by Gitano's voice, by the pony, by the Watchers, a very long trail.

They began the long scramble to the base of the bluff. The slope that led to it was a long patch of scree, not solid ground but loose stones that gave way under Travis's feet. With every step, he slid back down. The only way to make progress was to pump his legs like mad.

He stopped to suck in some air.

Oster was far ahead of him, nearly to the base. And he wasn't breathing hard; in fact, he was whistling.

Oster wasn't attacking the scree head-on. He walked zigzag up the mound of loose stones, cutting back on his path every six or seven steps. The scree held under his weight. It was a very Tortoise and the Hare moment for Travis.

Oster looked down at him.

"Walk like a cow," he said. "Or a goat. When cows go up a hill, they don't attack it, takes too much effort. They zigzag. Cows are smarter than they look."

And he went on ahead.

In one of those weird moments, Travis's brain connected this new piece of information with something very far away. Zigzag, that was Miss Babb's approach to saving the library. She wasn't running straight up the hill to knock down the people in charge. She was roaming from side to side, slowly and surely. She knew how steep the hill was.

"Wait for me." And, like a cow, Travis zigged and zagged up the scree in no time flat.

The view from the base of the bluff was, well, it was . . . Travis had run out of words. Not even *wow* fit this. The valley, the Corral, it filled the world. There was nothing else.

The sky was growing darker still, and the breezes up here cooled Travis. He ran his hands over the granulated limestone.

"Grab a handful of rocks," Oster said. "Let's pepper a few into the cave. Rattlers always like you to knock first."

They stood back from the edge of the cave's mouth and chucked in a few rocks. Travis heard nothing but pings.

Oster leaned in, shined a flashlight around, chucked more rocks. No noise, no rattle.

The entrance to the cave was about the size and shape of a man, easy to squeeze through. The actual cavern was larger, taller and wider, but it was hard to say how far back into the hillside it went.

Oster ducked into the cave, Travis followed close. Without thinking about it, he reached behind him and felt in his backpack for the cell phone. Just in case.

The darkness overwhelmed them for an instant, blacker than black and infinite. The flashlight beam swept across the cave, which was much bigger than Travis imagined, ten or twelve feet tall, and it went back into the hillside dozens of feet.

They both froze when they saw the man. He was enormous, silent and still.

Travis wanted to run but couldn't feel his feet.

"My, my," Oster said. "My, oh my. Scared the bejeezus out of me."

It wasn't a man, but a statue of a man. Travis laughed out loud.

"Will you look at that?" Oster said. He crouched, moving closer, but very slowly, toward the statue. "It's amazing."

The statue was made of hundreds of small flat stones, each layered upon the others. The stones were fitted so well, it was almost impossible to see them individually. All the little stones made one solid figure, and that figure seemed sturdy, unbreakable.

Travis stepped back. The stone man was well over six feet tall. His shoulders were as broad as two ordinary men. His legs were as round and solid as tree trunks, his hands were like catcher's mitts. The figure wore a plain shirt and pants, all made of stones. Even his bare feet were made of stones, each strange, square toe perfectly articulated.

What most struck Travis was the stone man's face. It was broad and flat, as wide open as a plate. The eyes were quiet, though, almost searching, almost glinting. There was a solid brow over the eyes. The hair was uneven, tousled, as if uncombed for a long time.

Oster put out a hand to touch it, but Travis grabbed it and pulled back. Sturdy as the statue appeared, Travis was afraid it might collapse.

"How did they do this?" Travis asked.

"Johnny Bear," Oster said. "It's Johnny Bear."

"What?"

"It's a statue of Johnny Bear. I'd recognize him anywhere. In *The Long Valley*, you know, the story 'Johnny Bear.' You remember, the giant simpleton? Strong as an ox. Has the power to recite any conversation he's ever heard. In the voices of, I mean, he does the voices perfectly."

"Yeah, I remember," Travis said. "But why? Who? Why up here?"

"I have no idea. But it's amazing."

The statue's open mouth seemed ready to speak.

"It is Johnny Bear," Travis said. "You're right. But I don't get it, don't get it at all." Travis sort of expected he'd be getting used to all these mysteries by now, but he wasn't. Each one he stumbled upon, or was called to, whatever was happening, surprised him still.

"And that, my young friend, is why they call it a mystery."

They pored over the statue with their eyes. Every detail was perfect.

There was nothing else in the cave, no signs of life—no bones, no scat, no nests. They agreed the cave was still being used by humans; otherwise, there'd be animal life, insect life.

It seemed safe enough for now, though, and a good place to rest. They sat at Johnny Bear's feet, and Oster served up a snack, fresh bread and cheese. Travis hadn't realized how hungry he'd grown.

"Who would do this?" Travis said. "It's beautiful, amazing. But why all the way up here where no one can see? Maybe we should tell Miss Babb. Might be cool publicity."

Oster pondered a slab of cheese on the blade of his pocketknife.

"You think? Just yet?" Oster asked. "I don't know.

Seems to me this is just the beginning. What was that voice? Why did it bring us up here? I don't have a clue. But I don't want to give up right now."

Travis told Oster all he knew about Gitano, where he'd seen him, what he found in *The Red Pony*. He promised to go looking for him downtown. Maybe Gitano would talk to him. Maybe Gitano could offer a clue.

They could see well enough in the cave now to stop using the flashlight. Even so, the hole of sky visible from the cave's mouth continued to grow darker.

"Is this place cursed, do you think?" Travis asked. "Not the cave, but the whole Corral."

A cursed valley? A mysterious cave? A crazy statue that seemed beyond any explanation? Travis thought he should probably be freaking out—totally freaking out—right about now. But the dark, still quiet of the cave hushed his nerves, cast a blanket of calm over him.

"I don't know. The more I learn about it, and being back up here today, I know even less. How can it be cursed? You saw all those houses, all those people living here now. It's a lovely piece of earth. Hard to see it as cursed."

"But . . ."

"I do know this," Oster continued. "Cursed or not, Steinbeck knew the Corral was special, different. And he knew reality wasn't as simple as it appeared. Not even nature was as simple as it seemed. Everybody calls him a realistic writer. They're wrong. He knew there was something like magic in the world, even if he never called it that. He knew, like we know now, that a whole town could simply disappear. He knew there were things in the world that were real but couldn't be explained. Couldn't be explained by science, or religion, not even by what most people think of as magic. And he knew that you didn't have to explain them. You simply had to live with them; understand them, not dissect them."

"Like this statue—Johnny Bear."

"Very possibly."

They sat in silence for a long while.

Just before he heard the sound, Travis smelled the change that would bring it. The air that blew in from the mouth of the cave was suddenly sweet, charged with some current, not the dust of the dying autumn, but a signal that the dust had been stirred by a new force.

Then he heard it. Rain. Tapping the scree, little sticks pounding little drums. It was slow at first, almost slow enough for Travis to count every drop.

"Well, I'll be," Oster said. "The first rain."

And the sky opened up, is what Travis thought when

he heard the noise, the crash of rain that pelted the world.

Travis and Oster stood in the mouth of the cave and watched the storm. The world had never smelled better.

"What is that smell?" Travis asked. "I can almost taste it."

"That's ozone, partly, flushed out from high in the sky. It's also the creosote in the manzanita and the madrone, an oil that protects the bark from the sun. It's the smell of stone wet again for the first time in months."

Nothing but rain.

"It's the smell," Oster said, "of the world coming back to life."

"Awesome."

They stayed in the cave for some time, waiting out the rain. They had planned to climb to the top of the mountain for the view from there, but the rain wouldn't end. It was getting late, and they had no choice but to leave. Oster left a heel of bread and the last of the cheese on the floor of the cave near the statue of Johnny Bear. Travis knew why Oster was leaving it, and he was glad of it. It was an offering of some kind, a way of saying, hello, if you're here, whoever you are, so are we.

They skidded down the scree, then hiked, almost at a run, down the ravines toward the car. The rain never let up.

When they reached the car, they were soaked through, their shoes and pants legs covered in mud. But it didn't seem to matter. All around they could hear the hard first rain gathering freshets in the hills.

Oster was urging Travis into the car when a voice rang out over the valley, like a bell, clear and true, loud above the rain.

"¡No, Papi, no! ¡Qué dejen!"

The voice called these sentences three times, then stopped. Both Travis and Oster knew that the voice had come from high up, near the limestone bluff.

Travis wanted to run after the voice, but knew he couldn't. It was dusk now.

"Your friend Gitano?" Oster asked.

"I don't think so. It's a little boy, can't you hear it? A young boy. What should we do? Shouldn't we call someone?"

"Do you really think someone is in trouble?"

No, he didn't think that. He knew what he was hearing, if not exactly where it came from. It was a voice from another time, a voice from Steinbeck's world. He knew it because he knew it, there was no other way to describe his certainty. This wasn't danger, not a warning. It was a call, a call for Travis to come back.

"No, no," Travis said. "It's not that. It's the next part of the mystery. Don't you think so? Can't you hear it?"

"I think you're right. But we better head on home now," Oster said. "We'll be back."

All the way home, they left the windows of the car open. They couldn't resist the smell of the rain-washed hills.

THIRTEEN

TRAVIS WOKE UP FEELING GUILTY ABOUT LYING TO HIL, SO HE CALLED HIM EARLY SUNDAY MORNING BEFORE HIL WENT OUT SOMEWHERE WITH HIS FAMILY. The lie—okay, lies, both of them—the lies he'd told had been small, Travis thought, but he knew Hil was hurt by the look on his face yesterday.

Travis wanted to explain everything—where he was going, who he was with, even what he'd seen—no matter how hard it might be. Travis knew he wouldn't be able to think straight about the Corral and the cave and Johnny Bear, unless he told Hil. In fact, he thought, maybe talking to Hil would help him understand the mysteries that had unfolded in the Corral.

Hil's mom picked up the phone; he was out for the day, she said, and she didn't know when he'd be back. Travis wanted to believe her, but she hesitated before she spoke. There was a loud TV in the background.

Travis stared out the kitchen window and waited for his cereal to get soggy.

The rains had continued through the night—their tap-tap-tap had lulled him to sleep—but the morning was cloudless and blue beyond blue. Everything was fresh.

He stared at the hills and saw that they were beautiful, but he was thinking only of the statue of Johnny Bear. Why would someone build such a thing? And why build it so far away, and inside a cave, where absolutely no one might ever see it? Most important, who was it—that voice—that had drawn him there?

In the car on the way home, exhilarated by the rain and the day's adventure, all Oster and Travis could do was go over what had happened, as if quizzing each other: remember when . . . remember how . . . did you see? Yes, they both agreed, everything they'd seen and heard was real. They both admitted, however, that they had no idea what was happening; all they knew was that they would have to go back again. Oster said they'd talk soon. In the meantime, he said, they should both do more research.

"Research?" Travis said. "You mean like reading more Steinbeck?"

"That. And anything else that strikes your fancy. I

gotta tell you, Travis, I'm stumped. We've got to look everywhere, anywhere. What we've found, it's huge. No telling where the answers lie."

His parents rustled their newspapers, slurped their coffee. Sunday on the couch. Every once in a while his father groaned for no particular reason.

Sundays were different when they lived in Oldtown. His mother was always in the garden on Sundays, in the front, tending to her poppies and wisteria and a thousand other plants. His father usually had a gig with the Not Band on Saturdays, which made for late nights, but on Sunday mornings he'd go to his music room to play and sing. Soft, stirring, Sunday morning songs. Almost a kind of church. Travis shuttled back and forth between them, helping his mom in the garden, plucking out a few chords with his dad.

Now they had a gardener, and his dad hadn't even unpacked his guitars.

"So, Travis, you all right?" his dad asked.

Travis spun on his stool.

"Yeah, you seem kind of blue," his mom said. "Why don't you call Hil?"

"I just did." He said this with a half-question at the end of it, an implied "duh."

"Okay," she said. "Sorry."

"Hey, what's wrong?" His father set the newspaper down.

"Nothing. I'm just tired. We hiked a long way yesterday."

"Yeah, how was that? Ernest show you around?" His parents had left a message for him last night. They would both be late. Again. He had no idea what time they came home.

"It was really pretty," he said. "Oster knows a ton about Steinbeck. And the Corral."

"So, what did you guys do?" his dad said. Travis spun on his stool and dived into his soggy cereal. "Hiking and stuff?"

"Yeah, you know, he just kind of showed me around. He knows everything you could possibly know about the Corral. I mean, he wrote the book on it, right?"

"You guys get along pretty well, that's nice," his mom said. "It's nice he's showing you all this stuff. I mean, just imagine, a letter from Steinbeck himself. How exciting."

"Yeah, it's great. I can talk to him about anything, and he really gets it."

"Well, you know," his dad said. "That's great, it really is. But you know you can still talk to us about anything, right?"

"Oh, I know," Travis said. But he also knew that he

wasn't ready to talk to his parents about everything. If they knew what he wasn't telling them, they'd flip out. He just couldn't. Partly it was what was happening, and partly he couldn't talk to them because, he figured, he was enjoying keeping this secret from them. But the biggest partly of all was that he wasn't sure he recognized his parents anymore. They were still the same people they'd always been, deep down, he knew, but it was harder and harder to remember that.

When, for instance, had his father started wearing fancy pajamas in the morning? It used to be his father only ever wore the same ratty old plaid flannel pants and some ratty old T-shirt or other, and he'd wear it all day if he could. But now, his parents not only got dressed up to go to work—ties for his dad, heels for his mom—now they were even dressing up for Sunday on the couch.

"Well, good, I'm glad you know that," his father said. "We're always here for you."

Oster had told him to talk to his parents, tell them everything about how he felt, everything that was going on, and he did want to. But how could you explain, over breakfast on a Sunday, that you were seeing ghosts, that characters from books were coming to life, that you were involved in a mystery that was completely mysterious?

Travis smiled weakly; his parents turned back to their newspapers and coffee.

✦ ✦ ✦

The morning wore on and turned into the afternoon. His parents could not be roused from their Camazotzian trances. All they wanted to do was chill, they said. The word *chill* scratched Travis's ear.

Finally, he thought the house might implode, collapse on itself, so he left. He took a basketball with him, as if that would answer any of his parents' questions. Apparently, it did.

He wandered around Bella Linda Terrace. Same as it ever was: cars being washed, lawns mowed, soccer played in the streets. Nothing had changed.

He ended up by the school, where he went to the far end of the playground and sat on his basketball, staring west. Past Salinas, to the Santa Lucias. The dark ridges of the mountains were in front of his eyes, but he saw through them into the Corral, into everything he'd seen yesterday.

If this were a book, Travis thought, if this were a book. If this were a book, he thought, I'd know by now who it was that was calling me. There'd be somebody, some one person, probably an archenemy, probably the dark lord of something or other, and Travis would know at least who to fight against. No matter how big or small the battle, how mysterious or straightforward the journey, there was always, in the end, one single person behind it all. Lord Voldemort, say, or the school bully. But this wasn't a book, and there was no archenemy. The mystery that was his real life was a mystery as big as the whole world. How do you research that, what spells could you cast?

He found a stick and made marks in the dusty lip of the basketball court; he drew a picture of the thread. He'd whispered the word *Camazotz,* gone to the library, seen Gitano, then Steinbeck's ghost—was it really Steinbeck's ghost?—found out about the library closing, came upon the Watchers, met Oster, saw Steinbeck and Doc at Cannery Row, then in the Corral encountered the red pony and the statue of Johnny Bear. That much was clear, each of these events led to the other. One big unanswered question: Why? No matter how hard he thought, nor how many diagrams he drew in the dirt, the why wouldn't come. But he kept thinking, even though it felt, as they say in the books, like hitting his head against a brick wall.

He really wanted to talk to Hil.

Time meant nothing. He might have sat there ten minutes or ten hours, impossible to know.

Without his noticing, it was already dusk. He figured he'd been sitting here forever, but no, it was only daylight savings time, "fall back." It was dark an hour earlier today, and it would only keep getting darker.

Later he called Hil again, sent him a couple of e-mails—no answer. After dinner he took a walk and went past Hil's house. All the lights were on; everyone was home.

He finished his homework, then read in bed. He read, again, the story "Johnny Bear." If the statue he'd seen in the Corral yesterday wasn't Johnny Bear, then nothing in the world made sense.

He was late to school the next morning. He waited at the usual spot, the corner of Harbor Mist and Narragansett, but Hil didn't show up. He waited much longer than he normally would have. Hil must have taken another way or gotten a ride; he must be really mad. Normally, Travis would have let it go, given Hil some time; friends, no matter how mad, at least a friend as good as Hil was, always came around sooner or later. But Travis felt like there simply wasn't time for waiting this time; he had to talk to Hil now.

All during school, Hil managed to be busy or someplace else. At lunch, he was deeply involved in a soccer game. Travis strolled close to the field a couple of times, but Hil ignored him, his head always turned the other way when Travis looked over. After school, it was as if Hil had used a transporter beam to get home—poof! he was gone.

Travis stalked around his own house, tried calling Hil. Nothing. He knew he was home; there was no soccer practice on Mondays.

Frustrated beyond all repair, he clomped the three blocks to Hil's house and pounded rather dramatically on the door.

The door opened.

"Yes, may I help you?" Hil spoke as if Travis were selling dead skunks door-to-door.

"I'm sorry," Travis said.

"Why did you lie to me, man?"

"I don't know. I mean, it's not a big deal. I just kind of messed up. I'm really sorry."

"Dude, what's up? That was so weird. Who was that guy?"

Travis tried his best to explain it all, but it was hard. The story of why he lied to Hil was a tangled ball of slippery threads. Just finding a place to start was impossible. But he managed to do it. He told Hil about Oster, about Oster's book, about Steinbeck and the Corral. He left out some parts—the statues, the voices. He'd save that for later, work up to it. He still wasn't sure Hil was ready to hear the stuff about ghosts and fictional characters coming to life. It felt good to be standing here talking to Hil again, and he wasn't ready for Hil to say, "Dude, you're crazy, get away from me."

"T," Hil said. "That sounds like a blast. Why didn't you just tell me?"

"I guess it was kind of a secret. Or I thought it was. I guess I wanted to go alone. I'm sorry, Hil."

Hil opened the front door a little more.

"Okay, I get it," Hil said. He was smiling now. "It's no biggie. But promise me two things."

Travis swore on it.

"Don't lie to me, man. That's bad. And someday, you take me up there with you. It sounds really cool. Okay, promise me *three* things. I really want to read those books, they sound awesome."

They both reached out for a Camazotz handshake, completed it, and then burst out laughing.

Travis followed Hil into the kitchen for cookies and sodas. Hil's mom always had the best cookies. She bought them from a panadería in Oldtown. These cookies were shaped like skulls, with pink and violet frosting outlines, and silver sugar balls for eyes.

"Day of the Dead cookies," Hil said. "My favorite. It's on Thursday. And that can only mean one thing."

"Uh?"

"Halloween's on Wednesday, dude. The great festival of candy."

Hil did a little dance around the table.

"What you are going as, Big T?"

Travis had seen the decorations going up. In his classrooms, in store windows, even at the library. But he thought maybe he wouldn't go this year. He was thirteen; maybe he was getting too big for Halloween. Other things seemed more important. All the same, maybe dressing up and begging door-to-door for candy would be a nice break from all the stuff swirling around in his head.

"I know, I know," Hil said. "But we can still pass. I mean, we're going, aren't we? I got a great idea. We go as hoboes, you know. Coupla old shirts, funky hats, shoe polish for beards. Easy. And we score huge candy. Yeah."

Travis looked at his friend. Hil's smile was irresistible. How could he say no? The candy alone seemed worth it. It was Halloween, and he'd never missed one.

✦ ✦ ✦

At nine thirty that night, Miss Babb called. Travis was as surprised as his parents. His mom yelled up the stairs,

"Travis, someone for you." When he took the phone from her, she wore a look that was half miffed—it's awfully late for a phone call, isn't it?—and half dumbfounded. "It's Charlene Babb. She says she needs to talk to you. Says it's *urgent.*"

He had no idea what could be so urgent, but he wasn't about to share this with his mom. He turned away from her, toward the wall. This was a private matter.

"Travis, hello." He knew instantly this was a good kind of urgency. Miss Babb's voice was jumping all around. "I'm sorry to bother you so late, but something's come up. About the library. Very exciting. And I need your help. I'm wondering if you'd be willing to start a new committee. I've got a great idea. It's about Halloween. Can you come in tomorrow? After school?"

"Sure." He'd go down there now if she asked. Work until dawn.

"And what about the rest of the week? Oh, Travis, we're so close. Will you really help?"

"I can come every day."

"Bless you, Travis. I'll see you tomorrow. Now let me talk to your mom. But first, how was the trip to the Corral with Ernest?"

"I'll tell you all about it tomorrow."

Travis handed off the phone and went to the refrigerator. He tried hard not to listen in, but he knew Miss Babb was talking about his parents allowing—*allowing!*—him to spend more time on the library campaign.

Travis grabbed a bottle of sapphire-blue liquid from the bottom shelf. The shelf was filled with drinks of surprisingly unnatural colors, neon crayon colors—hot pink, sizzling green, Valentine red, Halloween orange. Before they'd moved here, these kinds of drinks were never allowed. Now the place was overrun with them.

"Travis, Miss Babb says—"

"I know, Mom, I got it," he said sharply, and he loped up the stairs to his room. On the way he accidentally spilled some of the blue liquid on the bone-colored carpet. He left it there, soaking in, as purple as a bruise.

The library was packed. Not with committee members, not with reporters, but with readers. The checkout line was ten people deep. The career center's tables were all in use. Adults swam quietly through the main collection, and kids, tons of them, were doing their homework and reading and staring into space. It was as if everyone was trying to eat up the last of a wonderful dessert before the waiter took it away. Every last spoonful.

Travis and Miss Babb sat in little chairs at a little table in the kids' section. Outside, dark clouds had gathered; these clouds had traveled thousands of miles across the Pacific and down from Alaska. While Travis loved the hushed sense the sky brought to the busy library, he was worried about tomorrow's Halloween. It never rained on Halloween, at least not that he could remember.

"It's working," Miss Babb said. She had a thick file of loose papers on her knees. "That's the important thing. I want you to know that. Every little thing we've done, and everyone else has done, it's working. We may yet save the world."

Travis had to smile. He sensed from the way Miss Babb was talking that there was new, real hope for the library.

"All these," she said, slapping the file with the palm of her hand. "These are newspaper articles from all over the world about the library. And we helped. *You* helped. All those press releases you've been sending out, without those we wouldn't have these."

They looked through the file, articles from Iceland and Japan and North Dakota, and from unknown places in cyberspace. Miss Babb had been right, people did care about Steinbeck's library. Amazing.

"These are great," he said. "But what's the news? You said it was urgent."

"Okay." She sat up straight and took a deep breath. "The city council may take another vote. Hidalgo and Doyle, the council members? They both called the library, and the different committees, even ours. They say that the mayor and the council can be swayed. It's too embarrassing to them for the library to close. Thanks in part to all these articles. They think an election on a new library-tax measure would turn out differently now. And the best news of all: they'll keep the library open until after the election. Not dead yet."

"Awesome."

"That's where you come in."

"Me?"

"You have plans for Halloween?"

"Uh—"

"Listen. Here's the deal."

They needed to keep up the pressure, she said, get more people involved. Momentum was on their side. If Travis was going trick-or-treating, he could pass out flyers, let people know what was happening. He could collect donations, too, like UNICEF. Raise some money. Maybe get some other kids to help him. Get the word out, that was the phrase she kept using.

Would he sacrifice his Halloween?

"Even better," he said. "Hil will help. I'll make him, and I'll see if I can go from class to class tomorrow, get other kids to sign up."

The minute he said this, he knew it was a great idea. He also knew it was going to be embarrassing, standing up in front of all those kids. What was he thinking?

"Excellent, Mr. Williams." Miss Babb was almost dancing in her chair. "You do have the best ideas. Now, let's get to work."

In the A/V room, he and Miss Babb taped Save Our Library signs to the backs of twelve plastic pumpkins, the kind with handles, and stuffed each one with a hundred flyers. Miss Babb would drop the pumpkins at school in the morning, if he and Hil could meet her there.

While they worked, she told him in greater detail all that had happened with the library campaign. Money was pouring in from everywhere. Regular people had sent in checks for five and ten dollars, sometimes more. Bill Murray, the actor, had donated a "huge chunk of change," and other Hollywood people followed. Did he know who Bill Murray was?

Travis and his dad had watched *Ghostbusters*, *Caddyshack*, and *Stripes* over and over. Bill Murray was, Travis thought, the funniest human on the planet.

Oh, and the reading. She'd almost forgot. The reading would happen—Travis's idea, by the way—in November, downtown at the Maya Cinema. Laurence Yep had called that day to confirm; he was honored, he said, to be invited.

"And what about Mr. Oster?" she asked. "Have you convinced him?"

"I'm working on it."

"By the way, how was your trip to the Corral? Any more strange sightings?"

And Travis just opened up, told her everything about their trip. Telling her all this didn't help him solve anything, but he felt better having it out there. He asked her if she thought the statue of Johnny Bear might make good publicity for the library somehow.

"Travis," she said, "that is one of the spookiest stories I've ever heard. I mean, a real story. I don't think I could've done it. What do you think it is?"

He had no idea, he told her, and neither did Oster. But they were going back. They were on to something, that much was certain.

"Yes," she said. "It might help. We could tell everyone that it's Steinbeck's ghost come back to make sure we save the library. Wow, that'd be so great."

She said it, she said "Steinbeck's ghost."

"Look, you must have a cell phone," she said. "Take a picture when you go back. I'll think about it. There's got to be some way to use this statue. Plus, I'm dying to see it."

When they were finished, they stood together outside the library.

"Getting the word out," Miss Babb said.

"Consider it got out."

The clouds had pulled back a bit. A break in the lid of gray iron, north by Castroville, showed a patch of gold and orange where the sun reflected off the ocean.

Travis stood over his bike. It wasn't dark yet, technically, and so he didn't need a ride home. He and Miss Babb kept talking.

Gitano ambled out from the alley, crossed in front of them, headed toward Lincoln Street. His bindle bounced on his shoulder.

"Do you see that man?" Travis asked. He couldn't believe he'd asked her.

"Him?" she said. "He's harmless. He's been hanging around for weeks now. Seems to believe he lives here."

"That's Gitano," he said. "Remember, I just told you. I saw him here, and then in the Corral, we heard his voice. It was his voice we followed."

"Ooooh, aaaah. Did you feel that, just now? Goose bumps. Absolutely true, no doubt about it, not from some breeze kind of goose bumps. More like people-walking-on-your-grave goose bumps. Are you sure?"

"As sure as I can be. You should read *The Red Pony* again," Travis said.

"I will, I'll read it tonight. Oh, Travis, this is so weird."

Travis knew she believed him. He could feel her goose bumps across the space between them. They looked at each other with eyes as big as baseballs, but when they turned back to Gitano, he was gone.

When he got to the Steinbeck House, the sky had closed over again, blackened. Rain was coming soon; you could feel it.

He parked his bike across the street and looked up, and there was Steinbeck's ghost, seated at his desk in the yellow-lighted window. He was writing furiously, the pen bouncing along the page. Travis watched long enough to see him flip two pages worth of writing.

"I don't know why you're here," Travis said to the air. "But I'm glad you are."

That was when he figured out what to be for Halloween. The idea was too simple to pass up.

Crossing 101 on the way home, the sky blew open. The rain was intense, wind-thrashed, soaking. Travis couldn't have cared less. The world needed the rain.

FOURTEEN

TRAVIS WAS SURPRISED AT HOW MANY KIDS VOLUNTEERED TO HELP SAVE THE LIBRARY. After visits to five homerooms, three eighth grade and two seventh, all twelve pumpkins were spoken for. They should have brought more pumpkins. That was 1,200 flyers. He couldn't have done it without Hil.

That morning, Hil was waiting for him at the usual corner and immediately started to describe his grand plan. After Travis had called last night to ask for his help, Hil stayed up late working it all out. They'd go from room to room together and put on a little show. Make people laugh. Hil knew it was easier to get people to do things for you when they were laughing. By the time they got to school, they had it all sketched out.

Travis had almost fainted with relief when Hil volunteered last night on the phone. He couldn't really imagine doing it alone, standing in front of a bunch of kids he barely knew and asking them to sacrifice their Halloween, possibly their last Halloween ever, to help save a library. A dork. He would be a dork. A library dork. Fear of dorkdom wouldn't stop him, he knew that, he just didn't like the idea of being a dork on display.

It wasn't that Travis considered himself a dork, or even close to being one. He was a normal enough kid, which at school meant he had some friends, got along with practically everybody, and only got picked on as much as anybody else. But he also knew that the specter of dorkdom could strike at any minute, your standing could plummet in an instant. One good pantsing in front of a table full of girls, you were a dork. Suddenly finding a teacher calling on you to help with a project—dork. Worst of all, should the stomach flu hit, and you found yourself barfing in the cafeteria—dork for life.

He remembered a book he'd read late last year, another Miss Babb selection, *The Chocolate War* by Robert Cormier. Jerry Renault went to a scary private school, uniforms and all, and most of the time he kept his head underwater, just hoping to get by. But when the school's annual chocolate sale started, he rashly decided to go against the grain and refused to sell the chocolates. He figured a rebellion against the school's rather evil teachers would make him cool in the eyes of the students. But no, The Vigils, the school's secret society of upperclassmen bullies, decided Jerry's rebellion would not be tolerated, and Jerry became—at least for a while—the laughingstock of the school, the dork of all dorks.

The threat of dorkdom waited around every corner. You just had to be careful, part of you always on guard, and Travis was worried he might have set himself a dork trap. But he also figured that with Hil on his side, the chances of dorkdom would be lowered. Hil was too funny to be a dork.

Not only that, Hil was great with adults.

"Okay, Big T," Hil said as they approached the main office. "Let me butter him up."

Hil and Travis marched into the vice principal's office before the first morning bell, and by the time the second bell rang, the vice principal, the known-to-be-cruel Mr. Sdao, had agreed to let them skip class and go off on their merry pumpkin way. When they left his office, Mr. Sdao had an odd look on his face, as if his prized pony had been stolen and he couldn't be happier about it.

Miss Babb was waiting for them in the main office, the plastic pumpkins stacked on a rolling cart. She hugged Travis and Hil, and they were off.

The first class was their own homeroom, the mildly insane Mr. Brock. During his history classes, Mr. Brock was known for the use of a long wooden pointer, which he turned into a rifle or a spear or an oar or a telescope, whatever the lesson called for. He'd leap about the room, gesturing madly, trying to bring history to life, although most of the time he just looked crazy. Still, his classes were never boring.

A few weeks earlier, Mr. Brock had made the library closing into a manic play. He became Don Quixote tilting with his spear at the terrifying windmill monster. Don Quixote was supposed to represent the library, the windmill monster the faceless city bureaucracy. Nobody quite understood the play, but it was funny nonetheless.

When Hil and Travis rolled in the pumpkins, everyone was sitting up and paying attention. It was always good to have a break from the regular class, no matter how exciting the teacher.

Mr. Brock said a few words about the library, then introduced Travis. Travis stepped in front of Mr. Brock's desk, smiled. He thought he was going to be nervous, but found he wasn't. He guessed that if he could speak to the city council of Salinas in a jam-packed, overheated room, he could probably handle a bunch of eighth graders.

"Hello," he said. "Thanks for listening. I want to talk to you about the public library. I've been going to the library since before I could read. And I still go there today.

I bet a lot of you could say the same thing. Anyway, I could go on about all the reasons the library is closing, and how many different services the library offers"—Hil was making a silent blah-blah-blah gesture with his hands. Travis, as planned, shot Hil one of Mr. Brock's patented silence-ray gazes. It was a perfect imitation of Mr. Brock, and everyone laughed, especially Mr. Brock.

"But it's better to show than tell," Travis said. "So Hilario and I are going to show you. First, what the world would be like without libraries."

Hil and Travis faced each other, then slower than slow, went into an agonizing Camazotz handshake. After the handshake they went about their Camazotz day, but this world was so tedious, so gray, that soon both of the actors had fallen still in their tracks, unable to move.

Hil popped up, beaming.

"And now," Travis said, "what the world is like *with* libraries."

Hil and Travis met on the street again, with a hug instead of a handshake, and they mimed talking to each other with great animation about all the exciting things around them. Travis went off into his library day with a huge smile on his face, stopping now and then to stare into the future, pondering the bounties of the world.

But Hil. Oh, Hil. He was laughing and dancing about

the room like a ballet dancer who's had too much sugar. This wasn't Hil who was leaping about with the goofiest smile in the world, it was some other creature that inhabited his body. He was ecstatic. When he did a flirty, twinkle-toes pirouette right in front of Mr. Brock, the entire class lost it. Travis himself broke down in great gales of laughter, tears streaming from his eyes.

Hil and Travis took their bows. Mr. Brock was yelling, "Bravo, bravo!"

Travis made his pitch. He knew it was Halloween . . . the library needed . . . pretty simple . . . they'd still get a lot of candy.

Five people in their homeroom volunteered. After similar performances in the other homerooms, more volunteers stepped forward, and soon all the buckets were claimed. It was surprising to Travis who volunteered. It wasn't just the brainiacs or the wallflowers. There was a jock here, a cool guy there, a cheerleader, all over the board, a complete slice of the school's makeup. Travis knew that each of the volunteers had some deep tie to the library, deep enough to pull these kids from their otherwise unbreakable roles. And he knew what that tie was. No matter what role these kids played in their normal lives, when they sat down to read, the world cracked open for them, became more real than normal.

When school let out, every last bit of cloud had fled the sky, and the day was warm and toasty. A perfect night for Halloween.

✦ ✦ ✦

This was the first Halloween either of his parents had missed. Even when his dad was bartending and taking classes at the same time, he always arranged to have Halloween off. For the last few years, his parents didn't go trick-or-treating with Travis, but they did dress up—his dad was always a zombie rock star and his mom a zombie schoolteacher. They stayed home and gave out candy, and they were all together at the end of the night.

But there was another message on the machine when Travis came home from school. His parents had to work late again. They were so, so, so sorry, they said, they just couldn't help . . . But Travis deleted the message before his mom finished talking. He knew their apologies were sincere, but that didn't make up for them not being around, not even close. Ack! It was horrible; his parents had been turned into an answering machine.

Travis would not, he decided, "heat up something" as his mom suggested. He was going to eat nothing but candy all night.

In his room he stood in front of the closet mirror and considered his costume. Both he and Hil had changed their minds about being hoboes. The hobo costume was the easy way out, they agreed, and Halloween should be more fun than that. Neither Hil nor Travis would let on; both costumes were going to be surprises.

Travis had gone through his drawers and closets, and his parents' room, too, and found what he needed. He wore an old pair of blue jeans, some clunky, old-fashioned shoes of his dad's stuffed with socks, and a white shirt with black suspenders. He parted his hair in the middle and put gel on it to keep it down. It made him look old-fashioned. He looked exactly how he wanted to look. He was the ghost of young Steinbeck.

Of course he couldn't tell anyone that, it was too confusing a costume, requiring long explanations. Instead he'd tell everyone he was a ghostwriter. A ghostwriter was someone who did all the writing for someone who couldn't actually write, and Travis thought his idea was funny—ghost, writer, get it? Even if people didn't get the joke, the word *ghost* would probably be enough to satisfy them.

The only problem with the costume was the shirt. He found lots of white shirts, but they all had regular collars. Steinbeck's ghost wore a collarless shirt, and Travis knew that was the fashion of the time, almost a hundred years ago. He found a white, long-sleeved linen shirt in his dad's closet that was perfect except for the collar.

He took a pair of scissors and carefully cut off the collar. He was right: perfect.

But if Travis was going to be a ghostwriter, the shirt had to look like it belonged to a ghost who wrote a lot.

He found his old calligraphy set and smudged black ink all over the shirt.

He stared at himself as young Steinbeck for a moment longer, tried to see out of those eyes that looked out of the window, and imagined writing all those stories. Then he got to work on the makeup.

He made a pale wash of his skin with smudged clown-white. Then he darkened around his eyes with black eyeliner borrowed from his mom, bleeding it into gray on his cheekbones, around his nose, along the line of his jaw. Very ghost-ish, ghosty? No, *ghostiferous,* that was a good word. He smudged and tweaked until he had the makeup just right, until he was unmistakably a member of the undead.

The crowning touch: trickles of bloodred lipstick from the corners of his mouth.

He sprayed canned cobwebs up and down his body, over his head and arms. Newly risen from the crypt.

Last, he put his dad's best pen in his pocket, a fountain pen, and hung a composition book from a plastic prisoner's chain around his neck.

The only thing that would have made the costume better was if he'd been able to have the pen protruding from his cheek or neck, as if he'd been stabbed with it. He just couldn't figure out how to do it. His mom was good with stuff like that, she would know how. But.

One last glance. He was the ghostwriter.

Hil picked up Travis at six. They were in awe of each other's costumes, and overjoyed they hadn't given in to the easy-out of hoboes.

Hil was a perfect Day of the Dead figure, like one of the toy skeletons for sale at the mercados in Oldtown, skeletal bakers and musicians and priests. Hil's dad had turned his head into a sugar skull. Instead of blending the white and black to Travis's ghoulish gray, Hil's face and forehead were the brightest of whites. To emphasize the blocky shape of a skull, his dad used pure black under Hil's jaw, and on his temples and around the eyes. His father had drawn long teeth on Hil's lips, so that when his real mouth was closed, a skeleton's toothy grin showed. Pink-and-purple geometric patterns had been added for decoration, to complete the sugar-skull effect. It was hard to find the real Hil under the makeup.

He wore white jeans and a white shirt, over which he wore a black serape. On his feet he wore leather huaraches, and on his head a conical straw hat. He was a Day of the Dead Gitano.

In one hand he carried his plastic pumpkin, in the other an odd-looking garden tool.

"It's a short hoe," Hil said. "They're illegal now, but for years they broke the backs of farmworkers all over this valley. And now I have risen from the dead to wreak vengeance for my people."

Hil cackled and slashed at the air. He was actually pretty scary.

"I shall wreak the vengeance," Hil said. "And you, Señor Ghostwriter, you will create my legend."

Together they cackled and set out. Travis turned off all the lights, inside and out. He hoped this would prevent angry trick-or-treaters from too much tricking.

Dusk had already settled, purple-blue, but it was still warm out. The strong afternoon wind had died. The orange streetlights hummed. Travis stopped when they reached the sidewalk. Bella Linda Terrace had been transformed.

Across the street, Mrs. Juarez was putting up a string of orange lights around her front windows. Glowing purple bats hung from the empty branches of her little trees. A smoldering cauldron invited children to her porch.

Up and down the blocks, the houses were illuminated and decorated. Green and orange and purple lights shone on skeletons and headstones and giant spiders, on roofs and in front yards. In open garages, black lights and strobe lights hinted at spookier goings-on. It was a carnival, a carnival of the dead. Bands of costumed kids, mostly little kids at this hour, roamed from house to house. Bella Linda Terrace was almost beautiful.

"You know," Hil said. "It's like the Camazotz game out here. Except all the creatures from the hidden worlds have broken out of their prisons. Cool."

"That's what Halloween's about, right?" Travis said. "The mysterious world and the real world meeting. It's way cool."

They fell into the stream of the night, following trick-or-treaters from house to house, careful to not miss a single one.

They traipsed behind ninjas and princesses, vampires, Harry Potters, a few Hermiones, frogs and cats, mummies, ghosts, robots.

When they got to the second block, Hil started working the other side of the street. They'd never give out all the flyers working together.

That plan worked better, but as the blocks went by and the candy piled up in their pumpkins, it got harder to make their spiels about the library. More and more kids were out now, and they kept pushing past Travis to get to their candy. On one block they saw two other kids from school, duded up in serious Star Wars swag and toting their library pumpkins.

Travis pulled Hil to a streetlight on a busy corner.

"We're just going to the houses," he said. "But look at everybody else here. We're missing most of them, and there's a lot more trick-or-treaters than houses. If we stay here, they all have to walk past us. We'll get all the parents."

Without blinking, Hil began to shout, in a movie-newsboy voice. "Save our library, save our library right here."

In one hour they got rid of all the flyers, talked to hundreds of parents, even some kids, and collected a ton of money. And best of all, everyone dropped candy into their pumpkins. They each earned a mountain of tooth-melting sugar.

✦ ✦ ✦

They went to Travis's house, where they counted the candy and the money. They'd collected $212.37; Travis had 135 pieces of candy, Hil 177. An impressive haul all the way around. If each of the other pumpkins brought in close to the same amount of money, that would be over a thousand dollars. Better than the car wash. Maybe people were finally getting the message.

But they couldn't eat any more candy, and it was still pretty early, just after nine. It was Halloween! They couldn't stop now. So they went off in search of something spooky.

A smudged moon rose from behind the Gabilans. The streets were nearly empty, only a few knots of older kids here and there. Bella Linda Terrace was still lit up, though for the first time since he'd moved here, it looked tired to Travis, a bit worn. He couldn't explain why this was a nice feeling.

Hil knew a secret passage he'd been dying to show Travis. He led him to the bottom of Green Town Court, where between the last two houses on the cul-de-sac, a narrow alley opened.

"I think it's a maintenance thing," Hil said. "You know, so the gardeners and stuff can get behind the houses. They're all over the place, but this is the best one."

Travis had not noticed these tight alleys before, and he'd lived here five months. He needed to pay more attention.

The court was lit up but empty. They looked around, rather conspicuously, Travis thought, then whooshed into the alley.

The path was a thick carpet of new grass, pale blue in the moonlight. Hil might have been here before, but no one else had. This was unknown territory.

The stucco walls of the two-story houses—hard to know their color in this light—rose high above them, an impossible canyon. And higher still, the moon sat imperturbable in the sky, at its zenith, looking down on them, shining down on them. Hil crept along, bent low, as if he were a jewel thief on an escapade. All the white in his costume, his pants and skull and skeleton hands, was literally glowing. The black of his serape made him appear disjointed, floating. He really was a ghost.

Travis discovered that he was moving the same way, hunched over, stealthy.

"Hey," Travis whispered. "Why are we walking like this? We're not really doing anything wrong."

"I know," Hil whispered. "It's just more fun this way."

The alley continued between the high fences of the backyards, then opened up into a flat area between the backs of the fences and the stone wall that circled Bella Linda Terrace. This area was like a moat around Bella Linda Terrace, but instead of water, the moat was filled with plants and large river stones, a few spindly trees.

Travis realized for the first time that Bella Linda Terrace would be a much better place to live once the trees were fully grown. He could almost picture how the streets would look with big trees and their shade.

"No-man's-land," Hil whispered, spreading his arms. "And it's all ours."

"Yeah, great. I mean, it's cool and all. But what now? What do you do with a no-man's-land anyway?"

"You escape." Hil trudged off through the thick carpet of ice plant.

"We can't climb that wall. Look at the spikes."

"Aha," Hil said. "You are a wise man, ghostwriter. So, if you can't go over it . . ."

"You go under it?"

"Exactamente."

When Hil got to the wall, he pasted himself against it, like a convict during a prison break. Travis did the same. All Hil had to say was, "Well, Mugsy," and the two of them were on the ground howling, trying their best to stifle their laughter.

Hil led them, crouching, to a drainage grate below one of the wall's big pillars. He pulled up the grate and invited Travis to jump in.

"Dude, we'll get all dirty," Travis said, only half serious.

"We are ghouls," Hil said. "We do not concern ourselves with hygiene."

Hil jumped into the hole, and it splashed a little when he landed. His head barely reached the top of the hole. He waved at Travis, then ducked down and was gone. Travis heard another grate being lifted, then Hil's voice from the other side of the wall.

"Hurry up, ghoul-boy," Hil shout-whispered. "The spirits won't wait all night. Or will they?"

Travis jumped in the hole, ducked under the wall, and clambered out the other side.

"We made it, Mugsy," Travis snarled. "Free at last."

And they did the little dance of joy.

They moved to the side of Boronda Road, looked both ways—they were ghouls, not idiots—then zipped across the empty street. The whole way, Travis hummed the *Mission Impossible* theme. Hil joined in on the high-pitched doodle-oos.

Travis had stood here before, in front of the barbed wire fence looking up at the Gabilans. He'd always wanted to go beyond this fence.

He lifted his father's clunky old shoe and pushed down on the sagging wire between two barbs. Hil delicately climbed over. Hil held down the wire for Travis. They were on the other side.

They swished through the dry grass up the gentle slope of the hill, not talking. The farther they went, the louder the silence that swallowed them. They came to a dead oak trunk lying on its side and sat on it, looking out across the valley. There was Bella Linda Terrace, all lit up in Halloween colors, and beyond it, Salinas. In the moonlight, Salinas seemed more a reflection of the moon's brilliance than a city of its own.

"Now what?" Hil asked.

"I guess we wait for the spirits to rouse. Or something."

Because of the recent rain and the warmth that followed it, the earth beneath them breathed a sweet, soft smell into the night air. That smell was enough spirit for Travis.

They sat without talking. They didn't need to talk. Every once in a while, a car would come down Boronda. One car honked all the way, filled with screaming passengers.

"High schoolers," Hil said, and he spit in the dirt.

It was great just sitting there with Hil. Their friendship felt healed, back to where it should be. Maybe even further along.

Travis understood why he hadn't invited Hil to come along to the Corral with Oster, why he hadn't invited him to follow the mystery he was following. He was afraid. He was afraid Hil would think the whole thing was stupid, childish, insane. He was afraid Hil would turn away from him. Mostly, he was afraid that Hil wouldn't be able to see the things Travis saw. Oster saw them, yes, but Hil? Oster had his reasons for seeing all this. If Travis asked Hil to see what he saw, it would be a test for Travis, not for Hil. If only he could find the right moment to tell his friend everything.

Hil was talking about the Day of the Dead. He and his parents would go to the cemetery and offer sweets to one of his grandmothers—the other was still alive—and both his grandfathers. They would picnic in the cemetery, say some prayers, and talk to their ancestors as if they were still alive.

Travis felt something behind him. When he turned around, what he saw was more confusing than frightening. Orange lights bobbed in front of his eyes. Fireflies? No, there were no fireflies in California. And fireflies were green; he'd read about them in books. Then he realized the orange lights weren't in front of his face, they were farther up the hill. There was a ragged line of bobbing orange lanterns, twelve of them. No one held the lanterns.

"Hil," Travis whispered. "Do you see what I see?"

Hil turned, already starting to talk, but when he saw the lanterns, his mouth fell shut.

After a long time, he said, "I see them, Big T. But only if you see them. Do you see them?"

"I'm afraid so."

"Lanterns?"

"Looks like it."

"But."

"I know."

They stood at the same time, moved quietly up the hill after the orange lanterns. No matter how fast they moved, or in which direction, the lanterns stayed far away.

The lanterns moved to the top of the first ridge, spread out evenly along it, then disappeared over the other side.

"Whoa," Travis said.

"That about covers it," Hil said. "But let me repeat: Whoa."

They just stood there.

And then Travis did it. He told Hil all the rest—Gitano and the Watchers, and finally, Steinbeck's ghost. While Travis spoke, Hil stared up at the ridge where the lanterns had been.

Travis stopped talking; Hil was silent.

"Well, what do you think, Hil? Am I crazy, or what?"

"No, no, man, you aren't crazy. I don't know that I believe in ghosts, like out of books. But I know what I saw just now, and I know you saw it. And whatever is happening to you, with all this Steinbeck stuff, well, it can't be unreal."

"So, you believe me?"

"I have to," Hil said. "You're my best friend. And besides, I saw those lanterns, too. If you're crazy, then I'm crazy. And that's okay. At least we have each other to talk to."

"Really?"

"Really, man. No lie. But I swear, you have got to take me to the Corral with you."

Travis sighed. Finally, he'd finally told Hil. Travis's shoulders seemed to unscrunch; he seemed to be taller than just a moment before. Finally.

The world below them, the great and long Salinas Valley, seemed infinite.

The moon had moved past its zenith, west toward the

ocean. Without a word between them, the two friends turned and headed back down to Bella Linda Terrace. Every few steps, one of them would say, "Whoa."

Halfway down the hill, a thought flew into Travis's head: The moonlight was so bright he could read in it, write in it.

"Hold up," Travis said.

He opened his ghostwriter composition book, took out his father's pen, and scribbled these words: "The night so bright, even Bella Linda Terrace is beautiful. Halfway to home with a good friend."

He shut the book before the ink had time to dry. The words would be smeared, but that didn't matter. They were written.

FIFTEEN

FALLING ASLEEP ON HALLOWEEN, TRAVIS KNEW WHAT HE HAD TO DO THE NEXT DAY. And when he woke up on the Day of the Dead, that thought hadn't changed. He had to call Oster and see if they were still going to the Corral on Saturday, and if he could bring Hil along. Not only did he want to make it up to Hil for lying to him and not taking him to the Corral, but he sensed, deep down, that having Hil there would be a help. Hil saw what Travis saw, believed as he did. The lanterns last night had convinced him of this. If Hil also saw the statue, or whatever they might find in the Corral, then Travis would have another witness, and that would be a relief.

As soon as he got home from school that day, he called Oster. It was the Day of the Dead, the day after Halloween, the crux of autumn, Ray Bradbury season. Bradbury always seemed to be writing about this time in autumn, when the world shifted from light to dark, and the two mixed in spooky and beautiful ways. Just by thinking this, Travis could smell the sweet decay of fallen leaves.

"Yes, yes, I'll see you Saturday, of course," Oster said.

"Did you find out anything this week?" Travis asked.

Oster had been reading Steinbeck all week, he told Travis, and everywhere he turned, he found a reference to the Corral, and each of these passages was beyond mysterious. Then there was the letter, Steinbeck's letter to Oster: What had Steinbeck seen in the Corral that he would not talk about? Oster's letter wasn't the only one. In some of his other letters, he talked around the Corral, and was very vague about what he knew about it. Being vague was something Steinbeck rarely was, and Oster could only guess that he was covering up what he knew. Something strange had happened in the Corral. Maybe there *was* a curse.

Oster believed Gitano was the key. In *The Red Pony* Gitano spoke of having been in the Corral as a child, but after that he pointedly refused to go back. But Oster and Travis had heard him there last weekend. Or was it him?

What most disturbed Oster was the silence around the Corral, not just Steinbeck's but the world's. He'd spent hours that week at the library and in the hall of records at City Hall, just as he had over thirty years ago.

Nothing. Not one single mention of the town, as if it had never existed. Or had been erased.

Saturday, then, but would Oster mind if Hil came along? And could they wait until three? Hil had a soccer game. Oster didn't hesitate at all.

"The more eyes," Oster said, "the more we see. I already like the sound of this Hilario. Oh, by the way, how was Halloween? Miss Babb told me all about it."

"Have I got a story for you."

Travis told him about the orange lanterns he and Hil had seen bobbing bodiless through the hills.

"Oh, my," Oster said. "I know that story. I came across it yesterday. In one of the letters, Steinbeck writes about all these stories his mother used to tell about the Corral—she was a teacher there for several years, in the town we're looking for. He talked about those lanterns, just like you described. That's a hard one to get around. And Hil saw them, too?"

"Right, and I didn't say a thing to him, just said look, and he described them to me."

"Perfect," Oster said. "See you Saturday."

If he'd been reading the book of his own adventures, Travis thought, he'd be able to feel the end of story coming on, feel it with his fingers; there'd only be a quarter-inch of pages left to go.

Then Travis called Hil. He had loaned Hil his library copy of *Corral de Tierra* last night after trick-or-treating, and he had just started the first chapter.

"Dude," Hil said. "I'm only like this many pages into it, and I can't believe how good it is. You've been holding out on me. I'm sure I'll get it done by Saturday. I want to be ready for this."

"Oster says it's totally cool for you to come. I knew he'd say yes. Three o'clock?"

"Excellent."

Travis picked up the check his mom had made out to the Save Our Library committee, which made it easier than lugging all those coins. She'd also left a note. "We promise to be home for dinner. See you at six."

Travis scribbled a note for his parents. "Dear Mr. and Mrs. Williams, don't hold dinner on my account. I've got a prior engagement. I'll see you when I get home. Love, your son."

It was kind of a funny note, Travis knew, but a little bit mean, too.

✦ ✦ ✦

The library was practically empty. It was as if Halloween had taken the life out of everybody. Maybe they were communing with the dead. The cemeteries had to be packed.

Miss Babb was shelving in the kids' section.

"Mr. Williams," she said. "You have outdone yourself again. I heard from several of the other volunteers. You're well on the way to a thousand dollars. And all that money will go straight to the library. No more flyers."

"But we still need—"

"I know, calm down." She patted his shoulder. "It's better than that. We've got plenty of money for flyers. It's great news. I met with several of the other committee heads this morning. Get this: Altogether we've raised almost one million dollars. From corporations to piggybanks."

"Wow."

"That'll keep the library open for at least another month."

"A month? That's all?"

"Do the math, Travis. It's money. There's no mystery to money. But see: That means we're being heard. The word is out. I can feel it; we're gonna win. Our hours may get cut, but we'll be open."

"I didn't really believe you. I didn't think a lot of littles could add up to a whole bunch."

"Do the math, Travis."

And he reached over and hugged her.

"Gotta go."

Miss Babb was yelling after him as he ran out of the library.

"Don't forget next Tuesday," she called after him. "The reading committee. It was your idea. Where are you going? You never leave the library this fast."

✦ ✦ ✦

Clouds had come back in, though the day was still warm; the world was soft and gray. The dead leaves of summer rattled in the autumn breeze.

Gitano was nowhere to be found. The alley next to the library was deserted, and the lawns to the south of the library were oddly vacant of anybody, homeless or otherwise. Gitano was the answer, Travis was sure, and he had to find him.

He hopped on his bike and orbited the streets near the library, but no Gitano, no nobody.

He kept expanding the circle of his search until finally he was cruising down Main Street. Silent cars sailed by; here and there people stood alone and quiet under the broad eaves of the local shops.

There he was, Gitano, turning down the alley between Sheila's and The Swim thrift store.

By the time Travis turned into the alley, Gitano had assumed his usual stance. He squatted on his heels, his back against the alley wall. Gitano was rolling up tortillas and slowly chewing on them. They were fresh and warm, Travis could tell; he could almost smell them.

For a second he imagined flying up to Gitano on his bicycle and skidding to a halt, gravel flying. Like cops on TV. But that thought fled instantly; it would be cruel. Gitano had done nothing wrong. Travis got down from his bike, walked up the alley with soft steps.

"Hello," Travis said.

"Buenos días," Gitano said. He did not look up, although his voice was friendly.

"I'm sorry to bother you. But is your name Gitano?"

"I am Gitano," he said. He looked up at Travis, smiling. "And I have come back."

"Would it be okay if I talked to you for a little bit?"

He assumed he should be nervous right now, but strange to say, he wasn't. Gitano's dark eyes were not frightening at all. They were calm, inviting.

Gitano held out a rolled tortilla for Travis. He shook his head, but Gitano urged the tortilla on him, pushed it at him. Travis reached out for it, hesitated one short moment, then took the tortilla—it *was* warm. Gitano patted the ground next to him.

Travis lowered his bike and sat Indian-style next to

Gitano. The tortilla was sweet. He couldn't remember ever tasting anything better. He gobbled it down.

"Gracias," Travis said.

"De nada." He rolled another tortilla and gave it to Travis.

"Gitano," he said. "Why have you come back?"

"I am from here. I have come back because I am very old and I am ready to die. I must die here."

When he spoke, Gitano looked across the alley at the wall of Sheila's bar, but Travis knew his eyes did not see the white cinder block.

"Where is here?"

"Salinas. I was born here, and now I have come back."

"Where have you been?" Travis stared at Gitano, his brown and weathered face, the hatched lines around his dark, shining eyes.

"Down the valley. I have been working there. Nuestra Señora, King City, Soledad, Gonzales, Jolon. I have worked in the valley my whole life. And now I have come back. To die."

"To die? Really? Are you sick?"

"No, I am old, that's all. It is not bad. I am ready."

"When?"

"Soon."

"Can I help you?" Travis reached into his pocket. He'd brought along his saved-up allowance.

"Gracias, no. I am fine."

The sound of Gitano's voice reassured Travis.

"For you," Travis said. He laid the handful of bills at the old man's feet. "To thank you for all your work."

"Mi amigo," Gitano said, and he gave Travis another tortilla. Travis felt he could eat these tortillas forever.

Gitano scooped up the bills and stuffed them in the pocket of his denim jacket.

"Have you ever been to the Corral de Tierra?" Travis asked.

"¿Mande?"

"Corral de Tierra, Las Pasturas del Cielo. The Great Mountains."

"Ah, the Great Mountains. Yes, I went there once with my father, when I was only a child."

"What did you see there?"

"It was very beautiful there. Yes, Las Pasturas del Cielo."

"Anything else?"

"It was very beautiful. I remember."

Gitano spoke without looking at anything. It was as if he were still standing in the Corral, watching himself as a child.

"Did you ever go back?"

"To the Great Mountains? Never. Never."

"Didn't you ever want to go back?"

"No." Gitano's voice was suddenly hard. He said this with such authority that Travis stopped asking questions. The look on Gitano's face told him that his questions would not be answered. Gitano would not talk about it anymore.

Gitano packed up his tortillas, stood, and swung his bindle over his shoulder.

"Mi amigo," he said to Travis. "You must see these things for yourself. That is all I can tell you. And now, I must go."

Gitano whistled sharply, once, from between his teeth. From the other end of the alley, an old white horse clopped toward them. It wore no saddle. Gitano went up to meet it, and using a milk crate for a stool, climbed onto the old swayback. Gitano clicked once, pulled the reins to one side, and horse and rider turned away, headed west, toward the ocean.

Travis couldn't move for the longest time. When he finally did, he raced to the end of the alley, but both horse and rider were gone.

A horse? In Oldtown? Travis was ready to accept what he'd seen, if only because a bigger question was haunting him.

If Gitano was telling the truth, and he had never gone back to the Corral, then who had he and Oster heard last week?

✦ ✦ ✦

The first thing Travis saw when he walked in the house was his father's shirt. It was hanging off one of the kitchen stools, which had been placed squarely in the entrance to the kitchen. The shirt was obviously meant to be seen.

If this were a book, Travis thought, he would . . . But no, this wasn't a book.

The front door slammed behind him, pushed closed by the wind. He sensed, deep down, that his parents were waiting for him in the kitchen. Was it their breathing, the heat that came from the kitchen, made by their bodies? What sixth sense told him so? He froze in the front hall.

"Travis," his mom called. "Would you come in here." There was no question mark at the end of that sentence.

He'd never known that the front hallway was so incredibly long. Didn't know that the white, plastered walls were so fascinating.

But the hall did end, and there were his parents, seated on stools that faced the shirt, as if the three of them had been having a nice little chat. His mom and dad were each holding a coffee mug, a sign; whatever was coming was serious.

"Yes?" he asked. For now, the less said, the better.

"Travis," his mom said. She looked him straight in the eye. He tried not to look away. "What is this?"

"That's Dad's shirt."

He looked at his dad. It was no wonder his dad wasn't talking. He looked so tense Travis thought the coffee mug might splinter in his hands.

"Don't get smart with me," his mom said. There it was, proof. Trouble had arrived.

"It's my Halloween costume," Travis said. He looked at the floor. Where else could you look? "I'm sorry."

One long silence. Then the sound of his dad's coffee mug being set down, gently.

"Sorry?" his dad said. "Sorry? Is that all? Sorry? Well, I'm sorry, too, because sorry ain't going to cut it today."

Travis found it difficult not to laugh. But he managed.

He looked up, and as he feared, his father was glaring at him.

"I just—"

"Just nothing," his father said. Travis looked at the floor again. "You ruined that shirt. It was brand-new.

It cost seventy-four dollars. What were you thinking?"

What he was thinking was that his father would never have been so angry as he was now, not in the old days, not before the move. Not happy, sure, but this was beyond not happy; this was straight-up anger. And Travis couldn't believe his father had thrown the price of the shirt at him either. When they had no money, money didn't matter, but now that they did, it seemed way too important.

Travis waited. His father appeared to be done talking. For now.

"I needed a shirt for Halloween." He paused. Went on. "And this was the only one I could find that worked. It was getting late."

"Travis." His mom slipped in quickly. "Why didn't you ask us? We could've helped you."

He knew he shouldn't say what he was going to say. He knew the "discussion" would only get bigger and louder if he said it. But he couldn't help himself.

"Because you weren't here," he said. He wasn't looking at them, or at the floor. He looked past them, to the backyard. Dusk was giving way to true night. At least he'd made it home before dark.

"We were at work, you know that," his mom said.

"You can always call; we gave you the cell." She was trying to soften everything, but it was too late.

"I know," he said. "You're always at work. That's the problem."

"Now, sweetie," his mom said, softer than soft.

But his dad crushed all the softness in the room.

"No, no, no," his dad said. He stood up. "No, that's not the problem. The problem is, you weren't thinking. You ruined a perfectly good shirt, and there's no excuse for it."

His mom cut across his dad again.

"Travis, honey," she said. "You know we're doing the best we can. Yes, sometimes we have to work late, but—"

"No, not sometimes," Travis said, and he stared at his mom and then at his dad. "Every time. Every. Single. Time. That's all you do anymore. Work. This sucks."

His father took a deep breath.

"And who's going to pay for this house if we don't work?" His father sat down, trying to look reasonable.

"What does it matter?" Travis said. His arms were starting to wave about. "You have this big old house but you don't even live here. It doesn't make any sense."

"Travis?" His mom's voice was soft again. Maybe if she talked softly enough, Travis would stop waving his arms. "Don't you like it here?"

He didn't have to think.

"No," he said. Too late: He was shouting. "No, I hate it. I hate this stupid house. And I hate this stupid place. I mean, c'mon, Bella Linda Terrace? What kind of a stupid name is that? I hate it, I hate it, and I hate you."

And he was up the stairs and in his room, the only sound in the house the echo of the slammed bedroom door.

In books and movies at a time like this, one of the parents usually whispers, "Let him be now, he needs some time alone." But Travis's parents weren't like that. It was family policy during big arguments that the arguments get settled, talked out. No one got to hide.

Travis seated himself at his desk and opened *The Pastures of Heaven* to chapter twelve. He was pretending to read and doing a very poor job of it.

He didn't know how to feel. Part of him wanted his parents to stay away. That would allow him to get even angrier with them. There was a guilty pleasure in that feeling. But part of him also wanted them to come running up the stairs.

The echo of the slammed door died. Travis pretended to read one whole page of Steinbeck before he heard his parents' steps. They weren't running up the stairs, but they were coming.

They knocked on his door. He'd take that as a good sign.

"Come in," he said, but he didn't turn around.

His parents sat on his bed. He waited for them to speak first.

"Travis," his dad said. "Listen. Let's forget about the shirt for now, okay? I'm still mad, but we can talk about that later. There's obviously something else going on here. Bigger things. Can we talk about those?"

"Sure." He didn't want to be crying when he turned around, but he was. They weren't angry tears, though, these were tears of relief.

His mom and dad got up and came to him and hugged him. And it felt really great.

The three of them talked together for a long time. Travis told them everything he could, including things he didn't know until he said them. He told them all about Bella Linda Terrace and Camazotz. He told them how much he missed their old life; no, not the old life, really, just the being-together part.

His parents listened. Carefully, he could tell. And then they talked. They knew, they told him, that the move and everything else had been hard on him. But they hadn't realized how hard. In the end, they agreed with Travis. They were working too much.

And in the end, Travis agreed—surprising himself—that Bella Linda Terrace wasn't all that horrible. He was actually starting to like it. A little bit.

They had delivery pizza in the kitchen, and afterward, they sat out in the backyard on an old quilt and ate tons of Halloween candy. Travis told them all about Halloween with Hil, and their costumes. And about the library. And as the night moved on, he even told them about Gitano and the Watchers, and the Corral, what he and Oster had seen. He told them about Hil and lying to Hil and how everything seemed so much better now and how happy that made him. He even told them about Steinbeck's ghost.

Much to his relief, they didn't phone the loony bin and arrange to have him tucked away in some rubber-padded cell. His parents thought it was way spooky, and urged him to go back. If he felt that what he was doing was safe, and if Oster felt the same way, then, of course, they wanted him to go back, to unravel this mystery.

"Would you feel better if we went with you?" his mom asked.

"No," he said. "I mean, no thank you"—they all laughed—"but I think I better do this on my own. I mean, with Oster and Hil. But thanks. It'd be great, though, if you were here waiting for me when we got back. Just in case I have lost my mind."

"You know," his dad said. "I can't say why exactly, but it makes me feel better knowing that Hil is going with you. That's some friend you've got."

Later, they all ran out of things to say, but it didn't matter. Together, they watched the moon course through the sky. It was almost full tonight.

✦ ✦ ✦

The next morning the rains returned. The whole house smelled of rain.

When he went downstairs, his father was still in his old pajamas, making pancakes. His mom was there, too, being waited on and looking as though she were enjoying every minute of it. Neither of them was in a hurry.

"What's going on?"

"Well," his dad said, flipping a pancake onto a plate. "I called in sick this morning. I don't look well at all, now do I?"

"Oh, no," Travis said. "You look terrible. What about me? Do I look terrible, too? Maybe I shouldn't go to school."

"You?" his dad said. "No, you look fine. You're going to school. But your mom, now, she's gonna start looking terrible around lunchtime. I think she'll be completely under the weather by the time you get home."

"That's right," his mom said. "And your dad and I are both gonna be sick all weekend. Terribly, terribly sick. Not an ounce of work."

Something had changed. Travis knew it. This was no empty promise. The argument over the shirt yesterday, and the enormous one that followed, had helped his parents become unconfused. Travis saw it in their eyes, heard it in their voices. His dad was even wearing his ratty old pajama bottoms and an AC/DC T-shirt with great big holes in it.

The three of them ate breakfast together.

And when Travis came home from school, his dad was still in his pajamas and his mom was already home. She was in the garage planting bulbs in pots, and surprise of all surprises, his dad was in the living room playing music. He'd spent all day unpacking and arranging his gear.

"Jeez," his dad said, "these cathedral ceilings have great acoustics."

His dad showed Travis some new chords on the acoustic guitar, and they practiced Bob Dylan's "Shelter from the Storm," one of their favorites. His mom kept thinking up excuses to come back into the house and listen to them rehearse. She tracked dirt in from the garage.

Travis hadn't seen a living room this messy in ages.

SIXTEEN

THE FIRST PLACE THEY TOOK HIL WAS THE CASTLE. Oster pulled his old Dart into the country club parking lot again.

"But—" Travis said.

"You know," Oster said. "I was really mad the other day when that guy kicked us out of here. And I've been mad since. I'm not going to let these people own everything, and the view, too. We have a right to see it. And there it is."

The Castle hovered over the valley.

"Holy cow!" Hil said. He was sitting forward, his head hanging over the front seat. That huge Hil-smile.

They walked around behind the clubhouse, back behind the kitchen. No one would see them here, and the view was spectacular, unobstructed. Below them a foursome swung furiously at little white balls. None of the golfers looked up at the Castle, not once.

Oster was telling Hil about the sandstone, how the Castle was created. Hil was asking two tons of questions.

The rain had once again left the air clean, filled with the scent of new life. In one week, so much had changed. The native sweet grasses were already sprouting under the dead stalks of last spring's growth. The hills wore a thin but brilliant coat of new green. In a couple of weeks, with a little more rain, the color of the surrounding hills would put the fake-green of the golf course to shame. The rains were early this year, and heavy.

"Big T," Hil was saying, suddenly next to Travis. "We have to go up there, get close to the Castle. It's awesome."

"Can't," Travis said. "Look at all the fences. These people bought it all up, put fences around it, and now they play golf. Look."

Hil followed Travis's hand along the fence lines. The golf course was fenced in, and beyond that, ragged parcels of land were fenced in, one from another, the fence lines reaching up to the impossible sternness of the Castle's base. Everything around the Castle was owned, private property. But the Castle itself, it seemed, was too wild, too big to be tamed.

Hil was practically jumping up and down with frustration.

"It's not fair, man," he was saying. "Not fair at all. You guys are looking for a mystery, and there it is, big as a battleship. But it's all locked up. That's one gigantic gyp."

He put his head down on the fake ranch-style fence rail.

"Dude," Travis said, and patted him on the back.

"Gentlemen," Oster said. He made a clicking noise in his throat, like a rider calling his horse.

Travis and Hil looked up.

"It's true," Oster said. "It's not fair at all. But it happens all the time. They—whoever 'they' are, people with no imagination is my guess. Anyway, 'they' are always buying up the mystery and putting fences around it. They think they can own it, keep it all to themselves. And to a certain degree, they can, they do. I hate to say this, but it's been going on forever. So much of the mystery—the beauty and strangeness of the world—so much of it has been bought and fenced."

Travis thought of the stone wall around Bella Linda Terrace, how it kept things out and kept things in, too. The Corral, in Steinbeck's version, refused to be fenced in, and that was why, Travis knew, the lives of the people who'd come here, in the stories at least, had all gone wrong. It wasn't a curse that plagued the Corral, as much as the people trying to buy up and own—how did Oster put it?—the beauty and strangeness of the world. Maybe that was what was wrong with Bella Linda Terrace, the beauty and strangeness of the world hadn't found a way through the stone wall just yet.

The three of them leaned on the fence rail and stared at the Castle. In the shortening light of the November afternoon, the Corral was painted with a golden wash.

Travis looked up at the mini-mansion planted below the Castle. It was new and perfect and huge, and stood like a conquering hero. Except. Except that the wooden fence along the back side of the property, a brand-new fence, had already collapsed in one section, collapsed under the weight of a small rockslide. A fence was no match for the Castle.

"Bu-ut . . ." Hil said, stepping back from the rail. Both his hands were turned up, and he wore an expectant look. He was waiting for the punch line.

Travis and Oster stared at him.

"Bu-ut . . ." Hil said again. He was rolling his hands, as if that would get his friends started.

Oster straightened up.

"But," Oster said. He shot a finger at Hil, who smiled

and crossed his arms. "But a fence cannot stop the mystery. Right?"

"Right," Hil said. "Because you two guys . . ." And he rolled his hands again.

"We still found it," Travis said. "Despite the fences."

"Precisely," Oster said. "The way I see it, the people who put up the fences, because they've lost their imaginations, well, they only see the big things. They see the Castle and put a fence around it. And they forget to look in the small places. People like us, we know where to find the small places."

"Show me," Hil said. And they were off.

They drove through the Corral with the windows open. Hil, in the front seat now, was like a puppy out for his first car ride, his head hanging out the window.

They came to the end of the road, where they'd had lunch last week, but instead of stopping to eat, they hiked up the ravines toward the sandstone bluff.

Maybe it was the change the rains had brought, or maybe it was the fact that without a marked trail they wandered up a different series of ravines, but it all looked different to Travis today. The world was fresh, and the new green was everywhere.

They came to an open meadow high above the valley. There was a circle of gnarled oak around the flat expanse of the meadow, but in the center of that circle of trees, one lone oak stood straight and tall. The trees that ringed it were bent and shaped by the wind and the steep slopes from which they grew. The lone oak was unshaped by the world, and because of this, seemed powerful, magnetic, more alive.

Travis, Hil, and Oster, without a word between them, headed straight for this tree and planted themselves at its trunk. They opened their packs and shared a meal.

While they ate, Oster and Travis filled in more details for Hil. Hil ate and nodded, and drew on the ground with a stick, as if figuring out a math problem.

Then, as often happens during a shared meal, a comfortable silence landed among them. It was out of this silence that Hil spoke.

"I recognize this place," he said. "I've never been here before, but I know it. It's inside me already."

"The Corral can be like that," Oster said.

Travis was happy listening to the two of them, watching how they were getting to know each other, these friends of his.

"It's all your fault," Hil said, looking right at Oster. It was an accusation, but a warm one.

Oster pulled back, his eyes wide, his mouth stuffed with tortilla.

"Me?" he mumbled.

"Yeah," Hil said. "Your book. Travis made me read it. Finished it in one night. It's way cool. I loved it. And I know this place already because you showed it to me first. I know what can happen here—crazy frog hunts and gnomes in the woods, all that stuff. I've never been here before but it's familiar. Because of your book. I like that."

"Thanks, Hilario," Oster said. He looked away. "That means a lot to me. I guess it's why people write books."

"So," Hil said. "Why don't you write another one?"

Oster smiled.

"Well, I did," Oster said. "But it wasn't very good, I guess. I guess I only had one book. I'll take that."

"I know," Hil said. "Big T told me all about it. But that was stupid. Just because one person said so, doesn't make it true. It's like those fences. You let that one person build a fence around you. Not fair."

"Maybe you're right," Oster said.

Travis jumped in.

"Yeah," he said. "Why don't you write another book?"

"But I did," Oster said.

"Listen carefully," Travis said. "Why *don't* you? Present tense. A new one."

"What was wrong with that one anyway?" Hil said.

"They said—" Oster began.

"There's that 'they' again," Hil said.

"I think it was Steinbeck's ghost. I've been thinking about it lately. It was the ghost I got wrong. 'They' wanted something simple—a ghost story, a murder mystery. A plot with an answer. So I gave them one. A green ghost who floated around and looked like Steinbeck's corpse. Like Marley's ghost in *A Christmas Carol,* you know, a specter. An apparition. I gave them what they wanted and they hated it. It was all wrong, and I knew it. Even back then."

"How was it wrong?" Travis asked.

"Steinbeck's ghost would be different," Oster said.

"How?" Travis asked.

"His ghost would be bigger. He'd be a spirit, the spirit of this land, this valley. Or a tree, more likely. Steinbeck's ghost would be the spirit of a great tree."

They looked up at the tree.

"Like this one," Hil said, no question in his voice.

"That's perfect," Travis said. "Why don't you write that?"

"Maybe I will."

They packed up their picnic and litter, and got ready to move on. Hil was busy inspecting the tree.

"Uh, Big T," Hil said. "Someone named Jess has been up here. Look."

He was pointing to a spot on the tree where three initials had been carved: J.E.S.

"Can't spell his name either," Hil said.

"That's no name," Travis said. "Those are initials. John Ernst Steinbeck."

"Those could be his initials, I guess," Oster said. "He used to come up here all the time. It's possible."

"I don't think so," Hil said. "Look, these are fresh. Brand-new."

The wood where the bark had been scraped away was blond, still moist. The edges of the initials were sharp, clearly defined. At the base of the tree was a scattering of shavings.

"Cool," Hil said.

It was then they heard the dry rasp of the rattler's tail.

✦ ✦ ✦

The snake shouldn't have been there. It was too far from the rocks where it usually hid. And it was the wrong time of day, too early for hunting, and almost the wrong time of year, too late in the season. But there it was, not two feet from Travis and Hil. Much too close. Coiled and rattling. Anxious to strike.

Travis felt Oster's hand on his shoulder, soft, warning. He heard Oster's quick intake of breath, which, better than any words, urged him to keep still. He could not look at Hil, could only look at the snake. But all the same, he knew that Hil was frozen, too.

The tree breathed behind them. A cool breeze riffled the leaves. For a moment, even the rattler was quiet.

Travis's knee twitched; dead grass crackled under his foot.

The rattle shook to life again, quick-quick. The snake's head rose from it's coil, back at first, away from them. Then it would snap forward, Travis knew.

The rock thwacked the snake's head at that moment, the moment of lever, of swinging back to snapping forward. The snake fell away from them. Clearly dead.

It took several, well, seconds probably, but it felt closer to weeks, before Travis or Hil or Oster could move, turn to where the rock had come from. First they had to stare at the snake, watch its lifeless body sink into the dead grass and the new grass. Then they could breathe again.

They turned as one. The rock had flown in from behind them—they heard it smack the snake's skull before they saw it on the ricochet. They didn't have to think about where they turned to because something deep inside each of them, a deep and unthinking animal place, had perfectly reconstructed the rock's trajectory.

At first, Travis saw only a big rock, about twenty feet away. He tried to look around the rock, but did not realize that what he was looking around was what he was looking for. The rock was a man. And this was no statue either, but a living, breathing person.

"Johnny Bear," he whispered. "It's Johnny Bear." He spoke as quietly as if the man were as dangerous as the snake.

Hil said nothing, but Travis knew his brain was spinning.

Travis looked back to Oster, who turned to check that the snake was still dead, then turned back around.

"Thank you," Oster yelled over the still meadow. "Gracias, mi amigo."

"Sí, sí," Hil was saying now. "Sí, sí, muchas gracias."

Travis found it hard to speak. Not that he didn't want to, he was simply too surprised.

The figure before them was Johnny Bear, but the flesh-and-blood version of the statue they'd seen last week. His legs were bowed, shortish, but his arms hung long from his broad shoulders. His black hair was matted and messy, and on his face he wore a silly open grin, almost like a bear's. He swayed back and forth, dressed all in denim. In his left hand, he held the weapon, an ornately carved slingshot. Johnny Bear smiled and swayed.

And then he spoke, and what he said stunned Travis.

"Sí, sí. Sí, sí. Muchas gracias."

It wasn't what he said, but how it sounded. The voice that came out of Johnny Bear was not Johnny Bear's. It was Hil's, perfectly Hil's. It carried every tone and shade of Hil's voice, and with the sound of the words, Travis could almost see Johnny Bear become Hil.

Travis felt Hil shudder.

Johnny Bear spoke again, "Thank you, friend. Gracias, mi amigo." This time it was Oster's voice. Not an echo of Oster's voice, not an imitation: Oster's voice. He stood exactly like Oster when he spoke.

Travis knew now who had called them last week, the voice of Gitano, and that other voice, the one pleading for help.

A change shimmered over Johnny Bear. He seemed to shrink a little, turn his head in a feminine way.

A woman's voice, soft but firm. "Come, children, come now. It's time for lessons." A schoolteacher's voice.

Johnny Bear turned and shot up the hill, crashing through the thick oak and into the manzanita. Gone.

Travis and Oster bolted after him and had just got to the edge of the meadow, when they heard Hil.

"Wait, wait, wait. Wait just a minute."

His voice was a leash that pulled them back.

"Who. Was. That."

Hil stood with his hands on his hips. He wasn't so much looking at Travis and Oster as through them.

"We'll explain later," Travis yelled. "Come on. We've got to catch up."

"No," Hil said. "No, we don't. We have to tell me who—that—was. I'm totally freaked out."

"Okay," Travis said. "But then we go."

The three of them huddled in the open sunlight. Travis and Oster did their best to explain Johnny Bear. Again.

"So," he said. "This guy, the guy who just saved our lives, is a character out of a book, and we have no idea how that happened, and we're gonna go after him, and for all we know, there may be tons of other characters roaming around. Is that what you're trying to tell me?"

"Yes," Oster said. "That's about it."

"Cool," Hil said. "Let's get going." And he ran off into the manzanita scrub.

From a ridge not too far away, the schoolteacher's voice rang out.

"Come, children, it's time for lessons."

The golden afternoon was moving on, away from the hills, over the ocean, toward China.

SEVENTEEN

FROM THE BASE OF THE SCREE SLOPE, THEY COULD HEAR THE VOICES IN THE CAVE. But it wasn't until they'd reached the sandstone bluff and stood outside the cave's mouth that Travis could make out the words.

"Tularecito has escaped from Napa," a deep official-sounding voice said. "He'll come back here, you know he will."

"He's not dangerous, and you know that, Bert. We'll leave him be," a different voice said.

"He darn near killed me."

"You should have left his holes alone, Bert. He was just diggin' holes, looking for his gnomes. Gentle as a foal. Now, Bert, don't."

Travis and Hil and Oster had sidled up next to the cave's mouth. Travis peeked in. Johnny Bear stood over a small fire, speaking to himself, swaying. Thin gray smoke filled the upper aspect of the cavern and drifted into a deeper recess.

"Hello?" Travis said. "May we come in?"

He stepped into the cave. Oster and Hil followed.

Johnny Bear turned and grinned.

Across the fire from Johnny Bear was the rock-cobbled statue of him. It was such a precise likeness, Travis had a hard time knowing which was which. Hil went up to the statue and ran his hands over it.

Johnny Bear turned and grinned.

"Whiskey?" he said. "Food? Cheese?" This voice seemed to be Johnny Bear's own. It came from inside him and matched the expression on his grinning face.

He spoke again, this time in Spanish. "Está muerta la culebra, ¿no?" This voice, Travis heard in the words, came from a hundred years ago.

"The snake is dead," Hil said. "That's what he's telling us."

"Cheese," Oster said. "Yes. Cheese and bread."

Oster pulled packets of waxed paper from his knapsack and held them out to Johnny Bear. He took them gently from Oster's hands and offered a little bow.

"You know, Doc," Johnny Bear said. "I always say, 'the simpler the better.' Bread and cheese, ain't nothing beats it. Now, let's eat."

This voice was clear, full of laughter.

Johnny Bear sat in front of the fire. He held out the thick wedge of cheese to Hil. Hil sat, then Oster and Travis, too. Johnny Bear passed a crude knife to Hil, who hacked off a slab of cheese.

Travis remembered that in the story "Johnny Bear" from *The Long Valley,* Johnny Bear always had a story to tell. Sometimes the other characters bribed him with whiskey, and sometimes they just had to ask, but he always obliged.

"Do you have a story for us?" Travis asked.

In the light of the kindling fire, Johnny Bear's face flashed light and dark.

"All I got is stories, Doc. That's all there is," he said in the same voice as before, but which now seemed troubled, anxious.

Stories? Doc? Could this be the voice of Steinbeck himself? Travis wondered. The library had several audio recordings of Steinbeck reading his own work, but Travis had never checked them out. Now he wished he had. It didn't matter, really, for Travis knew what he believed. It wasn't his intuition that was telling him this was Steinbeck's voice. Johnny Bear's imitations were so precise, so chillingly perfect, that even here in the dark of the cave, Travis could almost see Steinbeck talking to his best friend Doc Ricketts. They were in Doc's lab.

Then there was silence in the cave, while the four of

them munched on bread and cheese. They watched Johnny Bear eat, looking back and forth from one to the other. Travis was a hive of questions, but he kept the silence. Now seemed the right time to listen. Dusk had come, and the fire in the cave was all the brighter for it.

Oster rustled in his knapsack.

"Whiskey, Johnny?" he asked. He held out a quart of Old Tennis Shoes. "Story, Johnny?"

Johnny Bear stood, took the bottle from Oster. He took a quick slug, offered it to Oster, who sipped at it. He took the bottle back and slipped it into his pocket. Johnny Bear's shoulders scrunched; he made himself smaller.

"I'll draw you a picture. A pretty picture. I draw real good pictures." This voice croaked, tinted with a Spanish accent. Then the voice changed when Johnny Bear coyly turned his head. The schoolteacher. "Come now, class. The lesson is about to begin, and we don't have much time."

There was a scrabbling sound from the rear of the cave, the sound of rock underfoot. It sounded to Travis like a hibernating animal stirring from a long slumber.

Hil put his hand on Travis's wrist, squeezed it. Oster sat up straight, his hand on his knapsack.

The man that emerged from the shadows was the

opposite of Johnny Bear. He was much shorter, though just as wide, and where Johnny Bear had short legs and long arms, this man's leg were lanky stilts, his arms stubby. But his hands, like Johnny Bear's, were large and powerful. He was dressed in little more than rags. His face was broad and flat and, when he stepped into the fire's glow, seemed as bland and simple as the face of a frog. He did not smile, as Johnny Bear did, but he was not frightening.

"You are Tularecito?" Oster asked.

The man nodded. "I am the little frog. I will draw you a picture. I draw good pictures, Miss Morgan tells me so."

"Tularecito is quite gifted," Johnny Bear said in the schoolteacher's voice.

In *The Pastures of Heaven,* Miss Morgan was Tularecito's teacher, the only one in the Corral who understood him. Johnny Bear's gift was mimicry; Tularecito's was art—painting, sculpting. Tularecito, it was obvious now, had created the statue of Johnny Bear.

Travis turned to Hil, but Hil put up a hand. "I know," Hil said. "At least I think I do."

Tularecito joined them by the fire. He stirred the outer ring of ash with a sharpened stick. He placed his hands into the ash, too, rubbed it into his fingertips.

"Why are you here?" Travis asked. "Why did you bring us up here?"

Tularecito looked up at Johnny Bear. The voice that erupted from Johnny Bear was the voice they'd just heard, the one Travis hoped was Steinbeck's voice.

"I can't tell that story, Doc, it's too awful, too horrible, I'm not ready."

Another man's voice came in. Doc's?

"You've got to, John, people need to know the truth, you know that. The truth matters."

"I don't think I can. I don't think I'm ready."

"Someday, John. Promise me. Someday you have to tell that story."

"Someday, Doc."

When he spoke, Johnny Bear became the people whose voices he borrowed, and Travis saw those figures as clearly as any photograph, perhaps even more so. He could see the worn-out chair and the green-shaded lamp in the lab, and the two men talking there. He was listening to Doc and Steinbeck.

Tularecito stood and moved to the blank cave wall. In one hand he carried a pile of ashes that he stirred with the other. Oster stoked the fire, and the cave was bathed in light.

Travis felt for the cell phone in his backpack. He

knew his parents were out there, in Salinas, knew the whole town was just over the ridge, not far away. But this cave seemed the only place in the world right now.

✦ ✦ ✦

The first few strokes of charcoal and ash were easy to make out, the silhouette of the Santa Lucias and then the Castle. While Tularecito drew on the cave wall, Johnny Bear spoke.

The first voice was in Spanish. "Ave María Purísima, por aquí se hallan las verdes pasturas del Cielo a que nos mandó el Señor."

Hil translated instantly. "Holy Mother, these are the pastures of Heaven, all green, where God is leading us to."

"The Corral," Travis said. "It's the Corral. He's the first Spanish soldier in the valley. From chapter one."

The drawings came more quickly. Each stroke of Tularecito's fingers seemed to create an entire world on the cave wall. The valley grew, became peopled, houses sprang up, farms flourished and failed.

Johnny Bear did all the voices, some in English, some in Spanish, some, it seemed, in German. Hil translated the Spanish as best he could. Oster and Travis called out the bits of *The Pastures of Heaven* they recognized.

The shape of a schoolhouse emerged on the cave wall.

A moon appeared, a band, people dancing outside in the night.

Johnny Bear hushed. Two voices, a boy's and a girl's, teenagers.

"No, Jimmie, I will not kiss you, my daddy says—"

"Oh, your daddy. Just one kiss, Alice, please, I do love you so. I won't tell."

Tularecito waved a rag-covered arm across the wall, and the drawing disappeared. The shape of another house, an orchard, the moon again.

Travis knew this story. Shark Wicks hated the thought that some boy might kiss his daughter and take her away. Shark Wicks, like everybody who moved into the Corral, wanted the world to stay the same forever. His daughter did not kiss Jimmie Munroe that night at the dance, but everyone in town told Shark she had kissed Jimmie, and Shark chose to not believe his daughter. He went after Jimmie Munroe with a shotgun, but the sheriff showed up in time, and Jimmie wasn't hurt. Travis knew this story already.

Johnny Bear crouched, his arms over his face, the voice of the teenage boy again, filled with fear. The voice sounded like quick water ran through it. "No, Mr. Wicks, I never did, please don't, please don't."

Another voice, ragged, terrifying: Wicks. "How dare

you, you little skunk, how dare you touch my Alice. I'll show you."

The next sound from Johnny Bear was tremendous, blew everyone back from the fire. A shotgun blast.

The figure of the murdered Jimmie Munroe appeared on the cave wall. Shark Wicks stood over him with a shotgun. Another figure, a sheriff, appeared next.

This was not how the story ended in the book.

Johnny spoke again. The sheriff: "Now, Shark, what are we gonna do with you? Why'd you have to go and do that?"

Shark's voice again, but no longer terrifying, rather terrified. "We'll take care of it, you'll see. Jimmie here, why Jimmie was just trying to protect my daughter from some Mexican and got himself shot. Why, he's a hero."

Tularecito erased the drawing, but another immediately took its place. A small house, but square, an adobe house, a stand of corn and beans next to it, a dog in the yard.

Johnny Bear threw his chest out. This voice had a heavy Spanish accent, but spoke perfect English.

"No, señor, no, you have the wrong man, señor. I do not know your daughter. Now leave my home, leave my family."

Tularecito continued to draw. A man in a sombrero

next, and then Shark Wicks again, his shotgun aimed at the man in the sombrero. And with the fewest of deft strokes, a crowd of men surrounded the one in the sombrero.

Johnny Bear dropped to all fours, his voice a growl.

"That's him, boys, that's the one that hurt my daughter and killed Jimmie Munroe. Here's the shotgun that proves it. Let's get him. Nobody'll ever miss another Mexican."

There were no more voices, no more sounds from Johnny Bear.

Tularecito worked in silence.

Travis could hardly stand to watch the images that flew onto the cave wall. But he could not look away.

Next to the adobe house, a tree appeared, and around that tree a crowd of men who carried torches. At the foot of that tree, a sombrero.

Off to one side, from behind the adobe, another man in a sombrero looked on. He was leading a mule on which a small boy rode.

There was no doubt at all who the boy on the mule was. It wasn't that the boy looked like Gitano, but that the story Gitano had told him in the alley now made sense. What Gitano had seen that long-ago day in the Corral, what had kept him from ever returning, was this story Tularecito and Johnny Bear were telling together. Travis got to his knees, reached for the cave wall, pointed at the boy on the mule.

"That's Gitano," Travis said. "This is what he saw in the Great Mountains. This is why he never went back. This is why he came to me."

Travis sat down. He looked at his finger. Where he had touched the drawing, a bit of the ash remained.

Tularecito's hand flashed angrily across the drawing, and when he stepped back, Travis saw the dangling, lifeless body of the farmer hanging from the tree.

Hil gasped. Oster was muttering. Travis's legs were shaking, his face was hot.

Johnny Bear straightened again, spoke one last time, Steinbeck's voice.

"There you go, Doc. The truth at last. The horrible truth. There never was a curse on the Corral. It's not an evil place. Not the place, Doc, the people. There's your story. Now what are you going to do with it?"

Johnny Bear took out the Old Tennis Shoes and drank deeply from it, then curled himself into a rough corner of the cave, turned away from them.

"Oh my God," Oster said. "Oh my God."

"Tell me what that was. Tell me what it means," Hil whispered.

Travis tried. The story of Shark Wicks wasn't as Steinbeck had written it. He had been afraid to write the truth then. The real Shark Wicks, at least the person he'd been based on, had killed Jimmie Munroe, and to cover it up, he and a group of white farmers from the valley lynched a Mexican farmer. They blamed him for killing Jimmie, who, they said, was defending Shark's daughter. Shark knew that back then, the law, and everyone else, would look away. They cared more about a white man's reputation than a Mexican's life. It was horrible.

The picture of the hanged man glowed on the wall.

The fire was dying out, and there was no more kindling. Tularecito had gone to the back of the cave and disappeared into whatever place he had come from. The cave seemed empty now, and cold.

"Why?" Hil said. "Why did they bring us up here?"

"I don't quite know," Oster said.

"The story," Travis said. "It's all about the story. I think Steinbeck had one more story to tell. At least the truer end of one story."

Hil stirred the ashes of the fire with a twig.

"It was real, wasn't it?" Hil said.

"We shared food with them," Oster said. "We shared

shelter with them. And the story, we shared their story. Is there anything more real than that?"

Hil and Travis shook their heads and stared into the fire. No, Travis thought, there was nothing more real than that.

"That story, the lynching," Hil said. "Mr. Oster, could that be true, could it really have happened?"

"Ernest, please."

"Ernest. Did things like that happen here?"

"I'm afraid so," Oster said. "People can be very cruel. Almost anywhere on this planet, not just here. They *can* be. That's why we have to tell such stories. To remember. To remind us that people *can* be cruel. But also that we don't *have* to be."

Travis looked at Hil. He wondered if it was any different for Hil to hear this story, because Hil's family was Mexican. He wondered if he would have felt differently himself if his family had been Mexican. Yes, Travis was white and Hil was brown, but they were more the same than they were different. Did it make a difference why someone was killed so viciously? No, the color of someone's skin, or the background of someone's family, had nothing to do with it. It was a cruel and awful story: men killing other men for stupid reasons.

Johnny Bear snored, turned in his deep slumber.

"But what do we do with it?" Travis asked. "Now that we've got the story. It was over a hundred years ago. What are we supposed to do with it all? We have no proof. Oh, sure, these characters came out of some book and told us this horrible story. No one will believe us."

Travis couldn't help it, he was pounding the ground with his fist.

"We tell the story," Oster said. "We write it down. We say, oh, this is just a story, and that way they'll believe it. We remember for everyone else. It's why we have stories."

Johnny Bear shook and grunted and rolled over. He got to his hands and knees, then ponderously stood.

"Whiskey?" he said.

He went to the mouth of the cave and looked out, took the Old Tennis Shoes from his pocket and drained the bottle in one pull. Then he stepped out into the night. He swung the bottle out over the hillside, sailing it high and far, and after a long time, there was the sound of it breaking on rock. Then Johnny Bear raced down the scree.

When he got to the cave's mouth, all Travis heard was Johnny Bear crashing through the undergrowth. He was gone.

It was night now, but still bright. The full moon had risen from behind the sandstone bluff.

The Watchers appeared on a faraway ridge; they

turned from Travis and disappeared into the west. He wanted to call to Hil and Oster, to show them the Watchers, but it was too late. Without being able to give a reason for it, other than he felt it deeply in the air around him, Travis knew he would never see the Watchers again.

Hil and Oster came up behind Travis. He took a last glimpse inside the cave. The fire was out.

"Jeez, you guys," Hil said. "We better book. My mom's gonna kill me."

Travis took out his cell phone and punched for his parents. They were glad to hear from him, and promised to call Hil's folks. Travis loved standing out here in the full-moon night, and he also liked hearing his parents' voices and knowing they were just on the other side of the mountain.

"A sugar moon," Oster said, pointing up. "That's what we used to call a moon like this."

Because the sugar moon was so bright, they did not need their flashlights to guide them down the ravines to the valley floor.

✦ ✦ ✦

During the drive back to Salinas, they talked and talked and talked. And, as people do at such times, they simply told the story of what had happened to them over and over again. To make sure they remembered it, to make sure it was real. It was real, they all agreed, everything they'd seen that day. They couldn't figure out why it had happened, but they knew it had. And they all believed it had been about the story; they all believed that Steinbeck had one more story he needed to tell.

Instead of taking the freeway around Salinas, Oster kept on Highway 68 and went straight through town to the Steinbeck House. He parked in front, and they all got out. Travis prayed that Steinbeck's ghost would be there; he wanted his friends to see it, wanted them to have that gift just once.

The attic bedroom windows were lighted yellow. Young Steinbeck sat at his desk, staring out the windows, a pen to his lips. He capped the pen and put it in his pocket, then closed the ledger he'd been writing in, stood up, and walked away from the desk. The yellow lights went out.

Every time he went to the library, for months after, Travis rode by the Steinbeck House. The windows were never lighted again.

EIGHTEEN

THE WIND HAD DIED. Outside Travis's window, the world was still, and quiet ruled the house. The Santa Lucias were a dark blue gash against the golden, ocean-inspired sunset. It was cooler outside, too. Travis could feel the first bite of true autumn hovering at his window. He knew his astronomy; the world had turned, and the shadows stretched ahead, and the days would be shorter.

At dinner he could barely keep his eyes open, and there was a moment when he thought maybe the mashed potatoes would make a nice pillow. It was just him and his parents, but they'd been up at the Corral all day, with Hil and his parents, Oster and Miss Babb. They had explored and talked, all of them together, and then they talked some more. When he and his parents got home, they had a lovely dinner—his mom's burgers were even better than Sheila's—and things felt pretty good. But there'd been so many words that day, so many stories, and he needed the quiet. His parents, too, Travis could tell, thought the quiet was pretty nice.

He excused himself and went to his room and sat at his desk in his window and enjoyed the silence for an hour. He looked out the window and stared at the Santa Lucias.

After some time his thinking slowed down enough that he could make out individual words and sentences, his brain no longer a whirl of voices.

He pulled open the top desk drawer, where he'd stashed the ghostwriter's composition book, and opened it to the first page. He read the words he'd scribbled on Halloween with Hil, the night of the floating lanterns. *The night so bright, even Bella Linda Terrace is beautiful. Halfway to home with a good friend.* He turned to the second page, where nothing was yet written.

He pulled out a black Pilot Rolling Ball, slid the drawer shut, then turned on the desk lamp, scooted in his chair, and began to write.

For no good reason at all, he began at the end. It seemed the best place.

"We all went to the Corral the next day," he wrote. "We had to. The minute I woke up, I told my parents we had to go back to the Corral. The night before, I told them everything that had happened with Johnny Bear and Tularecito, and the story of the Mexican farmer's lynching, and we stayed up for a long time talking about it. My parents didn't understand much more than I did about the story. So in the morning when I told them I wanted to go back to the Corral, they said yes, we had to, and just then Hil called and asked me if I wanted to go back, it was killing him, he was going to go with his parents no matter what I said. Then I called Oster and he practically shouted yes, and he said he'd call Miss Babb because she should come, too, and that was the best idea of a morning full of good ideas. Everyone needed to go there."

He wrote quickly, the ink flowing across the page, smearing, and he wasn't sure he'd be able to read it all, but it was important to get it down. He needed to write it down; he'd promised Oster he would.

"So we packed lunches and headed out to the Corral, to the same place Oster and Hil and I had stopped before, where we always stopped, the dead end. We drove in different cars but got there around the same time. We stood around the cars talking, and now that there were more of us, the talking couldn't be stopped. What happened in the cave, what did it mean, was it real? Everyone had to know. Then we hiked up to the cave, practically running up the ravines. We sort of looked for the plateau where we'd found, or thought we'd found, Steinbeck's initials carved in that one tree, but there wasn't anything like it, and we didn't have time to look harder. We knew that the answers—if there were going to be any answers—were hidden in the cave."

Travis looked at the white paper, its faint blue lines, watched the black ink unfurl from the pen like smoke from a chimney in a high wind. But that's not what he saw when he wrote. As he wrote the words, he saw what they'd seen that day, what they'd all said, the hillsides rushing beneath their feet.

When they got to the cave, it was empty. The fire pit was there, obviously fresh. But there were no other signs of what had happened. The walls of the cave, even under the gaze of several flashlight beams, looked like the walls of a cave, no sign of Tularecito's drawings. There were smudges, a few, but it was hard to tell if they were the ash smudges of Tularecito's drawings, or some other kind of smudge—cave smudge?

At first, Miss Babb, Hil's parents, and Travis's parents stayed near the entrance of the cave. Travis could tell they wanted him and Hil and Oster to have the first look. Then Hil saw the circle and pointed to it.

"But the only thing there, the only real evidence, was

this sort of lack of evidence, a big circle of swept dirt. Right where the statue of Johnny Bear had been—and where there was no statue, no leftover rocks at all—was a perfect circle swept into the floor of the cave, just the right size for the statue. It was too perfect a circle, you could just see that. Someone had left this circle for us. It was too perfect. We weren't disappointed at all."

When Travis saw the circle, he looked up at Oster, and then at Hil, and they were all looking at one another, and they were all smiling. In this perfect circle of nothing, they found all the evidence they needed.

As he wrote, his head was filled with a million other things he wanted to write about the circle, but he was writing too fast, didn't have time for it all. These words would be a good bookmark; he could come back to them later, he knew, and know his millions of thoughts would return.

He was writing so fast he felt like he wasn't moving the pen; the pen moved itself. The pages filled up.

They showed everyone else the circle, and they all agreed that it was a sign of some kind. Miss Babb looked positively giddy; Travis's mom looked a little freaked out.

All of them scoured the cave for more evidence, but there was nothing. Not a single footprint. And the back of the cave, where Tularecito had come from, well, that narrowed down to a crack about six inches wide. When Travis put his ear to the crack, he heard nothing but the whoosh of deep and dark spaces.

They left the cave and climbed to the top of the sandstone bluff, where the day was perfect and cool, and there were some nice big stones for sitting on, and they broke out their picnic. They ate and thought, and stared out into the Corral, and back toward Salinas. They could see everything from up here, the whole world. Then they talked.

Travis stopped writing for a minute. He smoothed down the page he'd been writing across with the palm of his hand, heard the crunch and swish of the half-blank paper. He wanted to remember as precisely as he could, what each of them had said. The pen moved again under his hand.

First, Miss Babb made them go over the whole story, from the very first visit with Oster and Travis, to the second visit when they took Hil along. So Oster and Travis, and then Hil, told that story. But then Hil made them all back up, and they had to talk about Gitano and the Watchers and, of course, Steinbeck's ghost. Hil's and Travis's parents and Miss Babb all had that look on their faces that you see when people are listening to . . . well, ghost stories. But this story, ghost or not, Travis knew, they believed.

"Then Hil's dad started to talk," Travis wrote, "and he told us stories his grandfather told him, about how badly the white farmers had treated the Mexicans when he was a kid, and even later. Then Oster spoke up, and he told us about his research into the Corral, and how he'd read newspaper stories of lynchings in and around Salinas. Some of the lynchings, he said, hadn't happened that long ago, just before World War Two. Then we all talked about the horrible things that people did to each other. Hil and I listened a lot during this part, all the grown-ups talking. And somehow the whole afternoon filled up with all this talking."

Travis looked down at his composition book. Then at his clock. Two hours had passed, and he'd already filled twenty-one pages.

He started to write again.

"Miss Babb finally asked the question everyone wanted to ask. We all believed this had happened, I could just tell, but she wanted to know—we all wanted to know—what did it mean? So Oster and Hil and me, we told them what we'd been saying all last night and all today. That Steinbeck had one more story to tell. We just couldn't figure out why us, what it had to do with the library, why now?

And none of us had any good answers. We finally agreed that we might never know. But we agreed it had happened. Then Miss Babb said the thing everyone was thinking. 'Well, you guys,' she said, and she pointed to me and Oster and Hil, 'you have to write it all down. We don't want to disappoint Mr. Steinbeck.'"

The sun had gone down, night was on, but Travis could still make out the rough silhouette of the Santa Lucias. He was suddenly tired, but he had to keep writing.

"So we went back to the cave, for just one more look, but just me and Hil and Oster, and we stood around the circle and made a promise that each of us would write down everything that had happened. We promised not to forget. Then we came home."

Travis didn't think he could write anymore. He knew it was late, he knew he had to get to sleep, had school tomorrow. He knew that this was just the beginning, too. It would take him a long time to write it all down, every single thing that had happened in the last few weeks, every detail. But he would. And not just because of the promise. Travis had made another promise in the cave, to himself. He would write everything down so that Oster could use it. He was going to make sure Oster would write his second book, make sure he'd use the story of Steinbeck's ghost, make sure it was never forgotten.

He started to close the cover of the composition book, but a word popped into his head, the word he'd been looking for when Miss Babb asked what it all meant.

"Silence," he wrote in clear, slow letters, and he hunched over the blank pages. "It's about silence. Steinbeck was silent about the real story he knew, and it haunted him. And there was this silence in Bella Linda Terrace that almost killed me, until I remembered the word *Camazotz*. And Oster, Oster let himself be quiet because someone else told him to be. And Hil and I were almost not-friends because I couldn't talk to him. My parents, too, they let the silence of their jobs shut up their real selves. And if the library closes, then all those books and all those words, they'll be silent forever. You can't let that kind of silence into the world. Make a noise."

He closed the book, but didn't put it in the desk drawer. He pushed it to one corner of the desk, where he knew it would be ready for him tomorrow.

Travis never expected the benefit reading to be the monumental success it turned out. The Maya Cinema donated one of its theaters for the evening, and all 250 tickets sold out the day they went on sale. People came from all over Salinas, and from as far away as San Francisco and Los Angeles. At a hundred dollars a ticket, and thanks to the sales of books after the program, the Save Our Library committee was able to donate $29,730 to Rally Salinas.

On the night of the reading, everyone had dinner together at Sheila's—Travis and his parents, Hil and his, Miss Babb and her husband and children, and Oster. "The whole gang," Travis wrote the next day in his composition book. Sheila picked up their tab. There was noise and chatter and laughing all during dinner.

Afterward, they walked down Main Street to the theater, where the marquee read, in huge letters: SAVE OUR LIBRARY. Four floodlights scraped across the sky. It was a gala, Miss Babb said, a regular extravaganza. She was glad so much attention was focused on the library, but she still thought it was a little too much fumadiddle for a library. She looked forward to the day, she said, when going to work wasn't about saving the world, but just another day at the library.

There were three special guests that night, authors of beloved books for younger readers—E. L. Konigsburg, Ursula K. Le Guin, and Laurence Yep, who, being from nearby Pacific Grove, was the headliner. Each of the writers had paid their own way to be part of the benefit.

But before the three main readers, there were two others, Hil and Travis. Miss Babb had asked them both if they'd choose a section from one of their favorite books to share with the audience. Travis and Hil pretended to be shy for about seven seconds each before they agreed to participate. Miss Babb wanted to thank them for all their work on the committee, and to remind everyone in attendance that the library was about readers.

Hil read the Camazotz section from *A Wrinkle in Time*, and even though it's not a particularly funny section, he had everyone in stitches. He had a magic voice like that. He made everyone in the audience see the absurdity of a world where everything was exactly the same.

Travis, of course, read from *Corral de Tierra*. He had tried and tried to get Oster to read, but there was no budging him. Oster told Travis he felt as if the book belonged more to Travis than to him anymore. He hadn't told Oster he was going read from *Corral de Tierra* until dinner the night of the reading, by which time, he knew, it would be too late for Oster to complain. Much to his surprise, though, Oster didn't object; in fact, he seemed delighted. Travis could swear that Oster was blushing.

The crowd that night seemed enormous from behind the curtains, but Travis wasn't nervous at all. He was holding the library's only copy of *Corral de Tierra,* which was now like an old friend to him.

He read two short sections, one about the frog hunt, which had people in tears with laughter, and the climactic scene when Steinbeck's sister Mary is bitten by a rattlesnake. During this section, Travis thought, If this were a book, you could hear a pin drop.

But he surprised himself by adding one section to the reading at the last moment, the book's last paragraphs. He made the decision while he was onstage, a sudden inspiration. These had always been among his favorite words in the entire book—Steinbeck sitting in his attic bedroom window and longing to go back to the Corral. After everything that had happened, it seemed impossible to leave this scene out. He was reading these words not so much for the audience, or for Oster, or even himself, but for something bigger. He was reading these as a tribute to the boy in the window.

"John regarded the books scattered around his desk, how much he had loved them all—*Le Morte d'Arthur, Treasure Island, The Aeneid,* the rest. No, these books were not life, he knew, and now that he'd seen life so much more close up, in the Corral with his sister nearly dying, he knew more than ever that books did not take the place of real life. But books were important, too.

Hadn't they taken him out of his quiet family home and led him into the real world? Without these books, he'd have never gone out there.

"Outside the window, the dark shape of the Santa Lucias called to him, quietly but powerfully. He would return there someday, and soon.

"John picked up his pen and began to write."

The audience loved it, and at the book table after the readings, people kept asking to buy *Corral de Tierra,* and seemed shocked that it was not available.

Travis was happy to be done with his part of the reading. That way he got to listen to the other readers.

Ursula K. Le Guin transported the audience to another world with an excerpt from *The Tombs of Atuan,* and E. L. Konigsburg delighted everyone with a few pieces of *From the Mixed-Up Files of Mrs. Basil E. Frankweiler.* At last, Miss Babb introduced Laurence Yep, who read from his novel *Dragonwings,* about Chinese immigrants during the Great San Francisco Earthquake of 1906.

Yep read the passage where Moon Shadow experienced the earthquake, which bounced him out of bed at dawn. Travis looked around the audience and saw people everywhere looking up and around during the reading, clutching the arms of their seats. When Yep read, the building seemed to crack and twist, the floor to heave and buckle. The earthquake was happening all over again.

Travis's only disappointment that night was that he hadn't finished the story for Oster. He wanted to hand over the composition book after the reading, a present for Oster, but he wasn't even halfway through. The more he wrote, the more he remembered. Just the night before, he'd remembered how he found Oster's phone number—right there in the phone book. This detail didn't change the story, he knew, but it was important to the story, and he was glad he remembered it.

The whole gang went to Marianne's for ice cream after the reading, where Miss Babb flat out asked Hil, Oster, and Travis if they had finished their stories yet. Each of them half mumbled that they were still working on them, and it was clear to Travis that they were. And that there was plenty of time.

Two weeks after the reading, Travis's dad's band played a benefit gig for the Save Our Library committee at Listen and Be Heard, an artsy coffeehouse out by the junior college. His dad had rounded up the Not Band for the gig; they hadn't played together in over a year, but every night for a week, they rehearsed in Travis's living room and were starting to sound pretty good.

Listen and Be Heard was filled with goofy-looking college students that night. The whole gang was there, too. Travis loved seeing his dad's old friends onstage again. They played the usual stuff, "old guy" music, they called it—Dylan and Neil Young and Joni Mitchell. And that night at Listen and Be Heard, they were hot. Ray Jim John punished his electric guitar, Cutlip Sam sang through the harmonica, Dave Tilton-Dave Tilton laid down the law on bass, and Big Gun Burge conga-drummed his way to heaven. Travis thought his dad's voice was as good as it had ever been.

For the last song, his dad brought Travis to the tiny stage. They'd been practicing a new piece together—Travis was really getting the hang of rhythm guitar and thought he might take lessons soon. The song was a surprise for his mom, "Luz de Mi Vida" by Los Lobos. Travis and his dad kind of lost their way in the middle for a few bars, but found their way back to the groove by the end. It was way cool.

When Travis came offstage, he sat with Hil alone at a table in the corner.

"You know, Big T," Hil said. "You play guitar almost as good as I play soccer. I had no idea. That rocked. You should have seen your mom. She was trying real hard not to cry. I hope you write like you play."

"You, too," Travis said. "So, you done yet?"

"You must be joking, Señor Weasel. I don't know about you, but the more I write, the more I write. It's weird."

"Tell me about it."

They stared at each other, knew what each other was thinking.

"Okay," Hil said. "As soon as I'm done, I'll show you. Ernie, too."

"Deal." They shook one more Camazotz handshake.

After the gig, Travis and his dad counted up the money in the tip jar. A whopping $212.79.

"There's got to be more," his dad said. "I mean, that's just not very much."

"Dad," Travis said. "That's not what matters. It's not this one thing that's gonna save the world. It's this one small thing and that one small thing, and all the others. This small thing here, it's part of something much bigger."

His dad had to agree with him.

On the first Tuesday in March, Measure V was passed by the voting citizens of Salinas, 67 percent in favor, 33

percent opposed, with a two-thirds majority required. Close but enough, and that was all that mattered. The city would increase its sales tax by one half of one penny, and the new money would be used to restore city services that had been cut. A large portion of the money, as written into the measure, would keep the library open.

The entire Save Our Library committee watched the election returns on TVs at the library. It wasn't until almost midnight that victory was assured, and when the announcement was made, a great whooping broke out. Travis looked around for Miss Babb, but she was nowhere to be seen. He found her a while later in the kids' section, curled up fast asleep in one of the old corduroy beanbag chairs.

The victory wasn't a total one, of course. The library would stay open, but with a greatly reduced staff and with minimal hours. But it would stay open, and they—the city, the librarians, the citizens—would continue to work on behalf of the library and its books.

"Whatever it takes, Travis," Miss Babb said. "We'll keep working. The fight's not over yet."

✦ ✦ ✦

Travis and Oster, and Hil, too, when he didn't have soccer, continued to work on the committee. Travis and

Oster both worked afternoons at the library as volunteer shelvers. Travis had never figured that putting books back in their proper places could be so much fun. He kept discovering books he never knew existed. He seemed to bring home as many as he shelved.

One afternoon, when they were both working in the kids' section, Travis picked up the library's only copy of *Corral de Tierra*.

"Look," he said. "You're popular again."

Oster laughed, looked away. He seemed embarrassed, which Travis thought was weird.

Travis needed to say something; he did.

"Remember," he said, "when we were up in the Corral, that day after. And we all promised to write down what we saw, everything."

"Yes." Oster kept shelving.

"So, have you been doing that?"

"Yes. Yes, I have." Oster stopped shelving and pointed a book at him. "And you, have you been writing it all down?"

"I have. Tons. But I'm not quite finished yet."

"Good. It's supposed to take time. I'm glad you're doing it, though."

Travis still wasn't finished with his version of what happened last fall, but he was close. He was dying to share it with Oster. Hil, Travis knew, was almost done, too.

"Remember," Travis said, "when you were talking about *Steinbeck's Ghost,* the book, your book, your *second* book, you said you'd got it wrong somehow. And Hil said you should finish that book, that he knew it'd be a better book this time."

"Yes, I remember."

"So? Are you working on that book, too? Are you gonna put the cave in that book? What happened to us?"

Oster grunted.

"So?" Travis asked.

Oster looked at him.

"Well," he said. "I have been. Writing, that is, *Steinbeck's Ghost.* I think I figured it out. What was wrong. I've been working on it a little bit. And yes, the cave's gonna be in there. After I check it out with you and Hil, of course."

"Why didn't you tell me?"

"Didn't want to jinx it."

"So how far—"

Oster put a finger to his lips.

"Don't want to jinx it."

That afternoon Travis and Oster said good-bye in the alley, and Oster drove off to Spreckels. Travis stood a long time in the alley, waiting for something. For what? It was too quiet out.

It was a sunny day, almost warm. The rains had been

thick and constant all winter, and the world was lush, exploding. The plum and apple and cherry trees had blossomed all at once, and the rain knocked those petals from the trees. The flowers were as thick as snow on the ground. The mountains—the Gabilans and the Santa Lucias—were so green the world seemed like a whole other planet.

Travis got on his bike and pedaled hard out to Spreckels, the afternoon wind pushing him all the way there. He knew he'd be late for dinner, but his parents would come pick him up.

Oster came to the door.

"So. You've been writing," Travis said. "I'd really like to hear some. Would you read me some? Some of *Steinbeck's Ghost?*"

"I don't know, Travis," Oster said. "It's kind of a private thing."

"A private thing?" he said. "Are you kidding me? Private? No, it's not. That's crazy."

There was a last silence.

"You're right," the writer said. "Come on in. I'll read you what I've got so far."

BIBLIOGRAPHY

If you're interested in reading Steinbeck, for the first time or the next, here are some of my favorites. Start at the top and work your way down. —L.B.

The Red Pony (New York: Penguin, 1993).

A short novel about Jody's pony, Gabilan, and Gitano, the old paisano. It's also included in *The Long Valley*.

The Long Valley (New York: Penguin, 2000).

All of Steinbeck's best short stories, and all set in the Salinas Valley, including "Johnny Bear" and "The Red Pony."

The Pastures of Heaven (New York: Penguin, 1995).

A novel told in stories set in the Corral de Tierra. In here, you'll find the tale of the talented outcast Tularecito.

Cup of Gold (New York: Penguin, 1995).

Steinbeck's first novel is a rousing pirate tale of adventure and treasure based on the myth of the Holy Grail.

The Pearl (New York: Penguin, 2000).

In this short novel, the discovery of a giant pearl in a small Mexican town brings out the worst in everyone who sees it.

Of Mice and Men (New York: Penguin, 2002).

Two itinerant ranch hands roam from job to job while working toward their dream of owning a farm someday. A heartbreaking tale of friendship and loyalty.

Tortilla Flat (New York: Penguin, 1977).

The Knights of the Round Table come to life as cannery workers in Monterey. Heroism was never so funny.

Cannery Row (New York: Penguin, 2002).

The "denizens" of Monterey's Cannery Row don't work too hard at much but having a good deal of fun. Includes Steinbeck's famous "Frog Hunt" sequence, where a pond of crazy frogs proves too much for Mack and the boys, a slapstick favorite.

Sweet Thursday (New York: Penguin, 1996).

This sequel to *Cannery Row* features an affectionate portrait of Steinbeck's closest friend, Edward "Doc" Ricketts, and the further misadventures of the Row's "denizens."

The Log from the Sea of Cortez (New York: Penguin, 1995).

A nonfiction account of Steinbeck's research voyage to Baja California with Ed "Doc" Ricketts. Steinbeck's love of nature, and his deep knowledge of it, glow from every page.

The Acts of King Arthur and His Noble Knights (New York: Viking, 2007).

In the 1950s, Steinbeck spent a year in England researching the myth of King Arthur and searching for the real Camelot. These stunning versions of the tales that inspired Steinbeck to become a writer are filled with magic and action.

The Grapes of Wrath, a Novel (New York: Penguin, 2006).

Steinbeck's most famous book is the courageous journey of the Joads from the Dust Bowl of Oklahoma to the fruit orchards of California. A great American novel.

East of Eden, a Novel (New York: Penguin, 2003).

A sweeping epic of early California, this novel is one part stories from the Old Testament retold and a history of Steinbeck's own ancestors.

About Steinbeck:

Catherine Reef, *John Steinbeck* (New York: Clarion, 2004).

A wonderful biography of the writer with lots of illustrations.

Thank you for reading
this FEIWEL AND FRIENDS book.
The Friends who made

Steinbeck's Ghost

possible are:

JEAN FEIWEL publisher

LIZ SZABLA editor-in-chief

RICH DEAS creative director

ELIZABETH FITHIAN marketing director

LIZ NOLAND publicist

HOLLY WEST assistant to the publisher

DAVE BARRETT managing editor

NICOLE LIEBOWITZ MOULAISON production manager

JESSICA TEDDER associate editor

ALLISON REMCHECK editorial assistant

KSENIA WINNICKI marketing assistant